5233 8141

P9-CLU-669

Skating

Under the Wire

Skating
Under the Wire

Joelle Charbonneau

Minotaur Books

A Thomas Dunne Book ⚞ New York

A THOMAS DUNNE BOOK FOR MINOTAUR BOOKS.
An imprint of St. Martin's Publishing Group.

SKATING UNDER THE WIRE. Copyright © 2013 by Joelle Charbonneau. All rights reserved. Printed in the United States of America. For information, address St. Martin's Press, 175 Fifth Avenue, New York, N.Y. 10010.

www.thomasdunnebooks.com
www.minotaurbooks.com

ISBN 978-1-250-01959-2 (hardcover)
ISBN 978-1-250-01960-8 (e-book)

Minotaur books may be purchased for educational, business, or promotional use. For information on bulk purchases, please contact Macmillan Corporate and Premium Sales Department at 1-800-221-7945, extension 5442, or write specialmarkets@macmillan.com.

First Edition: October 2013

10 9 8 7 6 5 4 3 2 1

For Max, who fills my world with laughter

Acknowledgments

I cannot begin to express how grateful I am for the opportunity to write this series. After four books, Rebecca, Pop, and the Indian Falls gang are still so much fun to visit, and I owe a great deal of thanks to all the readers, librarians, and booksellers who have supported these books. Also, thank you to my family, who encourage me every day to follow this strange and wonderful career path. I love you all!

My heartfelt thanks also go to the Thomas Dunne/Minotaur team, especially Andy Martin, Toni Kirkpatrick, Hector DeJean, David Baldeosingh Rotstein, and Doron Ben-Ami. Also, much thanks goes to the wonderful India Cooper for her copyediting process. I would not be able to do what I do without the amazing support and incredible talent of my agent, Stacia Decker.

Over the past couple of years, I have been lucky to come in contact with some incredible writers who have convinced me to always believe in myself. I can't name them all, but I do want to give shout-outs to Chuck Wendig, Adam Christopher, Nancy

Parra, Deb Gross, Erica O'Rourke, Steve Weddle, Thea Harrison, Scott Parker, Jay Stringer, Sophie Littlefield, Tracy Kiely, Brad Parks, Daniel Palmer, Chris Holm, Owen Laukkanen, Jamie Freveletti, Tasha Alexander, Andrew Grant, Linda Rodriguez, Donnell Bell, Jennifer McAndrews, Joelle Anthony, Sarah Anderson, and Heather Graham, as well as everyone on Team Decker. Thank you for the wonderful stories you create and your generous spirit.

Last, to everyone who picks up this book—thank you from the bottom of my heart.

Skating
Under the Wire

One

Nothing says romance like Bingo and Bengay. At least, I was telling myself that as I placed a token over the square marked "meat tenderizer" on my Bridal Bingo card. Pink and white crepe-paper bells hung from the ceiling, and every table in the senior center's recreation room was packed as the bride-to-be and one of my best friends, Danielle Martinez, held up the silver mallet for the crowd to admire.

I heard one woman say, "That should do the trick on a flank steak."

Personally, I thought the industrial-sized hammer would do the trick on just about anything—especially Danielle's controlling soon-to-be mother-in-law. Dressed in a flowing light blue skirt and high-necked white blouse, Danielle was the epitome of sweetness and decorum. However, the tire she had punctured on my car a few months ago knew better.

"Bingo." A hand shot up three tables back. "What do I win?"

"You don't win anything until the maid of honor checks your

card." Danielle pushed a lock of dark hair off her face and gave me a bright smile. "Right, Rebecca?"

"Right, Danielle." Actually, I had no idea this was part of my job, but I wasn't about to argue with a woman holding a meat mallet. Besides, because Danielle was marrying the pastor of the town's Lutheran church, the St. Mark's Women's Guild had relieved me of most of the shower-planning duties. Since I hadn't been required to do much up to this point, I wasn't in a position to complain.

The bottle-blond lady with the potential winning card eyed me with suspicion from under a flowery blue hat. Carefully, I checked to make sure each square was marked correctly. Each was, which meant the winner was now the proud owner of a Santa scarecrow crafted by Louise Lagotti, my grandfather's onetime girlfriend.

Everyone clapped for the bingo winner, and Danielle reached for her next gift.

"Oh, could you wait to open that one, dear?" Spritelike Ethel Jacabowski stood and gave Danielle an apologetic smile. "That's from Ginny and me. She went to the television room to get her glasses, but she's not back yet. I'd hate for her to miss the big moment."

Danielle put the silver-wrapped gift back on the table with a smile. "I'll wait to open it until Ginny gets here. How about I open this one instead?"

Ethel nodded and shuffled toward the door in search of Ginny while Danielle tore into a box covered in pink-and-white paper. Danielle held up a set of red-and-white Tupperware bowls, and everyone sighed.

I was heading back up front to do whatever else my maid of honor status decreed I do when I felt a tap on my shoulder.

"Rebecca? Do you have a minute?"

I automatically smiled as I turned. The smile froze and I started to sweat as I realized the tapper was none other than my high school English teacher, Mrs. Johnson.

I looked over at Danielle, who was happily tearing into another package. Since she didn't seem to miss me, I said, "Um. Sure, Mrs. Johnson." Was I eloquent or what?

Mrs. Johnson looked around the room and then motioned for me to follow her. Eek. Suddenly, I was back in the tenth grade, hoping she wasn't going to yell at me for dangling my participle. Not that Mrs. Johnson was ever mean. As a matter of fact, she was probably the nicest teacher I'd ever had. For some funny reason, though, she expected more from me than from the other kids in my class. Part of me was delighted someone thought I could do more than live in Indian Falls and help run my mother's roller-skating rink. The other part was terrified I'd disappoint. The terrified part couldn't help but wonder what Mrs. Johnson thought of my recent decision to pull the rink off the real estate market and stay in town.

We reached the back of the room as Danielle pulled his-and-her aprons out of a box. I tried not to fidget as Mrs. Johnson turned her attention from the gifts to me.

Her blue eyes met mine. "Your grandfather suggested I talk to you."

My stomach clenched, and I said a brief prayer that Mrs. Johnson wasn't one of my grandfather's girlfriends. Thus far Pop had limited his extensive dating pool to women old enough to cash in on the senior citizen discount. Mrs. Johnson didn't qualify. With shoulder-length ash-blond hair, a trim figure, and a flattering copper dress, Mrs. Johnson looked like she hadn't aged a day since my years at Indian Falls High School.

"Do you need to book the rink for a party?" I asked.

She shook her head. "No, although I wanted to tell you how much my daughter and I enjoy watching EstroGenocide. Renee's thinking about trying out for the team next season."

EstroGenocide was the rink's female flat-track derby team. Not only did the team pack the rink with fans for every bout, they'd also taken first in their season-ending tournament last week. Aside from a few glitches, letting the derby team become a member of the Toe Stop family was turning out to be the best business decision I'd ever made. "I'm sure a few of the team members would be happy to give Renee some pointers. Just have her come by the rink, and I'll make the introductions."

"I'll tell her." Applause for a set of CorningWare rang out. When the applause died, Mrs. Johnson said, "I have a problem, and your grandfather thought your unique skills would be helpful in solving it."

Unique skills? The only thing I was truly skilled at was getting back onto my roller skates after taking a spill. Somehow I didn't think my former teacher was looking for tips on how to pull splinters out of her backside. "What kind of problem, Mrs. Johnson?"

"Please, call me Julie." She smiled. I returned the smile even though I was pretty sure I wasn't going to be able to call her anything but Mrs. Johnson. "Have you heard about the Thanksgiving Day thefts?"

I nodded. With Thanksgiving less than two weeks away, it was hard to escape the speculation on which house would be hit this year. Especially around my grandfather. Pop and his friends elevated gossip to an art form. For the past ten Thanksgivings, thieves had broken into unattended homes. Jewelry, coin collections, cash, and other small valuables were taken. Televisions and larger items were always left behind. Not once had the thieves been spotted. Over the years the sheriff's department had investigated but had never come up with even one substantial lead. Rumor had it that this year Deputy Sean Holmes was making it his mission to catch the thieves and finally bring them to justice. Pop had started a pool betting on whether Deputy Sean would succeed. Unfortunately, the odds were definitely not in Sean's favor.

"Well, I'm sad to say, two years ago, mine was one of the houses broken into." Mrs. Johnson sighed. "I knew about the thefts, but you never think something like that is going to happen to you, especially since the police had made a point of putting six extra cars on patrol for the day. Renee and I went to a friend's house for an early dinner. We were only gone two hours, but when we came back the front door was unlocked and some of our things were missing."

"Bingo!" a woman yelled from a table in the middle of the room. I excused myself and wove around chairs to verify her card's win. Then I presented her with her prize—another scarecrow, this one dressed as a Pilgrim.

Danielle moved on to the next gift, and I walked back to Mrs. Johnson. "Have the police recovered any of your stolen belongings?" I asked. Pop had mentioned that a few of the stolen goods had been found on eBay or in consignment shops in Moline, Rockford, and Chicago.

"No. That's why I wanted to talk to you." She dug into her purse and pulled out a piece of paper. "I have a list of the items the thieves took."

Mrs. Johnson unfolded the paper and handed it to me. Silverware. Jewelry. A gold-plated serving set. A Waterford clock. Seven hundred dollars in cash. A large vase filled with loose change. Three pillowcases.

"Most of them aren't terribly important," Mrs. Johnson said. "Although I hate that someone took them. The two things I really want to find are my husband's watch and my great-grandmother's engagement ring. The ring's been passed down from daughter to daughter for over a hundred years. Now it's gone."

At the front of the room, Danielle held up a power drill. Not exactly my idea of a wedding gift, but I'd never been close to marriage. What did I know?

I looked down at the paper in my hands. The last item listed didn't seem typical either. "Why would the thieves take pillowcases?"

"Deputy Holmes speculated that the thieves used them as bags and carried everything out in them."

Made sense to me. What didn't make sense was why Mrs. Johnson was talking to me about this. "I'm sorry your house was broken into, but I'm not sure I'm the best person to help track down your great-grandmother's ring."

"Oh, I don't want you to track down the ring," Mrs. Johnson said.

Good, because I had no idea where to begin.

"I want you to catch the people who took it."

In high school, a lot of teachers had unrealistic expectations for students. Face it, not every kid was going to be the next Hemingway or Einstein no matter how much she studied. Mrs. Johnson was always careful to treat each student as an individual. What garnered praise for one was not acceptable work from another. Mrs. Johnson understood realistic expectations.

Which is why I must have misunderstood her request.

"You want me to *what*?" I asked as the crowd oohed over a taupe trivet set.

"I want you to track down and catch the thieves." She smiled as though this were the most obvious request ever made. "Sheriff Jackson and his deputies have been trying to catch the thieves for ten years. They haven't gotten close. They've never had a real lead. You've shown a knack for succeeding where the sheriff's department has failed. I'd like to see you show them up again."

Technically, I hadn't shown up anyone. While the town gave me credit for solving the two murders and the car thefts that had occurred since I'd blown back into Indian Falls, I knew better. Dumb luck factored heavily into my so-called crime-fighting accomplishments. So did a desperate need for self-preservation.

"I'm flattered, but I think you might want to hire a real private investigator for something like this." You know—someone who actually knew what he was doing.

Mrs. Johnson shook her head. "Your grandfather and I talked about that. We agreed—I need someone who knows the town and the people who live here. Besides, everyone already thinks of you as a private investigator. Why not make it official?"

I could come up with a very long list of reasons. The first would be Deputy Sean Holmes. Since I'd come back to town we'd had more than one run-in over my nosy nature. So far, he'd only threatened to arrest me for obstructing justice. I wasn't looking to give him a reason to make good on the threat.

Strange enough, though, the less than rational part of my brain was tempted to say yes. Running the roller rink was fun, but my skating-teacher-turned-manager and staff knew their stuff. Minimal supervision was required. So, while I was glad I'd decided not to sell the rink and move back to Chicago, I was starting to feel like I needed something more. I'd been toying with joining the derby team, but as a redhead I bruise easily. I wasn't looking forward to a life of Icy Hot patches and black-and-blue marks. Solving a ten-year-long breaking and entering ring sounded way less painful.

I looked at Danielle, who was still opening gifts. The mammoth stack she'd started with was down to five or six boxes. It would soon be time to serve the cake and the punch. "I don't know if I have the time. Danielle's wedding is in two weeks and . . ."

Mrs. Johnson gave me that look and my cheeks started to burn. It was the same look she used whenever I gave the wrong answer in class or tried to explain how the hamster ate my homework. The look stymied me. Kind of like it was doing now.

"Maybe I could talk to Deputy Holmes for you. He might be willing to . . ." I swallowed hard as Mrs. Johnson's expression grew more disappointed. My stomach clenched as she continued to watch me—waiting for the right answer.

Crap.

"I guess I could ask some of the other victims some questions. Maybe something new will turn up."

She beamed. "I knew I could count on you, Rebecca."

For a moment I basked in her approval. Then I realized I had no idea where to start.

Mrs. Johnson solved that problem by pulling an envelope out of her purse. "Your grandfather suggested I put together a list of all the past victims. The Buergeys moved to Michigan three or four years ago, and Matt McBride had that unfortunate incident with his tractor trailer. The rest are still in the area. I know they're as anxious as I am to find the culprits. A few of them even offered to help pay your fee."

8

"Fee?" What fee?

Only once had I been paid for my snooping. Since the client in question was a teenaged boy and my employee, he was willing to work off my fee with extra hours at the rink. During those hours he'd managed to stop up the toilet, cause a small fire in the toaster oven, and drop a quart of popcorn oil on the rink floor. Not getting paid would have been cheaper.

Mrs. Johnson didn't appear to notice my surprise. "Your grandfather quoted me your going rate. He also warned that you might have to charge more if the case gets too involved. The check is in the envelope with the list of names. If it isn't enough, I can write you another."

I could only imagine how much my grandfather thought my investigative services were worth. "I really don't think—"

"Your grandfather said you'd be uncomfortable taking money from me since I was one of your favorite teachers, but I insist." The steely glint in her eye said the subject was firmly closed.

Left with no real choice, I slid the envelope into my skirt pocket. "I don't know if I'll find the thieves, but I'll do my best." If I failed miserably, I'd comfort myself with the knowledge that Mrs. Johnson could insist only I take the check. She couldn't make me cash it.

Feeling slightly better about the situation, I asked a few more questions and wrote down Mrs. Johnson's e-mail address and phone number. After promising to give her regular updates, I skirted around chairs and tables to the front of the room, where Danielle was posing for a picture with a heart-shaped spatula.

There were only two gifts left on the table. I handed one to Danielle. My stomach growled in anticipation of the soon-to-be-served chocolate cake.

Danielle looked down at the box in her hands and frowned. "I don't think I'm supposed to open this one. Not until Ethel and Ginny arrive."

As though on cue, Ethel appeared in the doorway, looking a little unsteady on her feet. The walk to and from the television room must have worn her out.

"Is Ginny coming?" I asked.

Everyone turned to look at Ethel. She blinked twice at the attention. Then she shook her white, permed head. "No, dear. She's not going to make it. I'm afraid poor Ginny is dead."

Two

The party fizzled after that. Someone called the sheriff's department, which apparently was procedure when one of the visitors passed at the center, while someone else got Ethel a drink of water. Too bad this wasn't the kind of party where the punch got spiked. Ethel looked like she could use something with a kick. I would, too, if I found a dead body.

Even without the booze, Ethel was able to give everyone a rundown on her search for Ginny. Turns out Ethel found Ginny in one of the TV-room armchairs. A football game was on the television. According to Ethel, Ginny liked football because all the men wore tight pants. Sadly, Ginny was no longer able to enjoy the view.

After her story, Ethel assured everyone that the party should continue. Ginny would want it that way. Only no one felt right eating chocolate cake and constructing wedding dresses out of toilet paper. Not with Ginny eternally sleeping just down the hall. The partygoers said their farewells and told Danielle they'd see her at the wedding. Then they loaded up their to-go plates and headed for the exit.

After ten minutes, the room was empty of everyone but Danielle, me, and the mountain of shower gifts. Danielle drove a black Ford Focus. I had a yellow Honda Civic. We both got decent gas mileage, but our cars weren't big enough to get the haul to her fiancé's place. We needed help.

Lots of it.

"What happened to the party?"

Danielle and I turned. Limping into the recreation room with a frown was my grandfather. He was covered in gold lamé, white spandex, and a lot of rhinestones. The fact that I wasn't surprised to see Pop's fashion choices spoke volumes about my life. In the past couple of months, Pop's Elvis look had morphed from special occasion to personal style. More often than not, he wore his pants at least a size too small. Mobility took a backseat to pleasing his fans. Unfortunately, today his limp appeared to have little to do with fashion.

"Are you okay, Pop?" I hurried across the room and offered my grandfather my arm. He waved me away and stomped his right foot three times.

"I was waiting for my big entrance, and my foot fell asleep." He looked around at the empty room with a sigh. "That's the last time I take a gig that requires me to jump out of a cake."

"You were in a cake?" I shouldn't have been surprised, but still . . .

"Yeah." He leaned down to rub his calf, sending prisms of light dancing around the room. "It was pretty comfortable for the first twenty minutes, but then my butt began to itch. Do you know the lengths you have to go through to scratch the middle of your ass when you're stuck in the center layer of a cake?"

No, and I was pretty sure hearing about it would cause a lifetime of therapy bills. So I did what any person hoping to retain her sanity would do—I changed the subject. "What song were you going to sing when you leapt out of the cake?"

"'Burning Love.'" Pop grinned at Danielle. "We thought it would set the right tone leading up to the wedding. Louise even rigged the cake so it would light on fire for the big finale. I can't believe everyone left before we got a chance to bring the house down."

Something told me that everyone leaving was probably the only reason the Indian Falls Fire Department wasn't breaking out the hoses. Still, my heart went out to Pop, who was looking more than a little deflated at being left in the lurch by his fans.

"You can't really blame them for leaving. Ethel came in and told us Ginny passed away," I explained. "I don't think anyone was in the mood for cake after that."

Pop's eyes grew sad. Then he sighed. "Ginny was a feisty one. Since she refused to go out with me, you probably didn't know her. Every morning she'd walk five miles, rain or shine. She loved being outside, although she hated the cold. Once fall came, you'd find her walking on the treadmill, watching talk shows. Snow and icy rain are a pain at our age."

The winter weather in Illinois was hell at any age.

My grandfather shrugged and gave me a small smile, but he didn't have the usual sparkle in his eyes. Pop didn't do sad often. When he did, it knocked me for a loop. Kind of like now.

Putting my arms around my grandfather, I kissed his leathery cheek, careful not to dislodge the black pompadour wig. "Ginny was lucky to have you for a friend. I bet she made all the women crazy, turning you down."

Pop flashed a smile. "Yeah, I think she liked that part." He returned my hug and sighed. "I should probably go see how Ethel and the other ladies are holding up. We all expect to go at some point, but seeing someone like Ginny go—well, it makes you realize that you gotta enjoy life while you can, because you just never know." He walked toward the door, stomping his right foot every other step. "Let me know if you need any help getting those gifts home. My muscles could use a good workout."

Once Pop and his rhinestones were out of sight, Danielle sank into a chair with a weary sigh. "God, I never knew being polite and opening gifts could be so much work. Give me pole dancing any day."

I glanced around the room to make sure no one had overheard. Danielle must have been really tired to mention her past profession in a public place. She had reinvented herself when she moved from Chicago to Indian Falls, and she lived in fear that someone would discover she used to be a stripper. Especially her fiancé.

"You looked like you were having a good time."

She kicked off her strappy black heels and shrugged. "I preferred the shower you and the derby team threw for me last weekend."

"You liked the EstroGenocide dishes?" The girls had custom-ordered black dishes stamped with a silver and pink version of the team's logo. Skulls and crossbones were the epitome of class.

"The dishes are hideous." She laughed. "The people who gave them to me are wonderful, though. Most of the women today were here either to impress Rich or to see if I did something unworthy of a pastor's wife. They think their pastor is perfect, which means his wife has to be perfect, too."

"You're not having second thoughts, are you?"

14

"God, no."

The horror in her voice made me smile. On paper, the ex-stripper and the mild-mannered pastor looked like a mismatch, but as far as I was concerned, they were a perfect fit.

"I just wish we could have eloped." Danielle sighed. "Then I wouldn't have to worry about having the perfect dress and serving the perfect food. I was hoping having the wedding the Friday after Thanksgiving would make more people decline, but so far everyone's said yes. If I didn't have you helping me through this, I'd go crazy."

For a second, I wondered how Pop was holding up, but then I turned back to the problem at hand. "I guess we should think about moving these boxes to your place."

"Not in these heels." Danielle laughed. "Rich promised he'd move the gifts as long as he didn't have to come to the shower. You're off the hook."

Okay, the maid of honor handbook probably said I was supposed to turn down the offer of freedom and stay, but I did really want to check on Pop. I assuaged my guilty conscience by instructing Danielle to text me if she needed help—something she'd been doing more and more frequently as the wedding approached. Then I grabbed my coat and purse and bolted for the door.

Following the sound of voices, I walked through the center's blue-and-gray linoleum hallways, past rooms used for macaroni art and Jazzercise classes. During my mother's childhood, the building was home to the Indian Falls High School. By the time I'd hit the age of pimples and teenage angst, a new school had been built at the edge of town, leaving this one abandoned. Since the building sat next to the retirement home, the town's seniors commandeered it. Now it was a hub for bingo, backgammon, and gossip. If you wanted the skinny on anything Indian Falls, especially if you didn't care whether the information was one hundred percent accurate, this was where you came.

I found Pop in the workout room. He was consoling a cluster of distraught ladies huddled near a stationary bicycle. From the way the women were jockeying for position, I was guessing that not all of their distress was over poor Ginny's passing.

Pop spotted me, gave the tall brunette next to him a pat on the shoulder, and sauntered over. "Do you need a man to help lift heavy boxes? I've been logging a lot of hours on free weights."

My grandfather flexed his bicep. Rhinestones sparkled. The women behind him sighed. I pretended not to notice.

"Pastor Rich is coming to help, so I thought I'd ask if you need a ride home." I figured that sounded better than saying I wanted to see if he was an emotional wreck. I didn't want to ruin the macho mojo he had going on.

Pop shook his head. "My car's in the lot. Besides, I'm going to wait and see how Ethel's holding up before heading out. She's in the lounge, talking to Deputy Holmes."

Poor Ethel. I'd been grilled by Deputy Sean Holmes more than once since coming back to Indian Falls. Sean's interrogation style had all the subtlety of a sledgehammer. Ethel was going to need Pop's sparkly shoulder by the time it was over.

"Why is Sean talking to Ethel?" I asked. "Does he think there was foul play?"

"Nothing that interesting. I overheard the paramedics say something about a heart attack. Sean just needs something to write in his report."

"I guess that's good." I felt a knot of worry ease. Lately, too many of the deaths in town had involved foul play.

"Real good." Pop smiled. "Sean will be busy squaring away paperwork. That gives you time to get a head start on tracking down the Thanksgiving Day thief. Did Julie give you a list of the victims? If not, I probably remember most of them."

Oops. Ethel's surprise announcement had pushed my agreement to investigate off the radar. "Mrs. Johnson gave me the list, along with a check for my fee. What are you doing telling people I charge a fee?"

Pop's smile widened. "No one's going to take you seriously if you don't charge for your time."

No amount of money was going to make me a legitimate source of detective work. "I run a roller rink, Pop. That makes me qualified to burn pizza and schedule birthday parties."

My logic failed to impress my grandfather. "I called a couple of PIs in Moline and asked them what the going rate was. Then I knocked off twenty-five percent, seeing as how Julie gave you As in all her classes. I figured that was worth the discount."

I ignored the flash of indignation I felt over the implication I needed to buy my grades and focused on the real problem. "Pop, I can't charge for investigating crimes."

"Why not?"

"Because I have no training." Duh.

My grandfather waved off my concern with a flick of his wrinkled hand. "Training is overrated. I've never had a singing lesson, and look at me now." Pop gyrated his hips to the left, causing the women behind him to break into enthusiastic applause.

With all that sparkling it was hard *not* to look at Pop. I might even have been inspired by the comparison if Pop actually had talent. Pop's singing sounded a lot like a hedgehog in heat, and that was when he remembered the words. What he lacked in talent he made up for in shiny, tight clothes, unparalleled enthusiasm, and bribery. He gave away imitation silk scarves by the truckload. I had a closet full of them. Still, while lack of talent hadn't gotten in my grandfather's way, my pride wanted me to be good at what I did.

Pop finished one last pelvic thrust. Then he got back to business. "I can take a look at the list and give you background on the victims. Heck, I can even ride along when you interview them. With me helping, what can go wrong?"

I could think of at least a dozen things off the top of my head. Still, it couldn't hurt to get Pop's take on the victims, right? After all, I had promised Mrs. Johnson I would try to track down the thieves.

I pulled Mrs. Johnson's envelope out of my pocket and unfolded the sheet of paper inside. The list was long and arranged by the year of the theft. The most recent thefts were written at the top. In three of the years, more than one house had been hit. All combined, there were thirteen names listed. Something told me that if the thief had his way there would be fourteen come December. At least.

One of the names caught me by surprise. "I didn't know Annette was robbed. Mom never mentioned it." Annette was the owner of the town's hair salon and had been my mother's best friend.

Pop nodded. "For a while no one was certain whether the Thanksgiving thief cleaned her out or if it was her ex-boyfriend. The man was a skunk."

My mother had told me about the skunk. If she had mentioned the break-in, I hadn't been paying attention, which made me sad.

I quickly scanned the rest of the list. Some of the names—

Betsy Moore, Nan Thain, and Doc Truman—were familiar. The rest were not. Pop started to give me a rundown on the victims, but after hearing about Betsy Moore's controversial methods of inseminating a horse, I tuned him out. Sometimes too much information is a bad thing.

"So who are we going to question first? My vote is for Barna Donovan. Last summer he said one of his goats was eaten by an alien." Pop's eyes glittered with excitement, which was way better than the sorrow that had been there earlier. Too bad I was going to disappoint him.

"If I'm going to look like a professional investigator, I need to talk to victims on my own."

"You're probably right." Pop frowned. "We don't want to get your new business off on the wrong foot. Just keep me posted on how things are going. I have fifty dollars riding on you catching the crook before Sean Holmes does."

The women in the room stopped talking, and their eyes settled on something behind me. The hair on the back of my neck stood on end as I slowly turned around.

Well, crap. Leaning against the doorjamb, looking at me, was Deputy Sean Holmes. His ash-blond hair stood up as though he'd raked his hands through it a bunch while questioning Ethel, and his smoldering eyes had me ready to duck for cover.

"Where's Ethel?" Pop demanded. "We want to make sure you didn't rough her up."

Sean gave Pop a flat stare. "I don't rough up old ladies."

"Who are you calling old?" Ethel appeared behind Sean. Her eyes were swollen and her nose was red, but the way she was swinging her purse said she was ready for a fight.

The crowd of women near the bikes took a step forward. Pop

glared. Elvis and the septuagenarian Supremes were ready to rumble. Sean swallowed hard.

Call me crazy, but I decided this was a good time to clear out. I said good-bye to my grandfather, who was slowly advancing on Sean, skirted around the action, and headed out of the room. Shrieking voices and shouts for an AARP uprising followed me all the way down the hall and out the door leading to the parking lot.

The temperature was somewhere around freezing as I zipped up my coat and trudged to my car. Somewhere above the clouds the sun was probably shining, but it wasn't making its way down here. The mist of rain falling from the sky made me glad I hadn't walked the two and a half blocks from the rink to the center.

"Funky Town" was blasting from the sound system as I strolled into the rink. Kids and adults of all ages boogied counterclockwise on wheels while laughing, screaming, and inevitably falling. The smell of popcorn and pizza made my stomach growl, and I remembered I hadn't eaten since breakfast. After a quick talk with my staff, which today mostly consisted of responsible high school students, I decided everything was under control. I told them to call if they needed me and then headed back outside and around the side of the rink to the door leading to my second-story apartment.

The apartment was blissfully quiet thanks to Mom's decision to soundproof when she refurbished the place a few years ago. Kicking off my wet shoes, I made a beeline for the kitchen. I poured myself a bowl of Cocoa Puffs as my cell phone rang. Almost certain the call was my grandfather needing to be bailed out of jail, I dug my phone out of my purse. Then I smiled with pleasure as I read the display. Lionel.

I flipped open the phone, and a warm, sexy voice said, "Hey,

I'm sorry, but I'm running a little late. Mrs. Pendley's horse jumped a fence and hurt its leg."

Lionel was a large-animal vet. When he wasn't tending to the four-legged critters around town, the two of us were working to define our current relationship status. Lionel was the love, commitment, and marriage kind of guy. I was still trying to figure out what kind of girl I was. Right now, I was a girl who'd forgotten she had scheduled a date for tonight. Oops.

"Don't worry about it," I said. "We can reschedule for another night."

"I should be done here in another hour. Would you mind waiting a little longer to eat dinner?"

The idea of a real meal instead of a bowl of cereal had its lure, but I'd seen Lionel after one of his emergency animal visits. While nothing could detract from the appeal of his sculpted features and deep green eyes, dirt, blood, and manure were serious appetite suppressants.

"Why don't I meet you at your place?" I suggested. "That'll give you a chance to clean up before we eat." Plus, since one of last year's Thanksgiving theft victims lived just down the road from Lionel, I'd have time to pay her a visit. Could I multitask or what?

Plans made, I ate another handful of cereal, changed into jeans and a fitted blue sweater, and then rummaged through the end table in my bedroom for a pad of paper. In the movies, investigators wrote things down. Columbo, the *Law & Order* gang, Inspector Gadget—they all had pen and paper on hand when doing their work. While a spiral notepad wasn't exactly a stamp of legitimacy, it made me feel like I was at least trying to look the part.

Finishing the last handful of cereal, I brushed the crumbs from my sweater and shrugged into my white winter jacket. The coat was bulky and made me look like the Michelin Man. Perhaps not the look a person should go for when meeting the world's sexiest vet for dinner, but I didn't care. What the coat lacked in attractiveness it made up for in warmth. Anyone who'd lived through a Midwest winter would agree that warmth won out.

Checking to make sure my gloves were in my pocket, I opened the front door and walked smack into the chest of Deputy Sean Holmes.

The impact threw us both off balance. Sean staggered down two steps before regaining his footing and catching the back of my jacket as I started to sail past him. He hauled me onto the stair he was standing on, and for a moment we both looked down to the bottom of the steps, contemplating what might have happened.

Sean recovered first. After taking my arm, he walked me up the three steps to my apartment, pulled me inside, and closed the door behind us. "You can't stay out of trouble, can you?"

"I didn't expect you to be lurking behind my door." We both knew he wasn't referring to our close encounter of the almost painful kind, but I was hoping he'd believe I was shook up enough to avoid the other, less appealing topic.

No such luck.

"Your grandfather seems to think Julie Johnson hired you to catch the Thanksgiving Day thief."

My grandfather really needed a lesson on when to take his dentures out of his mouth. Without his dentures, Pop sounded like he was speaking Yiddish. I was faced with two choices: Tell the truth or lie. I opted for something in the middle. "Mrs. Johnson was at Danielle's bridal shower. The thefts might have come up in conversation."

He crossed his arms and stared at me.

The clock on the mantel ticked.

Sweat dripped down my back. Outside the coat would be perfect. Inside it was stifling. I tried not to fidget under Sean's unblinking gaze.

I failed.

Crap. "Mrs. Johnson really wants to know what happened to the things that were stolen. She asked me to talk to the other victims and see if I could uncover something new. Since I don't know much about the thefts, she thought I'd have a fresh perspective." I took a step back and braced myself for Sean's wrath.

"She might have a point."

Maybe I'd actually fallen down the stairs and was currently hallucinating. "What?"

Sean smiled, enjoying my confusion. "You have a disturbing knack for conning people around here into giving you information. It pisses me off, but I'm not above using it to catch the thief."

Huh. I was pretty sure I had just been insulted. I was going to complain when Sean added, "The victims are angry with the department for not catching the perp, and I can't blame them. If we have another burglary this year, the sheriff can kiss his job good-bye and I'll be demoted to dogcatcher."

Sentencing Sean to a life of yappy Pomeranians and annoyed pit bulls was appealing payback after his past threats to arrest me for obstruction. If it weren't for my promise to Mrs. Johnson, that image might encourage me to sit this one out. Oh well.

"So you aren't going to yell and threaten to arrest me for nosing into your case?"

Sean leaned back against the door. "Nope. In fact, I'm encouraging you to go out there and be your nosiest."

This seemed too good to be true. Maybe my luck in Indian Falls was changing. I should probably stop at Slaughter's Market and pick up a lottery ticket before it changed back.

"Just remember that you're required to report any new evidence to our office. Otherwise, I might have to revoke the nice-guy routine." Sean opened the front door and added, "I'd really hate to upset your grandfather by arresting you during the holidays."

"Wait. You're saying you want me to do the work and let you take the glory?"

Sean gave me a cocky smile. "That's exactly what I'm saying. Have a nice night." With a wink and a slam of the door, he was gone.

So much for thinking my luck had improved. Well, at least I wasn't alone. Sean had just ensured I'd do everything in my power to catch the Thanksgiving thief. If he thought I was going to give him all the credit, though, he was going to be sorely disappointed.

Fueled by righteous indignation, and a need to see Sean running after dogs with a net, I headed out the door to my car. It was time to question Betsy Moore and get this investigation started.

Three

The Moore farm was a fifteen-minute drive from downtown. Betsy had taken over the family business of raising horses and growing soybeans when her parents up and moved to Miami. She had been three years behind me in school, and the age gap had prevented us from being chummy. We still weren't what you would call friends—especially not since this summer, when she showed up on Lionel's arm at the town's dinner dance. Had a well-meaning person not shared her identity, I certainly would never have recognized her. The Betsy I'd known had had stringy hair and braces and was flat as a pancake. Postpuberty Betsy had perfect teeth, a great stylist, and a D-cup bra size. Lionel had picked buxom Betsy as his dinner-dance date to make me jealous. By the time the night was over, Lionel had defected from her side and she'd been consoling herself with the new lawyer in town. Word on the street said Betsy and the lawyer were still together. I hoped the gossips were right. Otherwise, this visit could get downright awkward.

The lights were on inside the house as I pulled into the Moores' long gravel driveway. I checked the dashboard clock. According to the bright green numbers, I had almost a half hour before I had to be at Lionel's.

In the dark it was hard to tell whether the rambling farmhouse was gray or blue. I climbed up the steps of the wraparound porch, rang the doorbell, and huddled into my coat as I waited for Betsy to answer.

I heard something thunk at the other end of the porch and squinted into the dark. Nothing there. Must be the wind.

Or not. Could the wind make scratching sounds? Or growl?

Yikes. Farmers had been complaining about the number of coyotes eating their chickens this year. I hadn't heard of any of the coyotes attacking people, but there was a first time for everything. I didn't want this to be that time. Questioning Betsy could wait until daylight.

The scratching sounds moved closer, and I edged slowly back from the door toward the steps. My heart banged against my chest as my feet prepared to run.

Just as I was about to bolt, the front door opened. Curvy Betsy Moore stood in the doorway, illuminated by the light of her living room. She took one look at me and pursed her lips. The scratching sound crept closer. Betsy cocked her head to the side to listen. I edged closer to the doorway as Betsy's lips spread into a wide smile.

"Homer, is that you?" She flipped a switch next to the door, and the porch burst into light. "I've been wondering where you got off to."

A large, fluffy raccoon stood ten feet away. The thing stood up on its hind legs, made what sounded like a purr, and waved its front paws. If I hadn't known better, I would have thought the raccoon was smiling.

Betsy laughed. "It's cold out here. You should come inside."

I wasn't sure whether Betsy was inviting me or the raccoon into the house. Either way, she was right. It was cold. I decided the invitation applied to me, too, and stepped past Betsy into the warm farmhouse with Homer scampering behind. The living room was decorated in silver-framed family photographs, blue gingham overstuffed furniture, and oak trim. The fireplace in the corner gave off a cheerful glow. The rocking chair next to the fireplace called my name, but I decided that might be pushing my luck.

Homer wasn't as concerned with social niceties. His furry body ambled across the room, and a moment later he was seated on the chair I coveted, warming himself in front of the fire.

"You have a raccoon for a pet?" I asked.

Betsy lifted her chin. "I know it seems strange. Not too many people know about Homer."

The animal in question curled himself into a ball and started to purr. My heart melted. I didn't think Homer was strange. Homer was cute. Then again, my boyfriend had a pet camel, and every piece of my grandfather's wardrobe was made out of Lycra. I was probably not the best judge of what was strange.

"I won't tell anyone about him. I promise." Betsy looked relieved. Homer just looked tired. "Do you mind if I ask how you ended up with a raccoon for a pet? I don't think I've ever known someone to invite one into her house." Raccoons were notorious for making messes.

Betsy smiled. "Technically, I didn't invite Homer. Last spring, his mother thought my chimney was a good place to give birth.

I called animal rescue to get mom and the babies out. A couple of hours after they left, I heard Homer scratching and crying. He'd been left behind. I couldn't just leave him there, so I put on a pair of oven mitts, fished him out, and bottle-fed him some milk."

"And you fell in love." The two of us looked at Homer, who was purring again.

"At first I told myself it was guilt over separating him from his mother. I planned on feeding him for a few days and then calling animal rescue again. Only I never did." Betsy walked over and stroked Homer's head. The purring got louder. "Homer uses the dog door to go in and out of the house, but I've been trying to keep him inside more now that it's hunting season on raccoons."

I knew about deer- and duck-hunting season. Half of the male high school population came down with the "flu" at some point in the winter months in order to go hunting with their dads. Teachers feigned deafness when the guys came back bragging about the bucks they shot. Never once did I hear a guy talk about the raccoon he took down.

"Doesn't Homer tear up your cushions?"

"He's pretty good. So far I've only had to replace a couple of chairs, two or three pillows, and a comforter. Oh, and a couch."

Homer looked up and cooed. Homer was proud of his destructive abilities.

Mentally crossing raccoon off the list of desirable pets, I said, "I stopped by because Mrs. Johnson asked me to look into the Thanksgiving Day thefts. She gave me a list of past victims to talk to, and you were on it." I hoped I sounded less foolish than I felt. In the past, I'd just steered the conversation around to my desired topic. The direct approach was going to take some getting used to.

Betsy nodded, walked across the room, and sank down on the

sofa. "Mrs. Johnson mentioned she planned on talking to you. She was hoping you might find something the cops missed."

Since Betsy didn't seem opposed to the idea, I sat in an armchair and forged on. "Can you tell me where you were last Thanksgiving when the thief broke in?"

"Miami. My parents insisted I come down for the holiday. I left Wednesday night. When I came home Saturday, I found the front door lock broken and stuff missing."

"What kind of stuff?"

Betsy sighed. "My jewelry. All of the good silver my Aunt Tina left me. DVDs. My laptop. And a lot of items my parents had stored in their old bedroom. My dad's collection of stamps and old coins was probably worth more than all of the other things combined."

Everything taken had been small. Just like the Johnson burglary. Definitely a trend.

"Did you tell anyone you were going to visit your folks?"

"Yeah." Betsy blew a strand of hair out of her face. "I know it seems stupid, but I had to make sure someone fed the horses."

I sat up straight at the prospect of landing my first suspect. "Who did you tell?"

"Lionel."

Drat. Not only was Lionel not a suspect because, well, I didn't want him to be, but he'd moved to town a few years after the thefts began. He was in the clear.

"Anyone else?"

"Lionel could only cover Friday's feedings, so I had to ask Mark Boggs to help out. He and his wife, Amy Jo, are pretty good friends of mine. They even know about Homer."

I reached for my notepad to jot down the names and realized

I'd left it in the car. So much for looking like a professional. Making a mental note to write down the names Mark and Amy Jo Boggs, I asked, "Did you recover any of the stolen property?"

"My father found my class ring on eBay and managed to get it back. The seller bought it at a church garage sale in Wisconsin. No one at the church knew who made the donation. They didn't keep records, which made Deputy Holmes angry. I was just glad to get the ring back. My parents bought it for my sixteenth birthday. Out of everything stolen, it had the most sentimental value. Although it would be nice to recover the rest of it. Having your stuff taken really sucks."

Yeah. That pretty much summed it up.

Racking my brain for something else to ask, I glanced at the clock over the mantel. Yikes. I was late. Time to clear out. "Thanks for your time. Would you mind if I contacted you again?"

"Stop by anytime. Do you want to pet Homer before you go? I think he likes you."

The feeling was mutual. I gave Homer a pat on the head, said good-bye to Betsy, and headed back into the cold, windy night feeling like Betsy and I might have just bonded over a raccoon. Was my life strange or what?

I cranked the heater and checked my phone for messages. Lionel hadn't called. At least, not that I could tell. The reception out in the middle of the cornfields and soybeans was unreliable at best.

Tooling down to Lionel's place, I tried to decide if I'd ever heard the names Mark and Amy Jo Boggs before. Nope. Totally unfamiliar to me, which meant they weren't part of Pop's social circle and they didn't come skating at the rink. Since they were willing to feed Betsy's horses, I was guessing they had livestock of their own. That meant they'd need a vet. I just hoped that vet wasn't angry with me for being late, meaning I wouldn't get a chance to pump him for information.

I pulled into Lionel's empty driveway and parked next to the house. Since even in the dim light Lionel's testosterone truck was impossible to hide, I was certain I'd gotten here first.

Climbing out of my car, I looked up at Lionel's house. The front porch light was on. It gave the green-and-white farmhouse a warm and inviting feel. Lionel had given me a key a few weeks ago—not long after my decision to pull the rink off the market and stay in Indian Falls. He said I could use the key if ever I needed a place to get away. Thus far, my key had gone unused. To use it implied a commitment level I wasn't entirely comfortable with—even now, when using it wouldn't imply anything other than sensibly getting out of the cold misty rain. Fortunately, I had another sensible option.

Huddled in my coat, I walked down the gravel path that led to Lionel's barn. This was better anyway, I thought as I opened the door and stepped into the warm, musky air, since the barn was home to my favorite four-legged friend, Elwood the camel.

The light was dim in the barn, and I squinted into the shadows. *Aha.* I heard the rustle of hay underfoot as the camel in question trotted down the center aisle of the barn wearing a Pilgrim's hat made out of black-and-white construction paper. At some point, Elwood had been part of a Blues Brothers circus act. His Jake died, and Elwood got sad. He gave up the circus for a home with Lionel, but he refused to give up the hats.

Elwood bumped my shoulder with his nose. This was a camel looking for attention, and I was more than happy to oblige. Careful not to dislodge his hat, I patted his flank, scratched under his chin, and rubbed his cheek. My ministrations were rewarded with happy camel noises.

I grinned. Life didn't get any better than petting a happy camel.

"Your hat is looking a little worse for wear," I said to Elwood, giving him one last pat. The construction paper was coming unglued at the top of the hat, and the brim had detached on one side. This was a problem. Elwood didn't like being without a hat. It made him cranky. Cranky camels spit. Hunting up a spare hat seemed like a good way to avoid a large dry-cleaning bill. "Maybe we should find you an Indian headdress or something."

"I'm saving the feather headdress for Thanksgiving Day."

I whipped around as Lionel strode across the barn toward me. I had just enough time to appreciate his long stride and the lines of his angular face before being yanked into his arms and kissed. My toes curled as his mouth slanted over mine, and little streaks of pleasure zinged up and down my spine. Lionel was a great kisser. It made me wonder how thus far I'd resisted enthusiastically jumping into his bed.

Lionel pulled back and gave me a slow, sexy smile. "Mrs. Rittle's first-grade class is going to be crushed to hear you don't like the hat they made for Elwood." Lionel walked over to a chest near the front door and rummaged through it. He pulled out an Elmer Fudd–style hunting cap and held it out to me. "Do you want to do the honors?"

Picturing flying camel saliva, I shook my head and took three steps back. Lionel laughed and with great efficiency removed the dilapidated Pilgrim chapeau, replacing it with the new one. Elwood snorted, but no spit. Success!

Pitching the paper hat into the trash, Lionel said, "Thanks for coming over. I hope you haven't been waiting too long. I know

I'm later than expected. Mrs. Pendley's dog went into labor as I was packing up, so I helped get Shadow comfortable and delivered the first puppy."

I smiled at the idea of a new, fuzzy puppy. Then I noticed a smear of something on the back of Lionel's hand. Ick! Lionel noticed it, too, and shrugged. "Give me a minute to take a shower. Then I'll feed you."

Worked for me.

Hand in hand, we walked toward the back of the barn, which Lionel had renovated after he bought the property. Now it boasted a full bath, which Lionel disappeared into. There was also a recreation room complete with a leather couch, an entertainment system, and a refrigerator perpetually stocked with beer, soda, and other goodies. The room was home to a weekly poker game that I had crashed when I first blew into town. Because Danielle needed me to help stuff purple feathers and sparkly gold swirly sticks into glass bowls that would serve as centerpieces for the tables at her wedding reception, I hadn't been able to attend last Thursday's game. Clearly, none of the guys who did attend stuck around to clean up. Pretzel and chip bags littered the floor. An empty pizza box sat open in the middle of the poker table, as did a bunch of crumpled napkins and more than a few beer bottles.

Since the couch was filled with debris, I shelved the idea of relaxing and started one of my least favorite activities—cleaning. By the time Lionel appeared in a fresh pair of jeans and a green button-down shirt, I had filled two bags with a variety of garbage, including a truly ugly potbellied pig-shaped ashtray that I'd wanted to ditch for months. What Lionel didn't know wouldn't hurt him.

"Sorry about the mess," Lionel said, plucking a piece of pretzel off the carpet. "The game didn't break up until after three. I meant to clean up this weekend, but things have been busier than expected."

I'd never seen Lionel blush. Funny, but I found his embarrassment endearing.

He took a half-filled garbage bag from me and gave me a light kiss. "I really owe you for cleaning up this mess."

"Good, because I need help with a project, and I'm not sure you're going to like it." Lionel's eyes lost the flustered haze. Before he could ask about my new venture and potentially forget about going for food, I said, "Why don't we talk about it over dinner? I'm starved."

There were only two restaurants open on a Sunday night in Indian Falls. One was the Hunger Paynes Diner, which was known for its greasy burgers, generous helpings of meat loaf, and ice cream confections. While a burger sounded great, the diner's acoustics encouraged eavesdropping. Since I didn't want half the town listening in on my conversation with Lionel, we headed for option number two—Papa Dom's Italian restaurant, which was situated on the far side of town. Papa Dom's was known for its fabulous tiramisu and award-winning red sauce. After the day I'd had, I was planning to indulge in both.

The restaurant was half filled with patrons when Lionel and I walked through the door. A brunette I was pretty certain I'd seen skating around the rink greeted Lionel and me at the podium and showed us to a booth in the back. Several people waved to us on the way to our table.

Once we were seated at the red-and-white checkered table, Lionel said, "Tell me about the project I'm going to be helping you with now. Then I'll know how much wine I need to order."

I probably should have been offended, but over the past couple of months I'd had more than my fair share of dangerous encounters. The potential need for copious amounts of alcohol was justified. So, instead of doing the injured female routine, I said, "Mrs. Johnson hired me to catch the Thanksgiving Day thief."

"And?"

No amusement. No anger. No reaction. Since I didn't know whether this was a good or a bad thing, I kept talking. "I stopped by Betsy Moore's place earlier and asked her about the break-in last year. She mentioned that Mark and Amy Jo Boggs helped take care of her horses while she was gone. I don't know them, so I thought you could fill me in on the pertinent details."

"Like whether I think they cleaned Betsy out?"

"That would be a good start." The hostess dropped off a basket of warm bread and a plate of seasoned olive oil. I tore off a hunk and dipped. "Betsy told them she was going to visit her folks in Miami over Thanksgiving."

"She also told me. Does that make me a suspect?"

"The thefts have been happening for ten years. You haven't lived here long enough. I don't know when the Boggses moved to town."

The waitress arrived and took our drink orders. I really wanted wine, but I figured I should keep a clear head, seeing as how I'd once again left the damn notebook in the car. I settled for a soda and took it as a good sign when Lionel ordered the same.

Leaning back, Lionel said, "From what I remember, Mark and Amy Jo moved here a year or two before I did. They raise pigs, grow corn, and are trying to adopt. I hope they do. Mark and Amy Jo are nice people."

The Boggses might be nice, but nice people had been known to do bad things. Running a farm was a healthy way of life, but rarely did it rake in the cash. Adoption was expensive.

"I know Sean questioned them last year when the thefts happened," Lionel added. "He questioned me, too. I wasn't able to tell him much. I'm guessing Mark and Amy Jo couldn't give him any leads either. You'll probably be wasting your time talking to them again."

Maybe, but it was my time to waste. Besides, I had to start somewhere, and the idea of succeeding where Sean had failed was just too tempting to ignore.

Our waitress arrived with more bread—I'd eaten it all—and to take our orders. Once she disappeared, Lionel changed the subject. We were now in the official date portion of the evening. He told me about his day and asked about the shower. I filled him in on Ginny's departure and Danielle's wedding blues. I decided not to tell him about my run-in with Sean. Our food had just arrived. Talking about Sean might kill my appetite, and it would be a sin to waste Dom's eggplant Parmesan. Instead, I asked, "Have you decided what you're doing for Thanksgiving?"

Up until last week, Lionel had been planning on spending the holiday in the Chicago suburbs with his parents. Then his mother had a falling-out with his great-aunt Natalie over the best ingredients for the stuffing and the family dinner was called off. He'd been waiting to see whether a truce was declared and dinner reinstated.

"I think so. Do you have room for any more guests at your table?"

I winced at the thought of my own upcoming holiday adventure. Somehow Pop had volunteered me to cook Thanksgiving dinner. He did a song and dance about how we hadn't had a real family dinner in years. How he missed the tradition. How he might not have many years left. I caved. What other choice did I have? Besides, I rationalized, how hard could cooking for my father and my grandfather be? Well, since I'd asked that question the list of guests had somehow grown to include my godmother, Annette; two members of Pop's mariachi/Elvis band; and Danielle and Rich. Although I cooked a dish every month for the meeting of the Indian Falls Gourmet Club, when I was left to my own devices my typical culinary achievements were popcorn and leftover pizza. This combined with the fact that I'd never cooked a formal meal for more than two people made the likelihood that my holiday dinner would bear a strong resemblance to the one in *A Charlie Brown Thanksgiving* pretty high.

Since I knew Lionel had a fondness for buttered popcorn, I said, "Sure. I think I can add another chair to the table." Maybe Lionel could help me keep the madness to a minimum.

Lionel took my hand and caressed my palm with his thumb. Now that I had eaten, I realized I was hungry for something else. Maybe tonight would be *the* night. He gave me one of his lazy smiles and asked, "Could you add a couple more?"

I blinked. "Are some of your college buddies coming to town?"

"No." His green eyes met mine. "My parents are."

Four

The soda I'd been swallowing lodged in my throat. I coughed.
I gasped. I wheezed. My eyes watered. Lionel didn't seem fazed.
He leaned over, whacked me on the back, and handed me a glass
of water.

I took a large drink, coughed one last time, and asked, "Your
parents are coming here for Thanksgiving?"

Maybe all the bread I'd consumed had caused me to go into a
gluten-induced shock. A visit to the hospital and lots of invasive
tests sounded far preferable to a visit from Lionel's folks. Not that
I had anything against them. I didn't. I'd never met them—and
while I was sure they were perfectly nice people, I wasn't interested in changing that anytime in the near future. Meeting parents
was a big deal. Cooking for parents, especially when I wasn't sure
of success, was even bigger. Plus, of course, spending holidays
with them implied a commitment level I wasn't sure I was ready to
admit to.

"My great-aunt threatened to disown anyone who didn't come

to her house this year for dinner. Aunt Natalie wanted Mom to bring her stuffing and allow the family to vote on which is superior. I've eaten my aunt's stuffing. Trust me, she would have lost. But my parents were given a stay of familial execution if they came to visit me. So, to avoid further family discord, Mom decided she and Dad are coming here for Thanksgiving. They're both excited to meet you."

Gulp. "I'm excited to meet them, too," I said, crossing my fingers under the table. It was childish, but it made me feel better about lying.

The waitress arrived with refills of our drinks. As she efficiently removed one glass and slid another into its place, I told myself not to panic. When the waitress disappeared, I had almost convinced myself this whole meet-the-parents thing was routine for Lionel's family. I mean, Lionel was in his midthirties. He'd dated lots of women over the years. This was going to be a piece of cake.

Forking up a piece of eggplant, I said, "Your parents have probably met a lot of your girlfriends, so this isn't all that big a deal. Right?"

"My parents met several of the girls I was involved with in the past." Lionel gave me one of his toe-curling smiles. I let out a sigh of relief and shoved food into my mouth, feeling pretty good about the whole thing. Then he added, "You're the first girlfriend my family has met since I moved to Indian Falls and decided this is where I want to settle down. Up until now, no one has mattered enough. You matter." The sexy look in his eyes was gone, replaced by one that was dead serious. I'd seen that look in Danielle's eyes when she fell in love with Rich and was hoping he'd propose. Most girls would jump for joy over that look. I was going to hurl.

Lucky for my clenching stomach and the other diners, Lionel changed the subject to something less nauseating if equally scary—my father. "I saw Stan earlier today. He wanted to know if I'd let him use my farm for location shoots. I didn't know your father was interested in photography."

My father was interested in anything that could be turned into a profit. Fake archaeological finds. Hot Chinese musical instruments. Stan would sell anything that fell off, or looked like it had the potential to fall off, the back of a truck. When I was a kid, my father traveled around the country, peddling whatever product he'd decided was going to be the next big thing. When I was nine, Dad took one of his trips in search of fame and fortune and didn't bother to come back. Growing up as the kid whose father had abandoned her spurred my desire to leave town and never return. Now I was back, and so was he. While much had changed, my father's dedication to the next get-rich-quick scheme hadn't diminished. This one involved cameras, locations, and lots of old people.

Sighing, I said, "Stan has started up his own modeling agency."

Lionel gaped. "Aren't modeling agencies typically located in or near cities?"

If they were actually making money by booking their clients, yes. Stan preferred charging for photographs, teaching classes, and talking a good game. Since I felt disloyal saying that aloud, I opted for "Stan thinks that the modeling world doesn't have enough interesting senior citizen faces to choose from and that the powers-that-be are willing to foot the bill for travel expenses in order to tap into a new talent pool."

"Do you think he's right?"

I thought there was a better chance of the Ice Capades performing in hell. "I guess time will tell."

"Who knows." Lionel laughed. "This time your dad might be onto something."

Oh, he was onto something, all right. I was just hoping he would leave me and my grandfather out of it.

By the time I climbed into Lionel's truck, my stomach was so full I could hardly breathe, let alone move. I definitely shouldn't have had the tiramisu, but no one turned down Dom's tiramisu. Especially not when Dom himself brought it to your table because you reminded him of his granddaughter.

Tomorrow, I was going to have to do dozens of laps around the rink to work off the calories. Otherwise, I'd risk not fitting into my maid of honor dress. Popping seams in front of the entire town wasn't my idea of a good time. As it was, Danielle was already obsessing over every detail of how I'd look. She'd picked out the shoes and the jewelry; she'd even booked an appointment for me tomorrow with Annette so she could see how different hairstyles would look. The woman needed Valium.

Although, now that I thought about it, the appointment with Annette was a fortunate coincidence. I would be able to question her about the thefts while she snipped, fluffed, and teased. Multi-tasking at its finest. Now I just had to figure out what a real private investigator would ask and I'd be set.

Hopping out of Lionel's truck, I turned to ask him what questions he'd ask and found my words cut off by his mouth. It was a hell of a mouth, too. The temperature might have been approaching freezing, but the way he nibbled on my bottom lip made me feel downright toasty. The minute he stepped back, I started to shiver. Either it was that cold or Lionel was that warm. When he nudged me toward his front porch, I decided science required an answer to that question and followed him up the steps and into his living room.

Since I'd come to Indian Falls almost seven months ago, Lionel and I had both danced away from acting on the chemistry between us. Me because I was planning on selling the rink and moving back to the city. Him because of my unwillingness to take the rink off the market and vow to stay put. Now that I'd decided to remain in town, Lionel was full steam ahead, and the way his hands peeled away my puffy white jacket and began exploring the body underneath made me wonder why I'd ever thought we should wait.

The jacket hit the floor. I unzipped Lionel's battered leather coat, and it joined mine on the ground.

Lionel's mouth trailed down my neck, making my body hum. His mouth was hot. His fingers slipping under my sweater, rubbing circles on the small of my back and dipping lower, were magic. We were standing here clothed, and the man couldn't have been sexier.

Okay. I was wrong. My fingers unbuttoned Lionel's shirt, revealing the hard, smooth lines of his chest. His mouth captured my bottom lip and tugged on it, ripping a gasp from my throat. Then, fingers entwined with mine, he led me toward the stairs.

This was it. If I wanted to put the brakes on, now was the time to do it. I had to make a decision. Did I want to sleep with Lionel and take the next, relationship-changing step? Or did I want to be smart and wait to sleep with him until I knew what my feelings were? I cared about Lionel. The way my body was tingling from his touch confirmed the attraction level. Lionel wanted more than affection and chemistry, though. He wanted picket fences and family. I wanted . . .

Nope. I had no idea what the hell I wanted.

Stopping in the doorway of Lionel's bedroom, I stared at the king-sized four-poster bed. A wave of panic hit me, followed by a wave of longing as Lionel's mouth worked its way from my neck to my lips. When his hands worked their way under my sweater, I had trouble forming a coherent thought. Which was okay, I decided, as I wrapped my arms around Lionel and held on tight. Thinking was overrated.

Wow.

I propped my head on Lionel's chest. His arm snaked around my shoulders and pulled me against his side. Just wow. Up until today, I'd only done the mattress machinations with two guys. Both promised to take me to the stars. Neither brought me to the promised destination before his rocket lost steam. The experiences led me to believe sex was not only overrated, it was downright boring.

Boy, was I wrong. Lionel's rocket not only got off the ground, it circled around the moon several times before coming in for a landing. My muscles were loose, my mind clear. I couldn't remember the last time I'd felt so good.

The sound of Lionel's heartbeat lulled me toward the haze of sleep. My fingers entwined with his. Vaguely, I wondered again why I'd waited so long to do something so fabulous with a guy this wonderful.

"I love you, Becky."

That's why.

I jumped as if I'd been bitten in the ass. Love had a way of doing that.

"Hmm . . ." I grunted and took slow breaths, hoping Lionel would think I was asleep. Asleep meant I could pretend he'd never said it. He would think I'd never heard those words. He wouldn't expect me to tell him how I felt about them, which was good because I doubted the right response to that declaration was hyperventilation.

To avoid the need for a paper bag, I slowly breathed in and out and worked hard to keep my expression slack. I even added some drool to the mix. When I was a kid, I did the possum routine all the time. Mom never questioned it. Maybe Lionel wouldn't question it now.

After several very long minutes, Lionel's breathing slowed and deepened. The arm around me loosened its grip until, finally, I was certain Lionel slept.

Hallelujah.

Careful not to jostle him, I slipped out of bed, ducked into the master bathroom, and locked the door behind me. Wrapping a towel around my body, I sat on the edge of the bathtub and put a hand on my jittery stomach. I needed to get a grip and think. In the past, Lionel had danced around the L-word. Now that he had said it aloud, I wasn't sure what to do about it. Chemistry was one thing. Love was something very different. I'd never been in love with a capital *L*. Not unless you counted the time Connor Sheppard gave me his last piece of Halloween candy when we were in the first grade. I mean, what girl could resist a snack-sized Snickers?

This wasn't elementary school, though. Heck, this wasn't even a college crush on the sexy debate team guy who used his powers of persuasion to talk me out of my clothes. This was Lionel. A man who was not only a great kisser but one of my closest friends. While I didn't want to lose the kissing benefits, I would hate to lose my friend more. Love made people do wacky things. Love created expectations. Those expectations meant people could get hurt. Badly. My ex-boss Neil proved that months ago. His belief that he was in love with me caused both emotional and physical injuries. And look at my former roommate, Jasmine. The phone call I'd received two weeks ago involved lots of tears, loud shouting, and even louder sounds of breaking glass. Jasmine didn't cope well with breakups.

Love, or unreturned love, could cause pain. I didn't want to hurt Lionel. Without having ever been in love, I was totally unqualified to understand my own feelings or deal with his. This could be very, very bad.

Of course, I thought, it could also be good. I mean, Lionel was smart. He was handsome, stable, and kind to animals. Heck, he even liked my grandfather—spandex, sequins, and all. Lionel was exactly the kind of guy I'd hoped to fall in love with. Who knows? Maybe I was in love and I just wasn't experienced enough with relationships to know it. If so, there was no need to panic.

Tiptoeing back into the bedroom, I slid under the covers and turned to look at Lionel's handsome face. What I needed was a sign. Something to tell me that I was in love. Lightning striking. A rooster crowing. Anything.

Lionel's eyes blinked open. "Can't sleep?" he asked.

"Guess not."

His mouth curled into a smile, and he pulled me close. "Well, let's see if we can't fix that."

Yowzah. Talk about a sign.

. . .

The problem with spending the night in a strange bed is that upon waking you have to deal with a strange toothbrush. It didn't matter that I'd swapped more than saliva with Lionel last night; the thought of using his toothbrush totally wigged me out.

After using my fingers and a wad of toothpaste, I went in search of the sweater I'd worn yesterday. Hmm . . . the sweater was wrinkled, dotted with red sauce, and ripped at the neckline where it had gotten caught on my watch. Not exactly the fashion statement I was going for. Figuring Lionel wouldn't mind my borrowing something of his, I slid on a deep purple dress shirt, tied it in a knot at my waist, and went in search of the shirt's owner.

The note on the table told me he was called away due to a heifer emergency and he would call me later. I felt a flood of both disappointment and relief that the note wasn't signed with the L-word. Was I screwed up or what?

Pulling on my puffy white coat, I grabbed my purse and ruined sweater and walked to my car. Yesterday, the weatherman had said today was going to be sunny and above freezing. The weatherman lied. Arctic wind howled. Sleet fell from the gray sky. By the time I opened the car door and slid inside, my teeth were chattering. Reminding myself I needed to buy a new pair of gloves, I slid my key into the ignition, cranked the heat, and waited until I could see past my frosty breath in order to drive.

I'd finally stopped shivering by the time I climbed out of my car and strolled across the parking lot of the Toe Stop Roller Rink. Every morning, I checked in with my unofficial rink manager, George. At least twice a week, I asked George to delete the unofficial from the title. For some reason, he was willing to handle most of the rink's day-to-day operations but refused to accept the moniker or pay raise that went along with it. George was afraid of commitment. I thought back to Lionel's declaration last night and felt my mind go fuzzy. Yep. George wasn't the only one with a fear of permanency.

The *Phantom of the Opera* soundtrack was blaring when I walked through the rink doors. George waved from the middle of the floor as Missy Boys did cross pulls to pick up speed. She approached the far end of the rink and then kicked her free foot forward and leaped off the ground. One and a half rotations in the air later, she landed on two feet before smashing to the ground.

Ouch.

George zipped to where she had fallen, made sure she was okay, and then watched her climb upright before he told her to try it again. Two weeks ago, George had convinced me to set up a big-screen television on the sidelines so everyone could watch the World Roller Figure Skating Championships. Since figure skating wasn't exactly a national pastime, I figured the rink would be empty. Imagine my surprise when the place was packed. I was even more stunned when George announced he was starting a figure skating club in order to train students to compete at the national level next year. So far, he had two dozen students working toward that goal. Missy was one of them.

Double ouch. Missy skidded face-first across the floor.

I winced, then watched with admiration as she scrambled back onto her wheels and immediately launched herself into the routine again. If all of George's students had her determination, the skating club would do well when they started competition in the spring. Only time would tell.

The music ended. Missy rolled to the sidelines for water and splinter removal. I waved to her and yelled to George, "Do you need me to handle anything this morning?"

"Not that I can think of." George executed a perfect T-stop in front of me. "I have three more private lessons before open session this afternoon. Oh, and Kristin Chapman's mom called to tell us Kristin can't work this week. Which is understandable, considering."

I blinked. "Considering what?"

"Considering what happened yesterday?" George frowned. When I didn't respond, he put his hand on his hip and stared at me harder.

Oh my God!

My cheeks started to burn as I thought about what had happened yesterday and once this morning. Had someone noticed my car at Lionel's place? Did the entire town know I was sleeping with him? Did Kristin's mother think I was a bad role model for her daughter?

The urge to stammer and run from the room was strong, kind of like the time my mother caught me and Michael Markson making out behind the snack counter.

When I didn't say anything, George sighed. "Kristin is Ginny Chapman's granddaughter. Kristin is going to watch her brothers and sisters while her mother makes the funeral arrangements."

Oh. My stomach clenched with sympathy. I knew what Kristin's mother was going through. A year and a half ago, I had to bury my mom. Not a day went by that I didn't wish for one more moment with her.

"Tell Kristin to take off as much time as she needs. Do you want me to cover her shifts?"

48

George shook his head. "You can't catch the Thanksgiving Day thief if you always have to be here. I've got it covered."

I was about to ask how he knew about my investigation of the thefts when the "Wedding March" blared from my cell phone.

The bride-to-be was calling and bubbling with happiness. Or maybe it was hysteria. Sometimes the two were hard to tell apart—especially when the person on the phone was speaking so fast she forgot to breathe.

Before I could ask her to slow down, Danielle said something about her mother-in-law and needing to change the appointment at Annette's. "Annette only has one time she can see us."

"Which is when?" I asked, taking advantage of Danielle's need to gasp oxygen.

"Well . . . um . . . now. See you in a few minutes."

Click.

Oy. Part of me wanted to call Danielle back and tell her I couldn't make it. After all, I had a life. I had responsibilities. Just because I signed on to wear an ugly dress didn't mean I had to drop my plans at a moment's notice. Of course, my righteous indignation would be better served if I actually had any plans to drop. Since my only plan was to question Annette about her unfortunate part in the Thanksgiving thefts, I didn't have much to complain about.

Yelling to George that I'd be back later, I shoved my hands into my pockets and headed back into the cold.

Shear Highlights was located a couple of blocks away on the north side of town. Annette had opened the place when I was in high school with the money she'd inherited from her great-aunt Alma. Mom had worried about Annette sinking every cent into the place. She'd thought it would be safer for Annette to open something smaller and save money for a rainy day. Annette thanked my mother for her concern and then turned around and bought not only the shop but the entire building. Annette said Aunt Alma would have approved. Since Alma's final moments involved a deep-sea diving expedition and a cranky shark, I was pretty sure Annette was right. Caution didn't rate high on Alma's list. Until I moved back to Indian Falls, I thought being careful rated high on mine. Of course, that was before the dead bodies, the exploding cars, and a sexy vet with incredible hands.

Thinking about those incredible hands was probably what distracted me as I walked into Indian Falls' only salon. Had I not been remembering the way he made my toes curl, I probably would have noticed the large purple roller before it hit me upside the head.

Five

"Direct hit, and there's more where that came from, you thief."

I turned toward the crackly voice and ducked. A large yellow comb sailed over my head and smacked into the wall behind me.

"Hey," I yelped as a group of senior women glared at me from under three industrial-sized dryers. Too bad my protest was drowned out by a shriek of "Get her!"

Yikes.

Pink and purple foam curlers flew from all directions. A gob of green goo splatted across the front of my puffy white jacket. Then another. Which is why I did the only thing any self-respecting person could do. I hid.

Diving behind the currently unoccupied receptionist podium, I yelled for everyone to stop. The curlers and combs kept flying. Whoever said aerosol hair spray was dangerous was right. These women had clearly OD'd on the stuff.

"Stop. Stop. Stop," a sweet but firm voice demanded.

"Violet—put down that brush this instant. You could hurt someone with it. What do you think you're doing?"

Now that the primping projectiles had halted, I braved a glance around the podium. Tiny Ethel Jacabowski stood in the center aisle, wagging a finger at her fellow salon customers. At least, I thought it was Ethel. The silver foil sticking out of her hair and the black smock around her neck made her look more like Frankenstein's grandmother than the woman I'd talked with yesterday.

A woman I assumed must be Violet put down a silver roller brush and frowned. "Nan said Rebecca was the Thanksgiving Day thief and we should all call the cops."

"I never said that." Nan ducked out from under a dryer and shook her curler-coated head. "You shouldn't eavesdrop on other people's conversations, Vi, especially when you're under the dryer with your hearing aid turned off. I was telling Ethel that Rebecca was going to catch the Thanksgiving Day thief and beat the cops." Nan gave me a small smile. "Sorry about the misunderstanding, dear. I hope you won't tell your grandfather."

Nan was one of Pop's admirers. She'd even taken up roller skating in order to snag him. A choice the rink's bank account appreciated even if my grandfather had failed to notice.

"I won't tell Pop," I assured her. I was about to ask her about her theft when I noticed the foam curlers in her hand. "But if you knew I wasn't the thief, why were you throwing things at me?"

"I thought this was a new wedding tradition like throwing rice. I didn't want to be left out."

I was about to point out that this wasn't a church and I wasn't the bride when Annette came hurrying out of the back of the salon. "What's going on out here? What happened to Michelle?"

Michelle was Annette's newest hire. From the look in my god-mother's eyes, I was guessing the HELP WANTED sign wouldn't be collecting dust for long.

"Michelle needed a smoke." Ethel took a seat in one of the red vinyl chairs and picked up an issue of *Cosmo*. "We told her we'd hold down the fort until she got back."

The bell on the door jingled, and the girl in question walked in. She took one look at Annette's face, glanced down at the curler-laden floor, and went racing for a broom. My assailants shrugged and went back to whatever they'd been doing before I walked through the door.

When Michelle returned with cleaning supplies and a contrite expression, Annette sighed and motioned for me to follow her down the salon's center aisle. "I'm sorry about your jacket. I should have known better than to leave Michelle alone with that group, but Danielle was so upset, I had to take her into the back to calm her down. Give me your coat. I'll run it over to the dry cleaners while you talk to Danielle. She's through there."

I handed the jacket to Annette, who gave me a firm shove into the back room before bolting toward the front of the salon. Sitting at a small table was the not-so-blushing bride-to-be. In her hands was a wadded-up tissue. Her hair was tangled, and her feet were sporting zebra-striped stilettos. Uh-oh.

"What's wrong?" I asked, sliding into the metal folding chair across from her.

Danielle looked at me with puffy eyes and a bright, albeit de-ranged, smile. "Wrong? Why do you think something's wrong?"

I pointed to her shoes, and Danielle's shoulders slumped as the shell of bravado disappeared. "This wedding is cursed."

"Just because someone died in the building where you were

having your wedding shower doesn't mean your wedding is cursed." At least I hoped not. The only thing I knew about curses involved voodoo dolls made out of Popsicle sticks.

"You're right, but losing a bridesmaid a week and a half before the wedding does."

"A bridesmaid died?" Yikes. While I didn't believe in curses, I was tempted to take several steps back. Death wasn't all that high on my bucket list.

"I wish." Danielle sniffled. "Rich's second cousin Sherilyn decided not to come to the wedding. She moved to Tibet in a quest for peace and harmony." The sniffle turned into a snarl. "Harmony couldn't have waited until after she'd worn her dress and walked down the aisle?"

I'd seen the dresses. As far as I was concerned, Sherilyn had made a good choice. Unfortunately, unless I wanted to move to Tibet, the only way I was going to find peace was to help Danielle with her crisis. "Just get married with one less bridesmaid."

Problem solved.

Or not.

Tears filled Danielle's big brown eyes, and her lip started to tremble. "I can't. Rich's mother said her family has always believed that a wedding must have an even number of attendants or risk inviting evil spirits into the marriage."

"So make one of the groomsmen an usher."

"Rich's mother says I'd cause irreparable damage to the family if I demoted one of Rich's cousins."

Rich's mother was starting to annoy me.

"Then ask someone else."

"Who?" A lone tear streaked down Danielle's face. "Most of my former friends are . . . dancers. I can't ask them. Not unless I want the church ladies to lynch me. Besides, they would never fit into Sherilyn's dress. I called Tilly at the dress shop, and she said she doesn't have time to do major alterations. So unless we can find an almost-six-foot-tall, large-chested woman who doesn't mind being second choice, my marriage is doomed."

"What about Erica the Red?"

Danielle looked up at me with horror. Or maybe it was hope. The suggestion to invite a Roller Derby girl with a penchant for tattoos into a Lutheran minister's wedding party could evoke either reaction. Now that I'd suggested it, I kind of liked the idea.

Aside from me, the other members of the wedding party had all been selected in an effort to please Rich's mother. Which meant they didn't know or didn't like Danielle—something they'd made very clear at the bridal shower they'd thrown a couple weeks ago. However, Erica and the rest of the EstroGenocide team were actually people Danielle hung out with. To top it off, not only would Erica fulfill the dress requirements, but she could body-check Rich's mother if the woman came up with any more doom-and-gloom predictions. Was I maid of honor of the year or what?

Before Danielle could think about what her mother-in-law would say, I pulled out my phone and dialed. Erica picked up on the first ring. "Hey, Coach."

I sighed. "I'm not your coach." At the moment, that job belonged to a very enthusiastic George.

"No." Erica laughed. "But 'rink owner' doesn't exactly roll off the tongue during team announcements. So Typhoon Mary decided we should call you Coach. Of course, if you pick a derby name, we can skip the whole coach thing."

Much to my dismay, I had attempted to come up with a derby name only to find that all the names I liked were already taken by real derby girls. Since I wasn't skating on the team, I'd given up on finding a name—something I'd have to readdress when I had hours to scour the Roller Derby Name Registry. For the sake of Danielle's wedding and my Thanksgiving investigation, I was just going to have to settle for Coach.

"One of Danielle's bridesmaids bailed on the wedding. Can you fill in?"

"Hell yeah." Erica let out a booming laugh. "Do I get to bring a date?"

"Bring whomever you'd like." If Danielle didn't want to pay for the extra seating, I would. How much could the caterers charge for a plate of cardboard-flavored chicken?

"Awesome. Tell me what you need me to do and I'll do it."

Since Danielle still looked torn between joy and dismay, I instructed Erica to meet us at Nothing Borrowed Nothing Blue later in the day to try on the dress. I hung up as Annette blew threw the door.

"Your coat will be ready by the time we're done picking hairstyles. They're going to bring it over." Annette put on her smock and smiled. "Are we ready to get to work?"

We both turned to Danielle. She closed her eyes and took several deep, long breaths. A tear leaked down her cheek, and guilt churned my stomach.

Eek! Maybe I'd gotten a little too carried away with fixing Danielle's problem. I wanted to help make Danielle's wedding better, not ruin the entire thing. Weddings were important. Just because I wasn't sure I ever wanted to have one of my own didn't mean I didn't understand that. I had to fix this. Now.

"I can call Erica back and tell her I made a mistake," I said, pulling my phone out of my pocket. "I'll tell her I misunderstood."

Danielle's eyes snapped open, and she snatched the phone out of my hand before my finger could press SEND. "Don't you dare! I'm crying because I'm relieved—and the best part is I can honestly tell Rich's mother I had nothing to do with inviting Erica. You are the best maid of honor."

Two hours later, I was ready to ditch my title. My hair had been washed, set, curled, pinned, sprayed, and pulled so tight my eyes looked as if I'd just had Botox. My hair wasn't merely teased, it was seriously pissed off. Worse, Danielle hadn't liked a single style Annette had tried. The upside was, if Danielle kept this up, I wouldn't have enough hair left to style and we could all go home.

Sitting at the back of the salon, trying to ignore the looks coming from the clients up front, I decided to concentrate on my other problem—tracking down a thief. "Annette, I had no idea you had your house robbed five years ago. Mom never mentioned it."

Annette poked me with a bobby pin and sighed. "Probably because whoever the thief was didn't take much. That's why I thought it was my two-timing ex, Keith Brennan. He was pissed I'd broken up with him after I caught him fogging up the windows of Valerie Parra's Ford Escort. The man had the nerve to say my work schedule made him feel neglected."

She shifted my head to the right and shrugged. "When I found both my house and salon had been broken into, I figured he had to be behind it. I mean, who else would break into a place just to swipe hair products, a few knickknacks, and a jar of spare change? Unfortunately, when Sean questioned Keith, he learned the jerk had an alibi, which meant the Thanksgiving thief was behind both robberies."

"The thief broke into the salon?" That seemed like something I should write down. For once I'd remembered to bring the notebook with me. Too bad the red plastic cape I was wearing prevented me from doing anything with it.

"The thief found my extra set of keys on the kitchen counter." Annette twisted a lock of my hair and looked over at Danielle, who shook her head. Sighing, Annette untwisted my hair and continued talking. "It was a good thing I put most of my smaller valuables in the trunk of my car before I left town for the holiday. The other people hit that Thanksgiving weren't so lucky."

Crap. I'd left the list of victims in my car. "Who else was hit that year?"

"Autumn and Jeremy Gullifer."

I ransacked my memory and came up blank.

Annette must have seen my confusion, because she said, "They live in the old Bower place. Autumn's an artist. She makes custom stained-glass windows and pottery. She had a booth at the St. Mark's Women's Guild craft fair the weekend before the theft and was in Moline the weekend before. With all the holiday bustle, she and Jeremy never had a chance to get to the bank to deposit the money. The thief walked away with several thousand dollars in cash."

Wow. My mother took a pottery class when I was in high school. The result was a brown and green vase that leaned precariously to the left. Something told me Autumn was a better craftsman than Mom.

"Did you tell anyone that you weren't going to be home for Thanksgiving that year?"

58

"A few of my customers asked if I had someplace to spend the holiday. After my breakup with Keith, I think they were worried I'd be eating processed turkey sandwiches alone at home." Annette grabbed the curling iron and began attacking the left side of my head.

I sat up a little straighter. "Do you remember who asked you about your plans?"

Danielle made an unhappy noise. The women up front stopped talking as they watched to see what would happen next. Annette sighed, put down the curling iron, and attacked my hair with a brush. Yeouch.

Finally, she put the brush down, poured some familiar-looking green goop into her hands, and continued talking. "I gave Sean a list of the clients who were scheduled to get their hair done. I imagine he still has it, but I can honestly say I don't remember which clients asked about my plans. The day before a holiday is always so busy it's hard to remember exactly who said what. To make matters worse, one of my suppliers showed up that day with a delivery, most of which was wrong. The supplier wasn't happy to learn about the mistake, or that the thief had helped himself to several of the boxes before it could be remedied."

"What was in the boxes?" I asked.

"Four mobile tanning kits, a dozen heated booties, and a case of aerosol hair spray."

"That's it!" Danielle's shout made Annette and me jump. "That's the perfect style for Rebecca and the rest of my bridesmaids."

I looked at the mirror and blinked. Other than being so filled with products that a strong wind couldn't move it, my hair looked exactly the way it had when I'd walked into the salon that day.

"Are you sure?" Annette asked. "I thought you said you wanted your bridesmaids to wear their hair up."

Danielle shook her head. "My mother-in-law was the one who wanted that. I was going to go along, but Rebecca reminded me that this is my wedding. What I want goes." The gleam in her eyes made me want to duck for cover. When Danielle got that look, scarecrows went up in smoke. This wasn't good.

Before I could say anything, Annette whipped off my cape and escorted Danielle up front to the manicurist's station to consult with Michelle on color choices. Grabbing my notebook out of my purse, I scribbled down the information Annette had given me. While considering my next investigative move, I studied my hair in the mirror.

Huh. Maybe I'd judged the style too quickly. Now that I really looked at it, I noticed the wave Annette had added. She had also encouraged one lock to skim across my forehead just above my right eye, which looked kind of sexy. Ever since high school I'd been called cute, spunky, and sometimes, on a really good day, pretty. Sexy was never on the list. Straightening my shoulders, I gave my head a toss—and sighed. Hair that didn't move wasn't sexy. It was downright creepy.

Making a note to take a shower before I saw Lionel, I grabbed my stuff and headed to the front of the salon, where Danielle was receiving wedding advice from several of Annette's clients.

"The silver polish will look wonderful with a white dress." This from a lovely older woman with tightly wound white curls.

Ethel shook her now perfectly styled head. "Mauve will give you a pop of color without making you look like a harlot."

"Men like harlots." Sweet-voiced Nan winked at Danielle. "Go with Rascal Red. Just make sure you file your nails down before the wedding night. I forgot to do that and made my poor Johnny bleed. The man was a tiger in bed. So don't be bashful about talking to me if you need any pointers."

"Or me," volunteered the white-haired lady. "My Matthew wasn't very big, but he knew how to use what God gave him."

A good maid of honor would rescue her friend from this trio of Dr. Ruth wannabes. I was making a break for it. My jacket still hadn't been returned, but one more word about Johnny's jackhammer move and I'd be psychologically scarred for life. Frostbite would be easier to treat.

Telling Danielle I'd see her at Erica's fitting, I put my head down and dashed into the icy wind. One good thing about living in Indian Falls was that its small size meant most businesses were located close together. So I was only partially frozen when I raced into Fast and Clean—the only dry cleaners located within a fifteen-mile radius.

The lack of competition meant job security and the customer base's willingness to put up with the company living up to only half of its name. Which is why I left the store with Mr. Bettis's flannel jacket and a promise my puffy white coat would be ready for pickup in twenty minutes. Enough time for me to stop for a quick snack at the DiBelka Bakery.

The bagels, croissants, and doughnuts were a bit picked over by the time I walked into the blissfully warm and fabulous-smelling bakery showroom. Still, the cinnamon coffee was fresh, and slices of apple coffee cake were on the counter for free sampling. Yum.

After scarfing down three pieces of cake, I selected a half-dozen Danishes to take to my next stop—the Indian Falls Sheriff's Department. Annette had said she'd given Sean the list of clients who had been in the salon the day before the theft. Sean wasn't the type to share information, but I was hoping his desperation for a break in the case combined with Mrs. DiBelka's award-winning pastries would loosen his tongue. If not, I'd have six Danishes to eat later. It was a win-win proposition.

Box in hand, I clutched my borrowed flannel jacket and raced to the building next door. No one knows if it was by design or chance that the DiBelka family established their bakery next door to the sheriff's department. Regardless of whether luck or business savvy played a role in the neighboring locations, both sides were delighted with the results. A cop's love of doughnuts was cliché, but Sean Holmes and the rest of the department staff proved clichés existed for a reason.

Teeth chattering, I pushed open the glass door, walked to the front desk, and peeked over the counter, looking for the receptionist, Roxy Moore. Since Indian Falls wasn't exactly a hotbed of criminal activity, Roxy used the downtime to practice her pedicure technique. Today, however, Roxy and her polished toes were nowhere in sight.

Buoyed by my good fortune, I walked down the hall to the offices, hoping my luck would hold and Sheriff Jackson would be seated at his desk. The sheriff wasn't always great at his job, but he tried. Better still, he liked me. He'd be more inclined to share information that Sean on principle kept to himself.

Drat. Sheriff Jackson's office was empty, but the light glowing from the office next door told me Deputy Holmes was in residence.

Taking a deep breath, I marched into Sean's office, took one look at his face, and fought the urge to flee. His cheeks were red. His eyes were narrowed. His hair was sticking straight up, or it would be when he stopped raking his hand through it in frustration.

All around the room was paper. In piles on the desk. In the trash can. Sitting atop the three filing cabinets lined up against the far wall, and poking out of folders stacked up around the floor. The only thing not coated in paper was the computer that Sean was at the moment calling a string of very colorful names.

"Troubles?" I asked.

Sean jumped, sending a folder perched near his elbow careening to the floor. "Crap."

He leaned down and gathered the papers that had slid out of the folder and shoved them back inside. Without looking up, he asked, "Do you need something? I'm kind of busy here."

I leaned against the door frame and smiled. "Did you decide to take up origami? If so, I might remember how to make a dog. Jack Gatto showed me how in Algebra."

"Jack Gatto was a dog."

Since the person in question got two girls pregnant at the end of his senior year, I couldn't argue the point. "So what are you doing in here? Shouldn't you be saving the world from jaywalking?"

"I could write you a ticket now, if you'd like." Sighing, Sean ran a hand through his hair and looked around the room. "Roxy reorganized the sheriff's case files. I'm trying to put them back into some logical order while she's out sick. I don't know what she was thinking when she set up the new system. It doesn't make any sense."

Something told me logical order wasn't on the top of Roxy's priority list when creating the filing system. Roxy had a serious crush on Deputy Sean, one he either didn't notice or chose to turn a blind eye to. Ensuring that Sean had to enlist her help whenever he needed to find a file would give Roxy ample opportunity to flex her flirting muscles. Too bad Roxy had called in sick or she could be milking the helping-look-for-a-file routine right now.

Since my mother taught me manners, I felt compelled to ask, "Is there anything I can do to help?" Tracking down a paper shredder or creating a bonfire seemed like good options.

Thank goodness Sean turned down my request, which allowed me to circle back to my purpose in coming here. "Annette said she gave you a list of the clients who were in her salon the day before her house was broken into. Could I get a copy?"

Sean raised an eyebrow and gave a pointed look to the explosion of paper on his desk. "You want me to find a file for you?"

I smiled and held out the Danishes.

Sighing, Sean took the box and said, "Tell you what, if you can find the file on Annette's robbery, you can read it. It used to be filed under *R* for Robbery."

Made sense.

As Sean dove into the Danishes, I took off the flannel coat, pulled open the first filing drawer, and began to search. After a few minutes, Roxy's filing system became clear. Public nuisance reports were filed under *C* for Cow Tipping. Automobile accidents were in the *F* drawer for Fender Bender, and all drunk-and-disorderly records were listed under *P* for Pete's Pub.

Mildly disturbed that I was following Roxy's train of thought, I dove into the *T* drawer. Eureka! There were the case folders for the Thanksgiving Day robberies. I found the file devoted to Annette's break-ins, flipped to the list in question, and felt my pulse spike.

There in the middle of the list was a name I not only recognized but knew had been connected to other thefts over a dozen years ago. Thefts Sean and the sheriff's department knew nothing about.

I had my first suspect.

Six

I copied the list into my handy-dandy notebook, refiled the folder, and slammed the drawer closed with a satisfying thud. It was time to hit the road.

Grabbing my borrowed coat, I turned toward the door and found my path blocked by a baffled, Danish-holding Sean. "You found what you were looking for? How did you manage that?"

"Maybe it was my keen investigative skills," I quipped.

"More likely it was dumb luck."

I wanted to be offended, but Sean wasn't far off the mark.

"If I didn't know better," he said, brushing Danish crumbs off his shirt, "I'd have thought you and Roxy plotted this whole files debacle just to drive me crazy. As it is, you drive me crazy enough all on your own." He took a step closer. "You have a suspect. Who is it?"

"I don't know what you mean."

He smiled and took another step toward me. "Your eyebrow goes up when you're lying."

Crap. I'd been trying to control that. Apparently, all my practicing in the mirror had yet to pay off.

"That's okay," Sean said, taking another step closer. "I'll find out who it is eventually. Just remember, Rebecca . . ." His eyes met mine. Sweat prickled at the back of my neck. Sean reached out and tucked a plasticized strand of hair behind my ear. His smile vanished. "I'm watching you."

Yikes.

Skirting around Sean and the piles of folders strewn across the floor, I headed for the door.

"Oh, Rebecca."

I stiffened and turned. "Yes."

"Nice shirt."

I looked down, remembered I was wearing Lionel's shirt, and felt my cheeks start to burn. My archnemesis knew I'd had a sleepover with Lionel. I wanted to scream or say something pithy that would wipe off the smirk that I was certain was gracing Sean's handsome, albeit annoying, face. Instead, I did what any self-respecting girl would do.

I bolted.

My face was still hot when I exchanged the flannel coat for my puffy one. I was thankful the weather made everyone in the dry cleaners think I was cold instead of mortified. To avoid future embarrassment, I steered my car to the rink. A quick shower and change of clothes later and I'd almost convinced myself Sean was simply complimenting my sense of style. While my lying needed work, my denial skills were coming along nicely.

Now that my hair could move and my clothes weren't broadcasting my newly rejuvenated sex life, I headed to the north side of town, where I was certain I'd find the person I needed to question: Doc Truman's nurse and all-around girl Friday, Eleanor Schaffer.

Sure enough, Eleanor was exactly where I expected to find her—soothing sick patients and handing out lollipops in the reception area of Doc Truman's office. A little blond girl raced around the room, singing at the top of her lungs, while Eleanor talked to her harried mother about a follow-up appointment to make sure little Bianca was no longer contagious and could return to school. The girl in question shoved her fingers in her mouth and then proceeded to rub them on the table, two of the four waiting-area chairs, the counter, and her mother's jeans. Little Bianca was an epidemic waiting to happen.

Once Bubonic Bianca and her mother were safely out of my airspace, I sat on a chair untouched by Bianca's slobber-coated fingers and waited for Eleanor to escort the remaining patient back to see Doc Truman. When she returned five minutes later, she gave me a weak smile and dropped her ample body into one of the waiting-room chairs with a thud.

"What a day. Our part-time receptionist just quit, and almost every second grader in Mrs. Malarky's class has lice."

"Lice?" I reached up and touched my freshly washed hair.

Eleanor waved off my concern. "Just make sure none of the kids take skating lessons until they've been cleared to go back to school and you'll be fine." She squinted at me from behind her fake eyelashes. "Speaking of fine, what are you doing here? I hope you're not sick. Not with the wedding only a week and a half away."

"I'm good." Ignoring the desire to scratch my scalp, I said, "Mrs. Johnson hired me to look into the Thanksgiving Day thefts."

Eleanor smiled. "Ethel said something about that this morning when she called to ask if I'd heard anything about Ginny's funeral service. Everyone I've talked to is heartbroken about Ginny's passing. Especially since so many of us talked to her at Danielle's bridal shower just before she passed on. She was so happy and energetic, talking about her upcoming trip. I guess it just goes to show that you have to live every moment to the fullest because you just never know when you're going to go."

I thought back to the last conversation I had with my mother. Mom talked about the new improvements to the rink and how she planned on celebrating their completion by coming to visit me. She wanted to see a play, kayak down the Chicago River, and go shopping on Michigan Avenue. We were going to have an entire week to ourselves. The next day she was gone.

Tears lodged in my throat and burned the back of my eyes. I couldn't help it. Not a day went by that I didn't miss Mom and wish she hadn't left me alone.

Swallowing down the lump of emotion, I changed the subject back to one that wouldn't evoke tears. "I've been talking to the victims of the robberies. Annette mentioned you were in the salon the day before her house was broken into."

"I've had my hair done the day before Thanksgiving for twenty years." Eleanor smiled. "My appointment for next Wednesday was made six months ago. Good thing, too. The salon has been booked solid ever since your father got everyone dreaming about being in magazines. I have my photo shoot scheduled for this Friday."

Of course she did. Biting back a sigh, I reached into my purse and pulled out my notebook. "Do you remember hearing Annette say that she was going out of town for the holiday?"

"Sure. I was relieved that she was getting out of town before her rat of an ex-boyfriend could sweet-talk her into thinking about reconciliation."

"Did you talk about Annette's travel plans to anyone after you left the salon?"

"Lord, just about everyone was talking about Annette's breakup and wondering if she'd take the skunk back. Annette has great business sense but terrible taste in men. I remember telling Joey that I was relieved she was leaving town. If she hadn't, I might have suggested to Joey that he ask her out."

Bingo.

"Joey knew Annette was going away. Did he also know where Doc Truman and his wife were spending the Thanksgiving holiday when their house was broken into?"

"Well, of course he knew. I asked him to help me water their plants and let their dog, Rusty, out when . . ." Eleanor's eyes went wide. "You think my Joey is the Thanksgiving Day thief? Sheriff Jackson and Deputy Holmes never questioned him, let alone said he was a suspect."

That's because the sheriff and Sean didn't know what I knew. One night when I was fourteen, I couldn't sleep and went down to the rink, hoping to raid the snack bar. Instead of indigestion, I found seventeen-year-old Joey Schaffer with one hand in the cash register and a bag of Fritos in the other. Faced with an intruder, I did the only thing I could think to do. I grabbed a nearby broom, brandished it like a sword, and screamed, hoping my mother would hear the sound from our apartment.

She did.

Twenty minutes later, Eleanor and her husband were standing next to their youngest son, begging my mother not to call the cops. They didn't want one mistake to ruin his chances of college and a good future. The next day, my mother installed a new lock on the front door, and Joey was shipped off to live with his grandmother for senior year.

"They might if I told them about the theft at the rink."

Eleanor glanced at the door to Doc's office and whispered, "You're not going to tell them, are you?"

In movies, private detectives were smart. They were ruthless. They demanded the truth. I wasn't up to demanding. Especially not when faced with tears and a quivering lower lip.

Sighing, I said, "I don't want to cast suspicion on anyone unless I know they're behind the thefts, especially not Joey. I like him." At least I did when we were in high school. Our paths hadn't crossed much since I'd returned to Indian Falls. "Does he have an alibi for the thefts? If so, he's off the hook. If not . . ." I frowned.

Eleanor sucked in air. We stared at each other, waiting to see who would blink first.

Eleanor did. She looked down at her hands as a tear streaked down her face.

"He doesn't have alibis. Does he?"

"I don't know," she whispered. "When Bernie died twelve years ago, I started spending Thanksgiving at one of my daughters' houses. Joey never wants to go. He prefers to pay a visit to his dad's grave and spend the rest of the holiday alone. Everyone around here just assumes he goes with me. I've never said different. At first because it was no one's business but Joey's, and then because I was worried."

"Then he might have something to do with the robberies?"

"No. Yes. I don't know." Eleanor pushed out of the chair and grabbed a tissue from a box on the counter. "Joey's always been my quiet child. With five older sisters, he never had a chance to get a word into the conversation. He broke into your mother's rink because he wanted attention."

"He got it."

Eleanor sighed. "Yes, he did, and he never lost it. He lives rent-free. He has a good job. Joey would have no reason to break into anyone's home and steal." She turned and looked me dead in the eye. "I promise you, Rebecca, my boy isn't the person behind these crimes."

Conviction filled her voice. This wasn't the same tone she used when snowing kids into believing that a shot wasn't going to hurt. I should know. Growing up, I fell for that line every time.

No, this wasn't Eleanor's vaccine voice. This was something different. Which made me wonder. "Did you search his room?"

"Yes." Her cheeks flared with color, but her eyes stayed locked on mine. "I also checked the trunk of his car, looked through the Internet search history on his computer, and peeked at his bank statements for large deposits. The victims of the robberies are my friends. If I'd found anything that hinted Joey took from them, I would have turned him in."

Crap. I believed her.

Trying not to be disappointed with the loss of my best and only suspect, I stood and asked, "Do you know if Joey is working at home today? Sean hasn't put Joey on the suspect list yet, but he might. If Joey can come up with an alibi for even one of the crimes, it'll help keep him in the clear."

Oof. I found myself squashed against Eleanor's ample chest. When she let go and I could breathe again, she said that Joey had been working in the home office when she left that morning. He planned on being there all day.

When I drove up to the Schaffers' sprawling brick ranch home, I spotted Joey through the large picture window exactly where Eleanor had said he'd be—sitting smack in front of a computer screen. The empty jumbo-sized coffee cup and the overflowing wastepaper basket filled with candy wrappers, empty chip bags, and scribbled-on Post-it notes told me he'd been there a while.

Joey was painfully shy when he invited me inside and asked if I was here for computer help. When I explained why I stopped by, his shoulders straightened. Under his shaggy blond hair, his brown eyes lit with excitement. Being a criminal suspect was clearly the most thrilling thing to happen to Joey in a long time. Too bad he had an alibi for the first five Thanksgiving Day break-ins. Otherwise, he might have marched himself down to the sheriff's office and turned himself in just to break up the monotony of his day.

"For those Thanksgivings I drove to Dixon and helped cook dinner at a homeless shelter."

Wow. Joey had just gone from shy and geeky to heroic and selfless in two seconds flat. "Why does your mom think you spent those Thanksgivings alone?"

He shifted his feet and shrugged. "Mom loves family holidays. I didn't want her to feel like she had to come with me. Before my dad died, he said we should volunteer at a shelter. Every year he said he was going to do it, but he never did. After he died, I decided to do it as a way of honoring him. It made me feel good about myself, so I kept going back."

Double wow. "Why did you stop?"

The theme from Pachelbel's Canon in D blared from my phone. Danielle had sent me a text.

"Sorry," I said to Joey as I pulled out my phone and looked at Danielle's text message.

I gave Joey an apologetic smile and typed back, I'LL FIGURE SOMETHING OUT. DON'T WORRY.

While the white frames with silver and gold etching were tasteful, they weren't exactly a big loss. Face it, no one *really* needed a three-inch by two-inch picture frame. Of course, now it was up to me to come up with something more interesting. Somehow I had a hard time believing real private investigators had to deal with this kind of crisis.

Flipping open my notebook, I jotted down a reminder to find an appropriate wedding giveaway before Danielle gnawed off her recently polished nails. Then I looked back at Joey, trying to remember what we had been talking about.

"Sorry," I said. "You were telling me why you stopped volunteering on Thanksgiving."

Joey frowned. "The shelter closed down due to lack of funds. Since then I've been spending Thanksgiving here. I guess that means I don't have an alibi for the last five years. Will that be a problem?"

"As far as I'm concerned, you're in the clear." And on his way to becoming a saint. "But why haven't you celebrated Thanksgiving with your family since?"

"I didn't know how to say I'd changed my mind without telling my mom about the shelter. I don't want her to think I chose my dad over her. You know?"

The logic was faulty, but the sentiment behind it was sweet. Unfortunately, that meant the poor guy was once again going to be alone on Turkey Day. The way his mouth turned down at the corners told me how he felt about that.

Before I could consider the implications, I found myself asking, "Would you like to come to Thanksgiving dinner at my place this year?"

"Really?" Joey gave me a toothpaste-ad-worthy smile. "Like a date?"

Yikes. "No."

His smile dimmed. "You probably have a boyfriend, right?"

"Boyfriend" seemed too casual a word after last night, but for lack of a better one . . . "Lionel Franklin and I have been seeing each other. His parents will be at dinner, too, along with my family and friends. It'd be great if you could join us."

By the time I climbed back in my car, I was up one dinner guest and down a suspect. Making a mental note to check how many place settings were in my cabinets, I flipped through my notebook and tried to decide what investigative path to take next. I had almost two hours until I had to meet Erica and Danielle for a dress fitting. Not enough time to go shopping for Danielle's wedding favor replacements, more than enough to question another suspect—if I had one. None of the other names on Annette's list made my Spidey-sense tingle.

Feeling bummed by my lack of detecting skills, I opted to drive the two blocks to my grandfather's house, hoping a snack would give my mental prowess a boost. At least it would stop my stomach from growling.

My grandfather's Lincoln Town Car sat in the driveway. Technically, the car was still registered in my grandmother's name. After she died, Pop pulled a tarp over the Town Car. Aside from seasonal checkups by the local mechanic, it remained unused for over a decade. It wasn't until after my mother died that Pop sold his vehicle and began using this one. The car guzzled gas, cornered like the *Titanic,* and, when Pop was decked out in concert attire, made him look like a geriatric broker of the world's oldest profession.

Pop normally parked the car in the garage. The fact that it was currently exposed to the damp cold made me believe that Elvis was in the building.

Sure enough, the minute I opened my car door I could hear the sounds of bass drum, electric guitar, and slightly off-key but enthusiastic singing. Pop and his band were in rehearsal.

Not wanting to ruin their musical mojo, I decided to wait until a break before saying hello and let myself in through the side door. The smell of coffee made my body quiver with happiness. I poured myself a cup from the pot sitting on the warmer, added two spoonfuls of sugar, and sighed as I took my first sip. Pop's culinary talents weren't much to speak of, but his coffee was legendary.

Fortified with caffeine, I rifled through the fridge for something edible. Not an easy task. Aside from a carton of eggs, milk, and a few stray veggies, the fridge was empty. When I first moved back to Indian Falls, the refrigerator was always stocked. Of course, that was before my father moved in and started mooching Pop's groceries. To make sure he didn't starve, Pop hid a small fridge in the garage and packed it with the good stuff he didn't want my father to know about. Unfortunately, unless I wanted to risk hearing loss or make a run to the store, I'd have to make do with what was here.

Ten minutes later, I was sitting down at the red Formica table with my investigator notebook, a pepper and onion omelet, and my third cup of coffee.

"Does something ever smell good in here."

Footsteps sounded on the stairs, and my father stepped into

view. With his perfectly pressed charcoal pants, off-white cable-knit sweater, and slightly graying auburn hair, my father looked both handsome and reliable. Proof that looks can be deceiving.

His deep blue eyes sparkled with happiness. "Hi, honey. What a wonderful surprise. Your grandfather didn't mention you were dropping by today, otherwise I would have cleared my afternoon. We haven't spent much time together lately."

Part of me wanted to point out that spending time together had never been a priority for Stan. In fact, since he'd blown back into town seven weeks ago, we'd spent more time together by accident than we had for the dozen years prior. The other part . . . well, Ginny's death and talking to Joey Schaffer about losing his father had me swallowing down my retort with a mouthful of eggs. Though I might not be thrilled with Stan's parenting, or lack thereof, he was the only parent I had left. The logical part of my brain told me I'd probably wake up tomorrow and find him packed and gone, but my heart desperately wanted him to care enough to stay.

Was it any wonder I had commitment issues?

Stan poured himself a cup of coffee to the muted sounds of "Battle Hymn of the Republic" and slid into the seat across from me. "Everyone's talking about your new business."

"This is just a one-shot deal," I said, ignoring the way my father was eyeing my lunch. "Mrs. Johnson asked me to do her a favor, and I didn't know how to say no."

"I wouldn't be surprised if lots of other folks start asking for similar favors. You've made a name for yourself in this town. Now's the time to capitalize on it." He sighed and leaned back in his chair as I put the last bite of omelet into my mouth. "Catching criminals is an exciting sideline. If I hadn't already started my own company, I'd be asking for a cut of the action."

I waited for a particularly loud drum solo to end before saying, "Lionel mentioned you wanted to use his farm for photographs."

Stan nodded. "The barn has good lighting. Shots of models sitting on hay bales or grooming some of the horses will look good on composite cards. I want all my models to be strong examples of healthy living to snag those AARP commercials."

He sounded confident and knowledgeable. It was easy to see how he convinced the senior population of Indian Falls that they were going to be the next big thing. Stan was an excellent salesperson, but I knew him far too well to buy what he was selling. "You know companies like AARP use established talent agencies in New York and Los Angeles. They aren't going to book models from an agency no one's heard of."

"That's why I'm starting small." He got up and poured the last of the coffee into his mug. "I'm tapping the local markets first to build a résumé for me and my talent. I've already booked Ethel Jacabowski for a photo shoot at one of those fancy retirement villages in Rock Island."

"Really?" Maybe this modeling agency endeavor wasn't a scam. "Congratulations."

"Thanks." Stan flashed his perfectly straight smile. "It took a lot of fast talking to get them to do the shoot before Ethel leaves town. I didn't realize when I signed her that she's one of the group that goes to Florida every winter. If I'd known that, I would have asked for a higher commission than twenty-five percent."

Wait. "I thought most agents took fifteen percent."

"Most agents aren't recruiting raw talent, training them from the ground up, and putting together portfolios. The coaching fees I charge cover only part of my cost."

So much for my father turning over a new leaf.

We both jumped as a high-pitched whine streaked through the air. There was a loud crash, followed by the sound of my grandfather swearing. Something told me band practice was over.

Shooting a look at the garage door, my father scooted back his chair, grabbed a set of keys off the table, and gave me a bright smile. "I hate to run, but I've got to get to a meeting with an account looking to score some fresh faces. Tell your grandfather I'll be back with the car in an hour or two. Oh, and if you don't mind, add one more plate to the table at Thanksgiving. Your old man is bringing a date."

With a wink, Stan disappeared out the door, leaving me gaping after him. Somehow Stan had just managed to turn our first attempt at a family holiday into his version of *The Dating Game*. Shaking off my disappointment, I started a fresh pot of coffee and washed the dishes. I had just sat down to review my investigative notes when the slamming of the garage door announced the arrival of my grandfather.

"Damn that man." Pop stormed into the kitchen, wearing blue suede boots and a fierce scowl. "I told him I needed the car to run errands this afternoon. Well, he's going to be sorry when he takes one of his marathon trips to the bathroom and discovers we're out of toilet paper."

Um . . . ick.

"Stan said he'd be back with the car later this afternoon." I hoped before using the bathroom became imperative. "He had to meet with someone looking for new talent."

I expected my grandfather to roll his eyes at Stan's new sideline. Instead he took a seat and sighed. "I guess I can't fault him for running down new opportunities. It takes time and dedication to build your own business. Just look at me."

The rhinestone-encrusted gold shirt made that hard to do without wearing shades. Still, though I didn't always understand my grandfather's passion for impersonating the King, I appreciated his perseverance and hard work. Two things Stan had spent most of his life avoiding. "This new business is probably just another one of his scams."

"That's what I thought at first, but I've changed my mind." The coffeepot burbled. Pop stood and rummaged through the cabinets for a mug. "I called the company that booked Ethel for her modeling job, pretending to be a hotshot Chicago talent agent. The guy on the phone asked me to send them my information for future consideration. He then said they'd just booked some local talent for their next shoot. I even snuck into Stan's room and took a look at the contract. It's legit."

"I thought Stan put a lock on his bedroom door." He claimed he wanted to ensure client confidentially. More likely Stan did it because sending the bill for the locksmith to my grandfather would drive Pop wild.

Pop grinned. "Your father doesn't lock his windows."

"You climbed through Dad's window?" My heart swooped into my stomach as I pictured Pop climbing through the second-story window.

"Are you crazy?" Pop sputtered. "Headliners never do their own stunts. I slipped Carlos twenty bucks to shimmy up the ladder and unlock your dad's door from the inside. Carlos learned more than how to play a rocking bass line during his stint in juvie."

I gaped at Pop.

He must have taken my stunned silence for criticism, because he explained, "I've always taught you to respect other people's space and property, but for most of his life your father has been a hemorrhoid on the butt of humanity. I didn't want him putting stars in my friends' eyes and then bilking them out of their Social Security checks. Now I know that he isn't. I honestly think your father's trying to do the right thing."

"Really?" I hated the hope I felt. Each time my father disappointed, my mother or Pop had to help me pick up the pieces and put them back together. If he disappointed me again, I wasn't sure I'd be able to get back up on my own.

Pop put a hand on my shoulder. "Your father has a lot to make up for. I have no idea if he can ever fix what he broke, but he has to start somewhere. Hanging around for the holidays and creating this business is that start." Giving my arm a squeeze, he said, "Speaking of the holidays, I've been thinking we should order some Pilgrims for Thanksgiving."

"Huh?"

"On Thanksgiving, some of the restaurants in the area make their employees dress up and deliver food. Having Pilgrims over for dinner has become the cool thing to do around here. I don't want to look like I'm behind on the trends."

Coffee cup in hand, Pop shuffled off, leaving me gaping after him. Flipping open my notebook, I tried to concentrate on the investigation. Still, my mind kept shifting back to what my grandfather had said about Stan. I wanted to believe he was right, that my father was trying to turn his life and our relationship around. Maybe this wasn't the way I'd choose for him to do it, but Pop was right. Everyone had to start somewhere.

Wait. That gave me an idea.

My eyes scooted down the list of victims. The crimes had been going on for so long it was easy to forget that there was once a time when Thanksgiving robberies didn't occur in Indian Falls. The thief started with one house. One set of stolen items. One set of victims. There had to be a specific inspiration behind that house being selected. If I was going to crack this case, I needed to figure out that reason. Starting now.

Seven

The first victims of the Thanksgiving Day thief were Seth and Jan Kurtz. All I remembered about them was that they gave out full-sized Snickers bars on Halloween. A serious craving for chocolate was the only reason my friends and I were willing to brave the Kurtzes' six German shepherds. Either those dogs were no longer in residence at the time of the break-in or the thief moonlighted as a dog whisperer. Pop might know, but he was busy belting out "White Christmas" while sudsing up in the shower. Since Pop had been known to perform entire concerts before drying off, I decided to pay the Kurtzes' farm a visit and see what I could learn on my own.

No one was home. Or, if they were, they couldn't hear the doorbell. The dogs could, though. Judging by the frantic barking, there were at least five or six of them attempting to gnaw through the door.

Vowing to bring a box of Milk-Bones when I returned, I hurried back to my car in case the dogs managed a breakout. Since I still had time before the dress-fitting appointment, I steered to the farm down the road, hoping my friends Bryan and Reginald would be willing to dish on their neighbors.

The baby blue farmhouse had already been decorated for Christmas. Icicle lights hung from the roof. White reindeer in various poses were perched near the house, and a sleek white sleigh trimmed with lights and evergreens was parked near the bottom of the lawn. Christmas might be seven weeks away, but that wasn't stopping Bryan and Reginald from decking the halls.

I couldn't blame them for their enthusiasm. The two had moved here to try their hand at organic farming and country living. The transition hadn't exactly been without challenges. While citizens around here had nothing against two men in love, it wasn't familiar ground for Indian Falls. Especially when one of the men had long black dreadlocks and was built like a Mack truck. His intimidating appearance and a brush with the law when he was a kid were the reasons Reginald had come under suspicion when someone was boosting cars a few months back. Reginald and Bryan already liked me before I helped convince Sheriff Jackson that Sean had arrested the wrong man. After Reginald was sprung, they elevated me to best-friend status. I was hoping that designation would encourage them to talk with me now.

"Rebecca, what a wonderful surprise." Bryan gave me a toothy grin when he opened the door and ushered me into the house. A large Christmas tree was standing in the living room with boxes of ornaments strewn around it. "Reginald is going to be unhappy to have missed you."

My nose twitched at the scent of chocolate chip cookies. Score. Bryan not only liked to bake, he was damn good at it.

"Where's Reggie?" I asked, following Bryan into the airy

country kitchen. On the counter were cooling racks filled with cookies.

Bryan handed me a still-warm cookie and took another for himself. "He's in St. Louis this week for a technology and farming conference. He hated leaving me alone to pack for our trip, but it's better this way. Reginald panics when he packs. He worries that he's going to bring the wrong thing and ends up taking every-thing he owns. No one needs ten pairs of shoes, especially ones big as boats."

"You're leaving town?"

"We're spending the week with Reginald's family. That's why I have the tree up already. I want it to be ready to decorate when we get home."

The cookie stopped halfway to my mouth. "You and Reginald aren't going to be in Indian Falls for Thanksgiving?"

I glanced around the kitchen. In this one room, I spotted a Waterford crystal mantel clock, a small, high-definition, flat-screen television, a laptop computer, and a jar that I'd witnessed Reginald throwing spare change into. If the thief caught wind of Reggie and Bryan going away, he'd cash in big-time.

"This is the first time Reginald's family has invited the two of us to spend a holiday with them." His elfin features were filled with a combination of embarrassment and pleasure. "This means they've begun to accept that we're a couple."

Yay for acceptance. Boo to the timing.

"Have you heard about the Thanksgiving Day robberies?"

Bryan brushed a lock of blond hair off his face and frowned at his cookie. "Jan and Seth mentioned the robberies when we told them about our trip. They offered to keep an eye on the place so what happened to them doesn't happen to us."

"Did they tell you how the thief broke into their place?" When he gave me a blank stare, I explained, "One of the other victims hired me to track down the person behind the robberies."

Bryan beamed. "That's wonderful. Not to add any pressure, but I'll feel better about leaving town knowing you're on the case. You'll probably have the thief behind bars long before Reginald and I hit the road."

No pressure. Right.

"Jan and Seth said they had an early dinner with friends," said Bryan. "When they came back to the house, it took them a while to realize someone had broken in. The dogs were sleeping in the living room. All the doors were locked, and there weren't any signs of forced entry."

So the dogs were there. Huh.

"Do the Kurtzes have a key to your house?" More important, did Reginald and Bryan have a key to theirs?

"Reginald gave Seth a key a couple of months back after he locked himself out and couldn't find the fake rock the spare was hidden in." Bryan's blue eyes went wide. "You don't think the thief will steal the key from Seth and Jan in order to break in here, do you?"

"Probably not." Although anything was possible. "Do you know if Jan and Seth trust a neighbor with their spare key?"

"I doubt it." He shrugged his slight shoulders. "Seth likes his privacy. He doesn't let many people come inside his house, and when he does they aren't left alone. Jan says not to take it personally, that he's always been that way, but I can't help being a little freaked out when someone follows me to the bathroom and stands outside the door to escort me back. Reginald thinks Seth must be hiding hot televisions or a serious S&M fetish. I think he's just plain old crazy."

Maybe. Or maybe whatever Seth was secretive about was the reason the thief had targeted him ten years ago. A few more quick questions gave me Jan and Seth's typical schedule. The two ran errands on Mondays. The rest of their week was split between walking the dogs and hanging out at the senior center, doing Jazzercise and playing Scrabble. Unless I wanted to help collect dog poop or brave being a doggy snack, I'd have to catch them during one of their forays to the center.

Armed with a plan and a tin of cookies, I headed for the Nothing Borrowed Nothing Blue Bridal Boutique. It was time to set aside my criminal investigation for something far more harrowing—a dress fitting.

The boutique on the north side of town was located on the same street as a weight-loss center, an attorney's office, and the building that was shared by a dentist and a shrink. A bride could get her teeth whitened, sweat off excess pounds to fit into that ideal dress, draw up the prenup, and have a breakdown from the stress all without moving her car. The only thing missing was a liquor store. For that you had to hoof it a few blocks. I guess the town planners couldn't control everything.

The store's owner, Tilly Ferguson, looked to be lamenting the lack of alcohol when the bell above the front door announced my arrival. The woman was dressed in the same colors as her store's decor—gray skirt, ruffled white shirt, and sensibly soled gray shoes. Between the clothes and her bouffant salt-and-pepper hair, the woman looked like a black-and-white movie begging to be colorized. Which is probably why Erica the Red sitting in the middle of the salon's gray couch had Tilly looking like she was going to pass out.

With her cascading magenta hair, Erica the Red lived up to

her name. The unnaturally red hair clashed violently with the pink-and-silver EstroGenocide T-shirt she was sporting, but Erica didn't seem to mind. Erica liked taking risks. No doubt that was part of her motivation for going into Roller Derby in the first place.

"Hey, Rebecca." Erica unfurled herself from the sofa. "How's the investigation? The girls are stoked that you've become an official PI. If you need a couple of bodyguards, let us know. Things have been a little dull now that the season is over."

My life had become entertainment for a group of girls who celebrated hip checks and fishnet stockings. How lucky was I?

"I should be okay on my own. The thief doesn't have a history of violence." Not to people, dogs, or property. Which, now that I thought about it, was kind of odd.

"Your grandfather seems to think the thief could change his pattern now that you're involved."

Sigh. "Why were you talking to Pop?"

She grinned. "He's working Halle, Anna, and me into his act as backup singers. None of us can sing, but that doesn't seem to matter."

Of course it didn't.

Before the conversation could disintegrate further, I asked, "Where's Danielle? We should get started on the fitting."

Tilly cleared her throat. "Danielle called a few minutes before you arrived. She had some kind of emergency and asked that we start without her."

I tried to decide whether I was worried or relieved that Danielle wasn't here to freak out about hemlines and broken frames. Since being worried would only result in my eating the entire tin of cookies, I opted for relieved and said, "Okay. Let's get to work."

Wow, was it work. My dress fit okay—if you didn't notice that the designer assumed I would be wearing stilts. Erica's dress was more of a challenge. While Erica had broad shoulders and the kind of chest most centerfolds paid top dollar for, my derby friend was still several sizes smaller than the original owner. The dress had enough excess material to reupholster the couch, which might not be a bad idea. The shiny, dark purple taffeta would look better as cushions than as a gown. On the other hand, the Hawaiian-looking floral pattern Danielle's mother-in-law had lobbied for would have been worse. If I was going to wear mutant flowers, I preferred to be doing it on a beach.

Erica stood perfectly still as Tilly poured all her alterations skills into making the dress fit. Tilly pinned, poked, pulled, and looked like she was going to cry on at least three separate occasions before the appointment ended. The only measure that prevented a full meltdown was a promise that my grandfather would drop by later to serenade her. Even though the female senior population's attraction to my grandfather wigged me out, I was not above using it to keep a grown woman from crying.

As soon as Erica was back in her own clothes, I made the next appointment and hustled us both out onto the sidewalk.

"Now what?" Erica asked as the door closed behind us.

"Now we give Tilly a couple of days to recover before going for the next fitting."

"I wasn't talking about the dress." Erica laughed. "What's the next step in the investigation? We have a thief to catch."

We?

Erica was an awesome skater and a great friend, but the last time she tagged along to help investigate, property damage was involved. We were lucky to escape without a criminal record after

I paid for a replacement window. Erica's assistance was expensive. With Christmas fast approaching, my bank account was strained enough.

"I have to get back to the rink," I said, huddling near the wall to avoid the wind. "We have two school groups coming in for holiday parties this week. I want to make sure everything is ready. Then I can focus on beating Sean at solving the case."

Erica smiled. "I bet the hunky defender of justice won't mind losing if it scores points with you. You're lucky. Two hot men to juggle. I have a hard time dealing with one. Although mine is worth the effort. Archaeologists really know how to use their hands."

Erica liked insisting that Sean's frustration with me was more sexual than job-related. Every time I tried to convince her she was mistaken, she described Sean's sexiest qualities. I blamed it on her day job. Erica wrote romance novels. After I found that out, I ordered all of her books. The woman was aces at describing the male anatomy, which was why I wanted to avoid another Sean dissertation now. Hearing about Sean's rippling abs freaked me out.

"I'm glad things are working out with you and Xavier. Is he going to be your date for the wedding?"

Erica's smile faltered. "I hope so. His team finished the excavation and is heading home. Without dirt to dig in, I don't know how much time he'll be spending around here."

Erica's head dropped, and my heart squeezed. Erica needed a distraction from her relationship woes. "Do you want to come back to the rink with me? You can skate while I get some work done, and then we can eat the rest of these cookies."

Erica's smile told me the answer was a resounding yes.

The rink was hopping when we arrived. Earth, Wind & Fire's "September" blared from the speakers as a large portion of the Indian Falls High School population skated counterclockwise while laughing, flirting, and falling. Erica raced to the locker room to shed her winter wear. When she skated onto the floor in her EstroGenocide uniform, the teens cheered.

Confident that Erica wasn't dwelling on relationship concerns, I dodged a couple holding hands and darted into the rink office. When I closed the door, the music muted, making me once again appreciate the renovations Mom had done a year before she passed away. When I was growing up, the warped office door frame and thin door made the decibel level only slightly lower in here than on the other side. Other than the door, Mom skipped renovating the rest of the office. She figured she had time to update the room later. Later never came. In a way I was glad. The scarred wooden desk, old trophies, and framed photographs made me feel as though Mom could walk through the door at any moment. On paper, the rink was mine. In my heart, it would always belong to my mother.

Sitting in one of the only additions I'd made to the room— a fake leather wheely chair—I fired up the computer and ran through the details for the upcoming school field trips. Once I knew we had adequate staffing and soda to keep the kids wired for hours of skating, I shifted my attention back to my investigation.

After flipping open my notebook, I ran a search on Seth and Jan Kurtz. There wasn't much to be found. Aside from the original article that appeared in the local paper after the theft (in which Seth was quoted as saying he hoped God struck the thief dead), I learned that Jan was a member of the quilting circle and that Seth habitually placed second in the Women's Guild's landscaping contest.

I jotted down the couple's hobbies and ran searches on the other victims. By the time I'd gone through all the names, I'd learned that a holiday tree-decorating contest had resulted in several small fires, an exposé of Barna Donovan's goat-eating alien had appeared in the *National Enquirer*, and Betsy Moore's neighbor and helper with horses, Amy Jo Boggs, was Ginny Chapman's great-niece. It was a small and peculiar world, especially when you lived in Indian Falls.

Since my Internet search had resulted in nothing more than my sending four Facebook friend requests, I picked up the phone and dialed my grandfather. While the World Wide Web was short on details on the upstanding citizens of Indian Falls, I was pretty sure Pop could tell me everything about them, including their favorite ice cream, how often they attended church, and who needed prunes to stay regular. The CIA, FBI, and Interpol had nothing on Pop and his friends.

Voice mail. Drat. Pop was probably too busy taunting my father with a roll of toilet paper to answer his phone. Leaving a message, I asked Pop to stop by Tilly's for a quick performance and to call me when he had a chance.

Deciding it would be best to wait to hear from Pop before questioning any more witnesses, I flipped off the lights and opened the door to the dance party on wheels. The new disco ball I'd purchased was spinning. Flecks of colorful light shimmered on the floor. The smell of pizza, popcorn, and sweat filled the air. Everywhere I looked kids were laughing, smiling, and having a great time. It was moments like these that made me understand why my mom loved owning The Toe Stop. This wasn't a business to make piles of cash. It was a place where a community could celebrate being together. Since I still wasn't sure what I wanted to be when I grew up, I figured this was a pretty good way to spend my time.

I spotted Erica in the center of the rink floor. Raising my hand, I started to flag her down before deciding against it. She was having the time of her life giving skating technique tips to some bourgeoning speed skaters. Erica excelled at speed. She crouched low and had good balance, strong leg pushes to the side, and wonderful recovery strokes. The woman was a natural. Hmmm. I wondered if her schedule was open enough for her to consider teaching a speed-skating class. With George booked solid for lessons, I was on the hunt for more instructors. I'd have to talk to her about that.

I asked one of my high school employees to tell Erica I'd gone upstairs when she came off the floor. Then I zipped up my coat and headed to my apartment for rest and relaxation.

I spotted the answering machine blinking on the kitchen counter, and my heart leaped. Lionel must have called. All day I'd been trying to keep my mind from drifting back to last night. Now that I was thinking about it, my stomach gave a giddy flip as I waited for the sound of Lionel's smooth baritone.

"Hey, girl." Not Lionel. I felt a wave of disappointment even as I smiled at the voice of my best friend and former Chicago roommate, Jasmine. "Pick up the phone. Damn it. I must have called your home line. Either that or you're outrunning madmen or getting shot at by camels. Whoever said city life is dangerous never visited your town. Call me back when you get this. Okay? I really need to talk."

Jasmine sounded sad. Jasmine rarely sounded sad. She was loud and brash, and she never allowed herself to get down. It was that over-the-top personality and downright cheerfulness that kept me sane after my mother died and kept me laughing even as I packed up my things and moved back home. Though I knew she was bummed I had to leave, she never once allowed me to see her unhappiness. She sounded unhappy now.

Worry gnawed at me as I picked up the phone and dialed. No answer. I left a quick message, making sure to give her my cell number, put the phone back in the cradle, and stared at it. Should I call Lionel? What was the protocol for the day after you spent the night with a person? Part of me wanted to pick up the phone. The other part expected Lionel to call and was disappointed he hadn't made the effort. After all, he was the one who used the L-word. Didn't that obligate him to call? Of course, there was the possibility that last night was less than he'd hoped for. I mean, I was out of practice—and while everyone said it was like riding a bike, I was the type who skinned my knees several times before I got the wheels zipping along.

I felt like I was back in high school. One would think I would have learned something about male/female relationships since then. One would be wrong. Good thing technology had evolved since the days of pimples and pubescent angst. If I'd been able to send text messages back then, I wouldn't have spent so much time sitting next to the phone.

Letting my fingers do the walking, I punched out what I hoped was a casual-sounding message telling Lionel my plans for the evening. Then I set the phone down to convince myself I wasn't waiting for Lionel's return message.

Five minutes passed. Ten. Fifteen. Nothing. No message. Not even one of those silly smiley faces to let me know my text had gone through. I gnawed on my lip, trying to resist the urge to pick up the phone and send another text. If he got the first text, the second would look desperate and clingy. Neither was a good look for me.

A knock on the door saved me from my insecurities. Erica was here. I sat the phone back on the kitchen counter and yelled, "The door's open, Erica. Come on in."

Putting a big smile on my face, I turned, walked out of the kitchen, and stopped dead in my tracks. Standing in my living room was a strange black-haired woman wearing a long trench coat. The moment she spotted me, her eyes narrowed.

"Are you Rebecca Robbins?" she asked.

"Yes."

Her lip curled into a snarl as she reached into her coat pocket and said, "The days of you causing trouble are going to end, and they are going to end right now."

Eight

I froze as I watched the stranger in my living room pull something out of her pocket. The glint of the recessed lighting against metal made my pulse jump.

A knife? A gun?

Whatever it was, I didn't plan on waiting around to find out. Over the last couple of months, I'd been shot at far more than I wanted to remember. I wasn't interested in adding to the count.

Leaping to my left, I dove behind the couch and then crawled to the end table. My hand felt around atop the table and latched on to an ugly metal statue of a roller skate. I heard footsteps shuffle on the carpet to my left. A moment later the black-haired stranger came into view. I cocked back my arm and was ready to let the statue fly when the front door opened.

"Mother Lucas, what are you doing here?"

Mother Lucas?

I peeked over the sofa and spotted Danielle in the doorway. Whether her red cheeks were from the cold, embarrassment, or anger was a toss-up. Something told me it was a combination of all three.

Mother Lucas slid whatever object she was holding back into her pocket and gave Danielle a wide smile. "Danielle, dear. After hearing so much about Rebecca, I wanted to stop by and introduce myself. It's such a pleasure to meet my son's friends, especially the ones who are going to be part of the most important day of his life."

"You broke into my apartment," I said, keeping a firm grip on the ugly bronze statue.

"Is that true, Mother Lucas?" Danielle asked.

The woman's eyes widened. "Of course not. My son is a minister."

What one thing had to do with another was beyond me. Clearly, the woman needed to brush up on her Bible studies. By my estimation, Rich's mother had put a dent in several commandments during the three minutes she'd been in my apartment.

"I didn't invite you into my house," I insisted.

"Of course you did, dear. I heard you quite clearly. You said to come in." She gave me a small, sad smile. "Why else would I be standing here? Danielle, why don't you get your friend a glass of water? She must have had a very long day between running her business and helping with your wedding."

This felt like one of the *Twilight Zone* episodes I used to watch when I was eight. Occasionally, the whole thing was a dream. Maybe if I pinched myself Mother Lucas and her alternate reality would go away.

Nope. Still here.

"Look," I said trying to ignore the bulge in Mother Lucas's pocket. "This is all a misunderstanding. My friend Erica was supposed to be here, so when I heard someone arrive, I thought it was her and asked *her* to come in. I never expected someone I hadn't met before to walk into my home." Or cause me to dive behind furniture. Speaking of which, ouch. I had a rug burn on my knee. When I was a kid, I thought being a movie stuntperson would be a glamorous career. Wow, had I been wrong.

Mother Lucas straightened her shoulders. "You have the audacity to question my manners? I'm not the one who was crawling around on the floor." Her nose wrinkled. "When was the last time you vacuumed?"

First she barged into my apartment. She then scared me with whatever was in her pocket, and now she was insulting my housekeeping skills! Enough was enough.

"I'd like you to leave."

"No."

I blinked. "No? What do you mean, no?"

Mother Lucas crossed her arms over her chest and sat on my chair. "You invited me into your home. That means I get to stay."

This was worse than inviting a vampire into your home. Something told me that garlic would only make her hungry. I needed something stronger, and only one thing came to mind.

Taking the route to the kitchen that kept me as far away from my unwanted guest as possible, I said, "I'm asking you one last time to please leave."

Mother Lucas shook her head.

"Okay," I said grabbing my phone. "You asked for it. I'm calling the cops."

Danielle gasped as my finger pushed Sean's number on speed dial. "That's not necessary, because we really have to get going," she said. "Mother Lucas, you and Rebecca can find a better time to get acquainted."

Like when hell froze over.

The phone started to ring.

Danielle looked at the phone in my hand, grabbed her soon-to-be mother-in-law by the hand, and tugged her out of the chair. "Rich is waiting in the car. He wanted to take us out to a special dinner to celebrate your early arrival. We don't want to keep him waiting. Do we?"

Mother Lucas gave Danielle's hand a pat. "Of course not. I'll be here from now until the wedding. There's plenty of time for me to pay Rebecca a call." She looked at me and smiled. "I'm very much looking forward to getting to know all about you."

With that threat hanging in the air, Mother Lucas walked out the door. Giving me an apologetic look, Danielle started to leave, then said, "I hate to ask, but have you come up with an idea for the new table favor yet?" When I raised an eyebrow, she said, "Why don't we talk about it tomorrow?" and closed the door behind her.

Hitting END on my phone, I decided I needed a drink. Or four.

Two steps away from the kitchen, I heard the door handle shift. Turning, I cocked my roller-skate-statue throwing arm back and stopped short as Sean Holmes asked, "What the hell do you think you're doing?"

Oy. Just what I needed. "I'm practicing shot put for the Olympic trials. What does it look like I'm doing?"

I waited for Sean to say something cutting. Instead he laughed. This day was getting stranger by the minute.

"Look, I've had a long day. Could laughing at my life wait until tomorrow?" I put down the statue, turned my back, and marched into the kitchen.

Sean followed. "I'm here because you called. Your phone calls often involve some kind of catastrophe, so I decided to drop by and see what was up."

Damn. I hated that he was right, about both the call and my life. I popped the cork on a bottle of wine and grabbed a glass. "The phone call was a mistake. Sorry to waste your time."

"It won't be a waste if you pour me a glass of that red."

"Isn't there a rule about cops drinking on duty?" As in, they aren't allowed to?

Sean smiled. "I'm not on duty." He plucked the glass of wine I'd poured for myself off the counter. "I only stopped here because I figured you needed help with your . . . investigation."

I felt the need to pinch myself again. "You're offering to help me?"

"You're trying to help Mrs. Johnson. I'm trying to help the entire community. I don't see why we shouldn't work together to put the thief behind bars." While I tried to recover from that shock, Sean took a sip of wine and added, "I heard you talked to Eleanor Schaffer today. I looked at the files. Her name was on Annette's list."

Technically Sean hadn't asked a question, so I didn't need to respond. I didn't know much about being an investigator, but I'd discovered that it was best to stay quiet and let other people fill in the silences. You learned more that way. Taking a wine goblet out of the cupboard, I filled it and took a big swig.

Sean studied me over the rim of his drink for a moment.

Then he put his wineglass on the counter and folded his arms across his chest. The movement caused his unzipped jacket to shift, giving me a good view of his holstered sidearm. Normally, this reminder of Sean's official authority would have worried me. Probably because most of the time in my quest for justice I tiptoed into the gray area of the law. On this occasion, however, I hadn't done anything to warrant concern. No breaking and entering. No obstruction of justice. Nothing that could allow Sean to throw his badge around and threaten to land me in jail. I was in the clear.

Giving him a big smile, I took another drink of wine and leaned back against the counter. If Sean thought I was going to be the one to speak first in this verbal game of chicken, he was mistaken. For the first time in our bizarre relationship, I was in charge—and I liked it.

Sean raked his hand through his hair and let out a sigh. "Look, I questioned Eleanor after Annette's break-in. She didn't have any information on the theft."

Still no question. Still no answer.

Sean must have figured this out since he added, "Did she remember anything new when you questioned her?"

"Nope. She didn't remember anything new about the salon." Oops. My system started to buzz in a way that told me to lay off the wine.

Maybe it was the wine, but I decided to cut Sean a break. "Eleanor told her son that Annette was leaving town for the holiday." Sean's eyes gleamed, and I shook my head before he could hurry to make a wrongful arrest. "Joey has a great alibi for half of the thefts. He's not the guy you're looking for."

Sean frowned and downed the rest of his wine. "No, but he could have been." His blue eyes met mine. "You did good work."

Pleasure streaked through me. "Really?"

He laughed. "As much as I hate to admit it, yeah. You found a lead and tracked it down. Too bad it didn't pan out. If we're lucky, the next one will."

Huh. There was that word again. We. As if the two of us were a team. Maybe pigs had grown wings and were flying over a ski resort in hell. Either that or the wine had also gone to Sean's head.

Regardless of the reason, I decided I'd better take advantage of his go-team attitude since I severely doubted it would ever come again. "I also stopped by the Kurtzes' house today. No one was home, but a neighbor mentioned the Kurtzes' dogs were in the house when the first theft took place. Don't you think it's strange that someone would break into a house guarded by a half-dozen German shepherds?"

Sean shrugged. "I wasn't part of the department when the first theft happened. Sheriff Jackson and Deputy Murphy were the investigative team. But yeah." He walked over and poured himself another glass. "I think it's strange the burglar chose a house with six large dogs. Especially since everyone around here knows the dogs are given free rein in the house when the Kurtzes aren't home."

"Were the dogs . . . you know . . . okay after the burglary?"

"They didn't need therapy, if that's what you're asking."

Sigh. "What I meant was, were the dogs sleepy or acting strange? Like they were drugged?"

Sean laughed. "This isn't a movie, Rebecca. In real life, people don't throw doctored steaks into the house and wait for the dogs to fall asleep."

The movies had to get their material from somewhere. Besides, from what I'd seen recently, real-life crime was far quirkier than the stuff I saw on the big screen. Sean's laughter grated on my nerves, but he had information I needed. Instead of a snappy retort, I dug my fingernails into my palms.

Sean tossed back the wine and glanced at his watch. "I should probably get going. There's a sexy nurse from Peoria who's waiting to raise my heart rate."

Oy. The man was a pig. Okay. Maybe pig was too harsh considering his recent streak of cooperation. Still . . . Men!

Rolling my eyes, I walked Sean to the door and said, "I hope you and your friend have a great date tonight."

He walked out the door and turned. "Your tone makes me think you don't approve of my date. Why is that?"

Because, whoever this woman was, she deserved better than having her potential sex life broadcast to the nearest listener.

"I don't know the woman you're going out with, so I have no reason to approve or disapprove."

Sean leaned against the door and grinned. "You know what?"

"What?"

"You're beautiful when you're jealous."

I didn't think. I just reacted. *Slam.*

"Ow." Sean yelped behind the closed door.

I threw the lock in case Sean decided to revoke his recent policy on not arresting me. Then I looked through the peephole in time to watch Sean retreat. Something told me he wouldn't be quite as friendly tomorrow. Then again, maybe he'd realize I'd done him a favor, since his date might need to employ her medical training.

As aggravating as it was to know Sean had gotten a rise out of me twice in one day, his visit had helped solidify my next investigative step. I was about to put in another call to my grandfather when someone knocked on the door. Erica had arrived, and she wasn't alone. Accompanying her were Anna Phylaxis, Halle Bury, derby captain Typhoon Mary, and three extralarge pizzas.

"Hey, Rebecca." Anna and her long legs made a beeline for

the kitchen. "Erica told us you wanted company for dinner, so here we are. Mary was supposed to bring soda, but she got a flat and had to tip the tow truck driver. If you want, we can go downstairs and buy some off the snack counter, or we can just drink whatever you have here."

Before I could answer, Anna returned with sodas, plates, napkins, and trivets.

There were only ten days until Thanksgiving. If I was going to solve this case, I needed to do it soon. Otherwise there was a good chance the thief would strike again. Unfortunately, if I wanted to get work done, I'd need to evict my friends. Past experience told me that I wasn't up to tossing derby girls out of my house. They were bigger, stronger, and really good at convincing me that they were only crashing my place for my own good. So, unless I wanted to call Sean (and I really didn't want to call Sean), or say something mean to make them feel bad (something I also didn't want to do), I would just have to eat pizza and wait until they left for practice to continue my investigation.

Or not.

As I took my first bite of spicy sausage and mushroom pizza, Erica said, "Everyone on the team is buzzing about your new career. Since Sherlene-n-Mean's memorial, there's been speculation about you pursuing a law enforcement career. The team thinks having a rink owner that doubles as a PI is great for our reputation."

Halle swallowed her pizza with a nod. "We all have your back. Just tell us what to do and we'll do it. The more of us working the case, the faster the crook is caught. Right?"

"Right." Anna, Erica, and Mary cheered and high-fived.

"So." Mary grabbed another slice of pizza and turned to me.

"What's the plan? Do you need us to do a stakeout or act as look-outs while you dig through people's files?"

"I'm not doing another stakeout." Erica frowned. "No offense, Rebecca, but my ass is still asleep from the last time."

"You're probably feeling last night's workout," Anna said. "My butt cheeks are still tingling. Those squats George made us do were brutal. I thought practices were going to get easier now that the season was over."

I heaved a relieved sigh as the derby girls exchanged complaints about George's painful fitness regime. Butts, abs, thighs, and boobs all ached. George was on a quest to get his team into top shape in order to kick butt on next year's circuit. He'd even given the team a list of eating dos and don'ts in order to ensure they built muscle tone.

"What list does pizza fall on?" I asked, watching Erica scarf her sixth slice.

"Pizza transcends lists." Halle smiled and patted her stomach. "But to ensure we get our vitamins, we ordered one vegetarian."

The vegetarian pizza box sat unopened. I guess the girls figured they could absorb the nutrients through inhalation. Who knows? Maybe they were onto something. Although I figured that would work better if they set the box on fire. I'd gone to enough college frat parties to understand the power of second-hand herbal smoke.

I was about to set a good example by opening the veggie pizza box when Halle asked, "So, what's our assignment, Coach? We won't leave until you tell us how we can help."

As far as threats went, that was a pretty good one. I'd had derby girls play sleepover at my place in the not so distant past. I still had the cracks and high-heel marks on my bedroom door to prove it. If I wanted to avoid further home repairs, I needed to come up with a task that would satisfy my friends and keep them out of my way.

"Do any of you own dogs?" I asked.

They looked at one another and then back at me with a shrug. Nope. No dogs here.

"Do you know anyone who owns dogs?"

They gave me happy smiles.

Phew. "Talk to the dog owners you know. Ask them if they've ever given their dogs over-the-counter medication to make them stop barking or go to sleep."

"You think the thief drugged a dog?" Anna's eyes widened. "That's just mean."

"It's a theory." One that I already planned to ask Lionel about, but it was the only task I could come up with to distract my team. "If the thief drugged the dogs, there's a chance he didn't use an animal-specific prescription. I want to know what kinds of meant-for-human medications animal owners have given to their pets without noticeable side effects. Send me a text or leave a note with George if you learn anything. This case will keep me too busy to spend much time at home."

I crossed my fingers behind my back and hoped they didn't know about the eyebrow raise I do when I fib. Hey, I might not have been lying. Between the wedding details, the investigation, and my recent upgrade in relationship status with Lionel, I might not be in my apartment much. I was a champ at rationalization.

Thank goodness either I'd learned to control my eyebrow twitch or the girls were too excited about their private-investigator-by-association status to care. They ate the rest of the nonveggie pizza, took their plates into the kitchen, and promised to keep me updated on their assignment as they tromped out the front door.

As soon as they were gone, I turned the dead bolt. I'd had enough guests for one night. Once the veggie pizza was stored and the plates stashed in the dishwasher, I looked at the clock. My heart dipped. It was almost eight o'clock, and Lionel still hadn't called.

I tried to tell myself that I didn't care. We were both mature adults who didn't need to check in with each other all the time. Come to think of it, too many phone calls during a day would feel possessive and annoying. Which we weren't. So this was good.

My stomach clenched. Nope. I wasn't buying it. Now that I was no longer preoccupied with murderous mothers-in-law and starved skaters, anxiety had taken hold.

To distract myself, I placed another call to Pop. Voice mail. I tried to call Jasmine again. Voice mail. I even called Annette, hoping my godmother would be willing to discuss the thefts some more. Voice mail.

Crap.

Unless I wanted to spend the rest of the evening feeling like the pizza I consumed was going to make a reappearance, there was only one thing to do. Sucking up my pride, I started to punch speed dial number 3 when "The Hokey Pokey" began to play.

Lionel was calling.

My blood buzzed with nerves and excitement. "Hey." Was I smooth or what?

"I hope you aren't mad at me for not calling sooner." Fatigue and tension resonated in his voice. "I planned to call this morning and surprise you with a romantic dinner at my place tonight, but something came up."

Emergencies were part of a country vet's life. Around here there were always cows in labor or horses twisting ankles. Throw in the stray call for a sick dog whose owner trusted Lionel more than the pet's typical vet, and rarely a week went by without a date being postponed or broken.

"Did something happen to Mrs. Riley's goat again?" So far the animal had eaten a pair of boots, a curry brush, six sponges, and an orange plastic bucket. Each dietary adventure caused severe indigestion and a panicked phone call to Lionel.

"Not exactly. Doc Truman called and asked for help."

Uh-oh. Doc Truman wasn't just Indian Falls' answer to sniffles and sore throats. He was also the coroner. Whenever he was on vacation or otherwise occupied, Lionel stepped into his shoes. "Who died?"

"Ginny Chapman. I needed to escort her to the medical examiner and wait for him to perform the autopsy."

Ick.

Wait . . . "Why does Ginny need an autopsy? I thought those were only performed when the death is unexplained or there's a chance of foul play." All those evenings vegging out in front of *Law & Order* had taught me something. "Ginny died in her sleep."

"That's what Sean thought. Doc was pretty sure that was the case, too, until he examined her. There's no doubt about it." Lionel sighed. "Ginny didn't die of old age. The medical examiner has ruled. It was murder."

Nine

"*Murder? As in someone intentionally* killed Ginny Chapman? How?"

Another sigh. "I'm not allowed to divulge details, and I'm pretty sure Sheriff Jackson and Sean haven't notified the next of kin."

Both fair points. Unfortunately, neither made me want the information less. After all, I had been in the building acting like Bridal Bingo's answer to Vanna White when Ginny was killed. I was a witness. I might have seen the killer.

As much as I wanted answers, though, I wasn't about to push Lionel. Not after a day of accompanying a dead body and observing while it was poked, prodded, and pierced. Ew. Lionel didn't need to relive that adventure. What he needed was food and a distraction. Lucky for him, I was happy to provide both.

Twenty minutes later, I was standing at Lionel's front door with a vegetarian pizza and a shoulder bag containing a change of clothes and my toothbrush. Just in case.

Lionel smiled when he saw me and the pizza. His jaw dropped when I took off my puffy white coat and revealed the low-cut, black lace bustier Jasmine had talked me into buying two years ago. I'd never had a reason to wear it and often complained that it was money wasted. Turned out I was wrong. Not only was that cash not wasted, it was quite possibly the best money I'd ever spent.

The next morning, I woke with the bustier on the floor and a smile on my face. Unfortunately, Lionel was once again nowhere to be found. This whole morning disappearing act was enough to give a girl a complex. On the plus side, coffee and cold pizza were waiting for me when I arrived downstairs. As were a text message from Danielle asking what I thought of bags of nuts for favors and a voice mail from my grandfather telling me to drop by his place pronto. He had news.

Since the nuts sounded, well, nuts, I vowed to come up with something better and sent my grandfather a text saying I was on my way. Then I burned my tongue chugging coffee and grabbed a slice of cold pizza for the road. It was time to hear what the Indian Falls Senior Center grapevine was gossiping about.

The minute I stepped into the kitchen, Pop announced, "Ginny was murdered."

"I heard."

Pop's face fell. "You heard? How?"

"Doc asked Lionel to observe the autopsy. He called on his way home to let me know why he hadn't been in touch."

"Why didn't you call and tell me?" Pop plopped a hand on his brown-velour-clad hip. "Ginny was my friend. I had a right to know."

"I was waiting for you to call me back. I left you a message."

Pop snapped his gnarled fingers. "I forgot about your message. Sorry." He poured a cup of coffee from the pot on the counter and handed it to me. "I had a date with Francine Holmes and meant to call when I got home, but one thing led to another. You know how that goes." He winked.

I winced.

"Since your father cramps my style, we went back to her place. That's the only reason I know about Ginny. I was Poligripping my dentures when Francine got a call from Nan, who just talked to Doreen, who heard from Eleanor that Ginny's death had been ruled a homicide."

My head spun trying to follow that game of telephone from hell. Not sure if the information was going to be any more accurate than when I played that game in elementary school, I asked, "Did Eleanor mention the cause of death? Lionel wasn't in the mood to share."

"He probably doesn't want you mixed up in another murder investigation, seeing as how the last murderer came after you while you were investigating."

Technically, the murderer was gunning for me all along and just missed the first time. I wasn't sure that counted. Still, Pop could have a point. During Sherlene-n-Mean's murder investigation, Lionel changed his mind about my selling the rink and suggested I leave town and go back to Chicago. He wanted me safe, even if that meant losing whatever we were building between us. His suggestion ticked me off then. Now the memory made my stomach all tingly. Relationships were weird.

Pop didn't notice my tingling. "Francine said Nan had a hard time understanding all the details, but according to Doreen, who heard it from Eleanor, Doc Truman was concerned about Ginny's toes." He shrugged. "Or maybe it was her nose. Whatever it was, Doc decided the situation was unusual enough to call for an autopsy. That's how we know Ginny died of insulin shock."

"Was Ginny diabetic?" Maybe this wasn't murder but a terrible accident. Maybe everyone was overreacting. After all, Indian Falls had seen more murders in the last year than it had in over a decade. Jumping to conclusions would be understandable given the circumstances.

"Nope." Pop burst my bubble. "Ginny eats sugar like a champ. She always wins the center's annual Halloween candy-corn-eating contest. Louise started a petition last year to get Ginny disqualified based on her lack of medical conditions. Thank goodness the board nixed that one or we'd have been eating leftover candy corn for weeks. That stuff is hard to pry off the dentures."

Before Pop could pull out his teeth and clean them in front of me, I steered the conversation back to the murder. "I'm surprised Eleanor told"—I blinked, trying to recall who Eleanor had talked to—"someone about the cause of death. Was the next of kin notified by the time she called?"

"Eleanor wouldn't have leaked the information before they were called. Normally Eleanor wouldn't have leaked it at all. You know how tight-lipped she can be unless she's provided with a big incentive."

I winced as a picture of Eleanor decked out in black leather flashed through my mind. Yeah—Eleanor kept her mouth shut unless she had a good reason not to. Last time her reason was an evening with Pop. "What was her reason for sharing information this time?"

"The cause of death." My blank stare made Pop explain. "Eleanor was concerned the murderer might have stolen someone's insulin prescription and swapped it with water or something worse. She's coordinating a medical task force to make house calls on anyone in Indian Falls who takes insulin and verify they have the right medication. I volunteered for the job, but Eleanor said watching *M*A*S*H* reruns doesn't qualify as medical training. She's probably right."

Pouring myself another cup of Pop's coffee, I asked, "Have you heard what Sean thought of the medical examiner's ruling?" Sean was the one who originally said Ginny died of natural causes. He wasn't gracious when proven wrong.

"Not a clue, but I'd imagine he's going to be too busy running down a murderer to catch the Thanksgiving Day thief. He must be grateful you're picking up the slack."

Sure, and Elwood might guide Santa's sleigh this year.

However, Pop's optimism made a great segue to the questions I'd wanted to ask yesterday. "Are you friends with Seth and Jan Kurtz? I went by their house yesterday to talk to them about the first theft, and only the dogs were home."

"I've known Seth for almost forty years, but I can't say he's my friend. He used to be thick with Paul Jacabowski, but the two had a falling-out. Since then Seth hasn't been much for socializing unless he's talking about dogs or plants. His main objective in life seems to be beating Sheriff Jackson for first place in the St. Mark's Women's Guild's Beautiful Garden Contest. Part of me thinks he keeps that many dogs just so he has enough fertilizer."

Interesting theory.

"What about Jan?"

Pop grabbed a box of Cocoa Puffs off the counter and frowned as he shook it. Empty. My father's appetite had struck again.

Pitching the box, Pop said, "Jan's a nice lady. She spends most of her time painting flamingos on ceramic bowls." When I blinked, Pop added, "She's trying to convince Seth they should go to Florida during the winter. A few of the folks at the center started a snowbird club. Every year they rent a house in Sarasota and spend their winter on the beach while the rest of us are up to our eyebrows in snow and cold."

"Why haven't you gone with them?" I asked. Pop's Elvis act would be a hot commodity among the senior Floridian set. Although just thinking about him being that far away for several months made me sad.

"I thought about it, but it's too much work finding someone to house-sit. Not to mention the packing involved. Packing sucks." Pop jumped, reached into his pocket, and pulled out his phone. "Ethel's calling. She's the branch above me on the center phone tree."

While Pop talked to Ethel, I snuck into the garage to raid Pop's secret food stash. Pop-Tarts. Score!

Careful to pull the tarp back over the small fridge and Rubbermaid container, I hurried back into the warmth of the kitchen and made a beeline for the toaster. I was just polishing off the last piece of the frosted imitation-strawberry treat when my father sauntered into the kitchen, wearing black denim pants and a beige sweater. ——

"Do I smell Pop-Tarts?" His nose twitched. "I didn't know we had those."

"I think I ate the only one in the house," I was able to say truthfully. The rest were out in the garage. "Sorry."

Dad shrugged. "It's probably for the best. Too much sugar creates wrinkles." Pop walked back into the room with drooped shoulders and a wistful look in his eyes. I might have imagined the sympathy that crossed Stan's face before he smiled and nodded toward my grandfather. "See what I mean about sugar causing wrinkles?"

Pop didn't even glance at my father. "Ethel said the murder ruling has thrown a wrench into the services. The wake has been moved to Sunday. The burial will be on Monday, weather permitting."

The weather report I'd heard said the first snow of the year might come as early as this week. Just thinking about it made me depressed. So did the dejected expression on Pop's face and his lack of reaction to Stan's jibe. Pop loved an excuse to fight with Stan. The fact that he didn't throw back an insult told me just how deeply Ginny's death had affected him.

I needed to make Pop smile, and I was pretty sure I knew a way. Tugging on my coat, I said, "I'm going to head over to the Kurtzes' place today to see if they'll talk to me about the theft. Want to come along?"

The investigation would be a good way to distract Pop, and his familiar presence could encourage the Kurtzes to talk to me about the break-in.

"Hey." Stan looked up from the coffee he was pouring. "Are you visiting Seth and Jan?"

I blinked. "You know them?"

"I ran into them at the center yesterday when I was doing a consultation." My father grabbed a spoon and ladled sugar into his mug. I guess he didn't care if he got wrinkles after all. "Seth has a distinguished look I can sell to advertisers. I planned to search for him at the center and make my pitch, but if you're going by his place I can just tag along for the ride. Maybe I can even help you with this whole investigation thing. Your old man's just as wily as your grandfather, you know."

I did know. How else could I explain the way he had neatly boxed me into letting him accompany me and Pop to question witnesses?

Pop made four phone-tree calls from the passenger seat while my father rummaged through his briefcase in the back. I couldn't help but note that Stan didn't make a single comment the entire ride. Either his work was that engrossing or he was being respectful of Pop and his feelings.

I parked the car in the middle of the long driveway and got out. Dogs came flying from around the side of the house, barking their heads off. Three ran for the front porch. The other trio stormed toward me.

Yikes.

The barking grew louder and angrier as I shrieked and dove back into the car. Getting mauled by dogs wasn't on today's to-do list. I grabbed the handle of the door and slammed it shut as a Cujo wannabe mashed his nose against my window, bared his teeth, and growled. Doggy drool smeared across the glass. Yick— but better the window than me.

I was about to put my key in the ignition and clear out when a loud whistle pierced the air. The dogs stopped barking. A second whistle had them bounding up to the porch, where Seth Kurtz was waiting. One by one they sedately padded through the front door.

Impressive.

Not impressive enough for me to get out of the car. Pop and Stan didn't feel the same. As soon as the dogs were out of sight, they climbed out of my Civic and headed up the walk. Crap. Unless I wanted to look like a total wimp, I had to follow.

"I don't believe you've talked to my granddaughter, Rebecca, since she came back to town," Pop said as I cautiously stepped onto the porch.

Seth shook my hand but didn't invite us inside. I didn't mind. Being outside was nice. Warmth was highly overrated.

Pop didn't agree. "Julie Johnson hired Rebecca to look into the Thanksgiving Day thefts. Since you were the first victim, Rebecca needs to ask you some questions. Can we come inside?"

Instead of answering the question, Seth folded his arms over his chest and nodded toward Stan. "What's he doing here?"

"I'm just along for the ride," my father answered. "I'd be happy to wait in the car if it'd make you feel better." He rubbed his hands together and stamped his feet in an effort to keep warm and gave Seth a tremulous smile.

"Seth, where are your manners?" a pleasant but firm voice said from behind Seth. "Invite them into the house. You're letting out the heat."

My grandfather didn't need to be asked twice. He gave Seth a big smile and marched into the house. Stan followed. I paused at the door and cocked my head, listening for the sounds of Cujo's second cousins.

"I put the dogs in the basement, dear." Mrs. Kurtz smiled her understanding. "They wouldn't hurt you. My boys aren't biters, but they do get a bit overenthusiastic when visitors drop by. Come in from the cold. I have hot tea and sugar cookies waiting in the kitchen."

A gust of wind and the promise of cookies chased me inside. After hearing so much about Seth being protective of his home, I expected something . . . different. Flashier. More expensive. Not that the house wasn't lovely. It was. The honey-colored wood floors were polished. The walls of the living room we passed as

Jan led us down to the back of the house were painted a warm, muted yellow that complemented the comfortable-looking deep blue sofa and chairs. The pale green-and-white kitchen was stylistically dated, but inviting. If it hadn't been for the scratching and whining coming from a door on the other side of the room, I would have felt very much at home.

As it was, I took the chair closest to the exit, just in case the dogs managed to gnaw their way through the processed wood. Not the most heroic gesture, but I figured Pop had a full plate of turkey-shaped cookies in front of him that could be used to distract the dogs.

Seth took the seat closest to the scratching door, while my father helped Jan set milk, sugar, and a pretty blue-and-white flowered teapot on the center of the table.

"I can't thank you enough for dropping by." Jan smiled at me as she passed me a cup. "The entire center is talking about your investigation into the thefts. Ours happened so long ago, I doubt there's any chance we'll get any of our things returned, but I'd sleep better knowing the person responsible has been punished. Right, Seth?"

Seth shrugged and grabbed a cookie. "I sleep plenty good, and it's not like anyone's going to rob our house again."

"Because of the dogs?" I asked.

"Those damn dogs didn't stop the thief the first time." Seth frowned as his wife took the cookie out of his hand and replaced it with a cup of tea.

"Doc Truman said you've been eating too many sweets and fatty foods." She patted his hand and took a seat. Turning to me, she said, "We always thought owning so many large dogs would be a deterrent for thieves. Once we learned our mistake, we had an alarm system installed."

"Makes sense." Pop nodded. "You can't be too careful these days. I've been thinking about installing a security system at my place. Music equipment is expensive, and it never hurts to have additional protection against enthusiastic fans."

I wasn't sure Pop's secondhand amplifiers and microphones would fetch much of a price on eBay. True, Pop owned lots of gold chains and impressive-looking watches, but they were made of materials that tinted skin green. If a thief broke into Pop's place, the best he could do was lift a couple of cases of fake silk scarves and three black pompadour wigs.

Huh. As Seth went into detail about his alarm, I glanced at Jan. She was wearing a faded pink sweatshirt advertising her awesomeness as a grandmother. Jeans. A pair of small gold hoops decorated her ears, and a simple wedding band adorned her left hand. Nothing that suggested she and Seth had a stash of artwork or cash to protect. From what I'd seen of the house, they weren't interested in priceless antiques or other expensive knickknacks either. Yet the system Seth had installed included motion sensors and cameras. I understood being nervous after the break-in, but having every sniffle and sneeze caught on camera seemed like overkill.

When the boys took a moment to savor their tea, I asked, "Did anyone know you weren't spending Thanksgiving at home?"

"I did," Pop said through a mouthful of cookie. "Jan announced it at Friday night bingo."

Jan's shoulders drooped. "I won the final game of the night. The prize was two hundred and fifty dollars. I was so excited. I'd never won before, and I told everyone how I was going to splurge and buy every flavor of DiBelka pie to take to my son's house for Thanksgiving."

Great. The entire senior citizen population of Indian Falls knew the Kurtzes were going to be MIA for the holiday. Which meant the rest of the town probably knew about the promised pie purchase by the end of church services on Sunday. So much for pinpointing a suspect.

"Was this the first time you went away for Thanksgiving dinner?"

"Goodness, no." Jan smiled. "We have four grown children with families of their own. All of them live less than an hour's drive away. So for the past twenty years we've celebrated Thanksgiving and Christmas at one of their houses."

Which meant there was a good chance the thief knew the Kurtzes' house would be vacant long before the bingo bucks bonanza.

"When did you report the break-in to the police?"

"Saturday morning." Seth leaned back in his chair with a frown. "Neither of us noticed anything funny when we got home Thursday night. We let the dogs out for a crap, put the leftovers in the fridge, and went to bed. The next day, I noticed a couple of things weren't where they were supposed to be, but I just thought it was those senior moments everyone harps about."

Pop sighed. "I hate those moments. Just last week I misplaced my teeth and found them sitting on a shelf in the refrigerator."

I glanced at my father, who had suddenly developed an avid interest in the linoleum. Making a mental note to address that later, I asked, "When did you realize someone had broken into the house?"

"Friday afternoon," Jan explained. "When I saw my mother's silver candy dish was missing."

"Good riddance. The thing was ugly as sin."

Jan shot her husband a stern look. "It was a wedding present."

"That doesn't make it less ugly," Seth said. "It just makes it impossible to get rid of."

Wait. "If you noticed the candy dish was missing on Friday, why did you wait until Saturday to call the sheriff?"

Seth shrugged. "Didn't seem much point in talking to Sheriff Jackson until we knew what exactly was missing. Wasn't like the crook was still lurking around, waiting to get caught. Right, Jan?"

"That's absolutely right."

Although the reasoning made sense, I wasn't buying it. Both Seth and Jan were trying to act casual, but the furious pace at which Seth was tapping his foot made me question his calm expression, and if Jan twisted that wedding ring any harder she'd do permanent damage to her hand. If they ever came to Lionel's weekly poker game, they'd lose their shirts. Unfortunately, while I was certain the two were hiding the real reason for their delay in reporting the incident, I had no idea what that reason was.

"Could you tell me what went missing from the house?" I asked, pulling the notebook from my purse. "The sheriff's department is in the middle of reorganizing their records. Otherwise, I'd ask Sheriff Jackson for his report."

"Well, there was my mother's silver candy dish." Jan sent her husband a look that, if directed at me, would have made me squirm. Unfortunately, or maybe fortunately, the recipient of the look was wiping tea off his pants. "My jewelry box, all the watches our kids have given Seth over the years, a silver clock we kept on the mantel, his mother's gold-plated flatware, and my entire collection of the new United States quarters. I still haven't been able to replace Maine and Mississippi."

My father and Pop dug into their pockets and picked through their change while I added up the value of the items and came up confused. Unless Seth's other watches weren't Timexes or the gold-plated forks had originally been used by Henry VIII, the value of the items taken didn't seem worth the risk of prison or rabies. There had to be another reason why the thief targeted this house and started the Thanksgiving stealing in the first place—and whatever was taken had to have provided enough value or thrill or a combination of both to prompt the robber to strike Barna Donovan's house the following year.

"Did you notice if the dogs were behaving any differently, or have a vet check them over?" I asked. "It just seems like the dogs would have scared the robber off or bit him."

Jan sighed. "Our dogs are excitable, but very sweet-natured. King, Princess, and Lady were puppies when the robbery happened. The other three we had then passed several years ago, but none of our animals have ever bitten anyone who's dropped by the house. Not even the mailman. I probably should have had the vet check them over, but other than not being interested in the turkey leftovers I put out, they were perfectly fine."

By the time we climbed back into the car, my father had gotten Seth to agree to a photo shoot, Pop had eaten through the entire plate of cookies, and I was no closer to finding the thief. On top of it all, I needed to pee and had been unable to do so at the Kurtzes', since Seth claimed one bathroom was being renovated and the other had a toilet in need of plunging.

Right.

Shifting uncomfortably in my seat, I pointed the car toward town and hit the gas. Further investigation could wait. I needed a bathroom. Now.

By the time I got close to town, Pop and Stan were also feeling the effects of Jan's tea and doing the bathroom boogie. Since Pop's house only had two stalls, I zipped past his place and headed for the rink. Without waiting for Pop and Stan, I hopped out of the car and dashed to the ladies' room. I heard George yell a greeting as I streaked past.

Feeling much better, I walked back into the rink and waved as George circled the floor with one of his best artistic skating students. Josie was home from college and working hard to improve in hopes of making it onto the World Artistic Team next year. I watched her execute a flawless triple toe loop/double toe loop combination as my father joined me on the sidelines.

"I remember standing in this very spot, watching you do that," he said.

Josie performed a beautiful spiral, pivoted, and launched herself into a triple lutz.

"I was never that good," I said.

"You could have been. Your mother said you could've competed with the top skaters if you'd practiced more."

Practicing jumps resulted in lots of falls. With my red hair and fair skin, hitting the ground meant lots of bruises. Even at the age of eight, I understood black-and-blue wasn't a good look. I'd tried, though, because my mother's belief in me made me have faith in myself. Too bad our combined belief couldn't make me more graceful on or off four wheels. Back then I'd shrugged off the disappointment. Now remembering how I'd let my mother down just made me sad.

"Seth told some lies today," my father said.

Thankful for the subject change, I swallowed down the memories and nodded. "I know. He fibbed about the reason they waited to report the crime. Unfortunately, without putting Seth on the rack and torturing the reason out of him, there's no way for me to learn the truth."

"You could if you search the basement."

"Why? What am I going to find in the basement?" Other than big angry dogs?

"Got me." Stan leaned back against the wall that separated the skating floor from the sidelines. "I just know there's something more than dog drool lurking down there."

"How do you know that?"

"Every time the dogs scratched and whined, Jan flinched and Seth pretended he'd lost his hearing."

"Maybe Jan was worried the dogs were making a bad impression and Seth is so used to hearing the commotion he doesn't even notice."

My father shook his head. "Cons can spot another con a hundred feet away, and those two are amateurs. Seth's hands clenched every time the dogs made a noise, and when your grandfather mistook the basement door for the exit, Jan almost passed out. So on the way out I peeked in one of the window wells. The glass is blacked out." He smiled. "Trust me. The reason they waited to report the break-in is still in that basement."

Wow. Stan's logic was hard to dispute. Who knew having a crook for a father would finally pay off?

"Too bad there's no way to get a look down there."

Stan patted my arm. "Sure there is."

"Seth wouldn't allow us to use the bathroom. He's not going to let me tromp down the stairs and poke around."

"Well, of course not. You'll have to do it when he isn't home."

"When who isn't home?" My grandfather joined us. "What did I miss? My pipes don't work on command the way they used to."

"Rebecca needs to break into Seth and Jan's basement."

Pop's eyes brightened. "Do you need a lookout?"

"I don't need a lookout because I'm not going into Seth and Jan's house. Even if breaking and entering wasn't wrong, they have six German shepherds and a security alarm." Thus far I'd managed to stay away from dog bites and handcuffs. Two streaks I intended to continue.

"The alarm is bogus."

I blinked at my dad. "They have a sticker on the door and a blinking box on the wall."

Stan grinned. "Those things are there because Seth and Jan used to have an alarm. Seth was telling the truth when he said he installed one after the robbery, but I'm betting he got annoyed by the expense and decided it wasn't worth it. People do that all the time."

True enough. "But how can you be so sure Seth and Jan are those people?" Not that I was considering breaking into their house. I was just curious.

Stan shrugged. "I sold security systems a few years back. The system Seth was bragging about is at least a decade old and has had mandatory updates two or three times since. When I asked Seth if his system ever required updating, he said no."

"Maybe he just forgot." I could never remember if I'd gotten the most recent Windows update for my PC.

Stan smiled. "Maybe, but I doubt it. The keypads in the kitchen and near the front door are coated in dust. Trust me, Rebecca. No one has set that alarm system in years. If someone wanted to take a peek inside the house, and I'm not saying that someone is you," he hurried to add, "that person would want to slip into the house while Seth and his lovely wife were busy getting their photographs taken. The photographer might even suggest they bring along their dogs to be in some action shots with Seth for the composite card."

"Hot damn. That's good." Pop slapped Stan on the back, and the two turned and gave me brilliant smiles in tandem.

Call me crazy, but my father and grandfather bonding over criminal activity was just plain weird.

I was about to burst their collective bubble when my cell phone rang. Unknown number. I considered letting it go to voice mail but then changed my mind. Being harassed by a telemarketer was preferable to dealing with Indian Falls' answer to Bonnie and Clyde.

Hitting TALK, I blinked as I recognized the voice on the other end as Erica the Red.

"Rebecca, could you drop by the sheriff's office when you have the chance?" she asked. "Mary, Halle, and I have been arrested."

Ten

Whoever decided to paint the holding cells at the sheriff's office hot pink must have anticipated the arrival of its current occupants. Aside from the color and the people sitting in the two metal-bar-lined cells, the rest of the room remained unchanged since my last visit. Same narrow cot beds. Same ugly orange plastic visitor chairs. Same fluorescent strip lights. Between the paint choice and the accoutrements, this room didn't scream comfort. Perhaps that was the point.

Erica the Red and Typhoon Mary were in the cell closest to the door. Halle graced the one nearest the window. Either Anna was a faster runner or she hadn't been part of their adventure.

Halle gave a finger wave. "Hey. Sorry to make you come down here. We normally call George in these situations, but he didn't answer his phone."

I blinked. "You've been arrested before?"

Mary had the decency to blush. Halle and Erica smiled.

"The after-bout parties can get a little boisterous." Erica

shrugged. "As long as we pay for the tables we break, the owners are willing to drop the charges."

Yikes.

"You didn't break any tables this time, did you?" They shook their heads, and I took a seat in one of the orange plastic chairs. "So what are you in for?"

"We were scoping out the over-the-counter sleep aids at the pharmacy to see if any of them could have made a bunch of dogs sleepy," Erica explained. "If a person didn't want to get fingered for buying the drug, we figured she'd steal it. I said it wouldn't be hard for someone to walk out of the store with a box of Unisom. Halle thought a small-town store would be harder to shoplift from than one in a bigger town. To prove who was right, Mary suggested we act like real investigators and run a reenactment."

I sighed. "You shoplifted a box of sleeping pills?"

"Technically, Mary shoplifted." Erica smiled and patted her red-faced team captain on the shoulder. "Halle and I are accessories to the crime."

Mary nodded. "The kid at the counter has good eyes and excellent reflexes. She had the cops on the phone before I ever saw her move. If she can skate, I think she'd make an excellent jammer."

"You're right." Erica beamed. "Once we get out of here, we should give her a call. Rebecca, do you think you could ask the drugstore's owner for the girl's phone number?"

"Wouldn't you rather have the number for a good lawyer?"

"Why?" The three blinked. I sighed. Leave it to my derby girls to worry more about new recruits than losing their freedom.

"Let me talk to Sean," I offered. "With everything going on around here, I'm betting the department isn't concerned about one shoplifted box of sleeping pills." The flush on Mary's face told me there might have been more than sleep aids in her pocket. I thought about asking and decided sometimes it was best not to know.

Promising the ladies I'd be back with news, I went in search of Indian Falls' finest. I found him seated at his desk, frowning at the phone.

"Yes, Mrs. Ellis. We're doubling the patrols on Thanksgiving." Sean's voice was calm, but the red tint to his face told me he was about to blow. "No, the sheriff won't sign a document that assumes liability if your house is robbed. If you are concerned about your property, the department and the mayor are recommending you stay home for the holiday or work with your neighbors to form a watch system. Both are deterrents against home invasion."

The squawk from the receiver told me Mrs. Ellis was less than impressed.

"I'm sorry you had to cancel your plans." Sean clenched his jaw. "No, the sheriff can't reimburse you for your plane tickets, but I'll let him know you called."

The phone clattered as Sean smacked it back into its cradle. Then his frustrated eyes turned to me. "Roxy's here, but she can't talk because she lost her voice. The sheriff is taking a personal day, and I'm up to my neck setting up interviews and fielding freaked-out phone calls." He frowned. "I don't have time for games, so let me guess. You want to talk about Ginny's murder."

No. Although now that he mentioned it . . . Since the derby girls hadn't appeared all that distressed by their current location, I decided to walk through the door Sean had opened. "I heard Ginny died from insulin overdose."

Sean crossed his arms over his chest. "Insulin overdose is almost impossible to detect without an autopsy. There was no reason to believe it wasn't natural causes until Doc Truman examined her and had the cause of death determined by the medical examiner. Anyone who says different doesn't understand what they're talking about."

The snotty tone irritated me. I started to come up with a zinging retort, but then I realized the flush on his neck wasn't from temper. Sean was embarrassed he'd ruled the wrong cause of death. I tried to imagine the guilt that came with making that mistake, and my heart melted. Sean had earned a lot of karmic kicks, but this wasn't one of them.

I took a step into the room and said, "The killer planned the murder to look like natural causes. The town should feel lucky that you and the sheriff work so closely with Doc Truman. It's because of your team that we know someone took Ginny's life and a murderer is on the loose."

Hmmm. When I put it that way, maybe the town wasn't so lucky after all. People were already panicking about the Thanksgiving thief. Add a syringe-wielding maniac to the mix and mayhem was bound to ensue.

As if the holidays weren't stressful enough.

Sean rolled his shoulders and gave me a small smile. "Thanks. It's nice to know someone in this town isn't ready to lynch me. Ginny's family wants me removed from the investigation, and a representative from the Indian Falls Senior Center's activities board is threatening to lead a protest against the sheriff's department. They say the last two murders were identified as such on sight and Ginny's death was mislabeled due to assumptions made because of her status as a senior citizen. In short, she was discriminated against because of her age."

The last two murders involved a roller-rink toilet and electrocution in a dunk tank. Not exactly covert. The insulin overdose, however, was sneaky. Well planned. Designed to be written off as death by natural causes just as Sean had done.

"If an insulin overdose is almost impossible to diagnose by sight, why did Doc Truman suspect Ginny didn't die of natural causes?" I asked.

Sean studied me for a second and then rubbed his forehead and sighed. "I might as well tell you. You'll end up hearing it anyway. Ginny's pupils were dilated, and Doc spotted a hint of blood inside her nose. The combination made Doc suspicious. He looked for signs of an injection and found one on her right upper arm."

Huh. "Did Ginny take medication that required a syringe?" If so, the killer probably swapped the two.

"Not that Doc prescribed. Before you ask, I checked her apartment and talked to her family. Ginny didn't own or use syringes."

Which meant the killer had to administer the overdose. But how? It was pretty hard to jab someone with a needle without them feeling it. Most nurses, including Eleanor, claimed shots didn't hurt. They lied.

Before I could ask Sean his theory, he asked, "If you're not here to harass me about the murder, why did you drop by?"

"I need to spring Mary, Erica, and Halle."

Sean shook his head. "Can't do it."

"Why?" It wasn't like they'd killed someone. Call me crazy, but next to murder, the whole pills-in-the-pocket thing was minor.

"The sheriff thinks letting your derby girls go without charging them sends a bad message to the community." Sean shrugged.

"With Thanksgiving coming up, he doesn't want to be accused of condoning theft."

While Sheriff Jackson wasn't as sharp as he had once been, I had a hard time faulting his logic. Still, I had to try. "The derby girls weren't actually stealing."

"Mary put a bottle of pills, baby oil, and two boxes of condoms in her pockets and walked out the door without paying. What would you call it?"

I'd call it way too much information.

Taking a deep breath, I explained, "The girls honestly weren't trying to shoplift. They were doing me a favor."

Sean's eyebrows lifted, and the corners of his mouth twitched. I felt my face start to burn as I realized he assumed the items they pocketed were for me.

Certain my cheeks now matched the color of my hair, I said, "The girls were helping investigate the thefts. They were supposed to research which over-the-counter sleeping pills are safe to give dogs. In their enthusiasm, they decided to take it a step further. The other items . . ." Sigh. "You'd have to ask them about those."

"Okay." He leaned back in his chair. "I'll bite. Why did you want to know what sleeping pills could be used on dogs?"

Grateful he'd stopped talking about the other items on the derby girls' shopping list, I explained my theory about the Kurtzes' dogs.

"So the thief was prepared to keep the dogs out of his hair for the time it took to steal whatever specifically made him select that house. Is that your theory?"

"Yes." I straightened my shoulders.

"That doesn't suck."

I blinked. "Really?"

"Yeah, really." He grinned. "Still, unless the Kurtzes plan on giving us information that wasn't in the official report, your investigation is out of luck."

"Pop and Stan have a theory that a clue to what they didn't report might be located in their basement."

"You took your grandfather and Stan with you to question witnesses?" Amusement, disbelief, and what looked like disappointment flickered across Sean's face. "I thought you were trying to look professional. Professionals don't bring their family members along on assignments. Especially not when their family members wear Elvis wigs and scam old people into thinking they're going to be discovered by Hollywood."

I stiffened at the insults but found the shimmer of condescension in Sean's voice strangely comforting. Too much basic human decency made me wonder whether an extraterrestrial had taken over Sean's body.

"You ask questions your way." I crossed my arms. "I ask them mine. Bringing Pop and Stan instead of a badge and an attitude made the whole thing feel like a friendly visit. Without that, I doubt I would have gotten through the front door."

That was my story, and I was sticking to it.

"My methods might be unusual, but they get results. Did Seth and Jan ever tell the sheriff or Deputy Murphy about the dogs feeling too tired to eat turkey?" I asked, knowing full well the answer was no. "The thief drugged Seth and Jan's dogs in order to break into the house. I know it."

At least, I thought I did. Which amounted to the same thing. Right?

Sean leaned forward. "You might be right. The sheriff's report says all six dogs were acting normal when the Kurtzes arrived home. When I took over the investigation, I did a follow-up with Jan and Seth. They never said anything about the dogs not having an appetite."

The phone rang, and Sean let out a sigh. "I have to get this. Let me know if you talk your way into the basement and figure out if the thief took something that was never reported. Just don't do anything I have to arrest you for in the process, or you'll end up handcuffed to my spare bed. The jail is full up as is."

Eek! I started to hightail it out of the room and then realized I hadn't addressed the problem that had made me come here in the first place. "Wait," I said as he picked up the phone. "Are you going to spring Erica, Mary, and Halle?"

"Tell you what," he said with his hand over the receiver. "If you convince the folks at the senior center not to picket the department, I'll get the charges dropped and set them free. Deal?"

"Deal."

"Good. Indian Falls Sheriff's Department. How can I help you? Sheriff Jackson isn't in the office right now, Mrs. James, but I'd be happy to address your concerns."

Leaving an exasperated Sean, I went back down the hall to inform the derby divas they'd be sprung soon. Then I headed out of the station, determined to follow through on my promise.

Simple as that seemed, though, I knew that cool reason was rarely enough to combat the rallying cries of the town's seniors when they were riled. Just last month, Zach Zettle, Indian Falls' answer to all things automotive, complimented Roberta Stringer's newly styled white hair. He then went on to suggest that the cracked taillight, scraped passenger door, and broken rearview mirror on her Chevy Malibu might be a sign Roberta needed to turn in her driver's license. Instead of heeding his advice, Roberta turned the compliment on her coif into a rallying cry. The next day, the center faithful arrived at Zach's garage sporting cardboard signs with slogans like GRAY'S THE NEW BLACK and WHITE IS BRIGHT. Even after Zach convinced them of his good intentions, it took two days for the seniors to leave. Protests and picketing were more exciting than pinochle any day. With everything else going on, two days of honking horns and snappy slogans would send Sean over the edge. To make sure that didn't happen, I needed more than a logical argument. I needed a secret weapon. I needed my grandfather.

"What do you mean he's not here?" I asked George as he skated off the rink. "Pop and Stan were supposed to wait here for me."

George wiped his sweaty, red-splotched forehead with the back of his hand. "They must have gotten tired of waiting. One minute they were sitting on the sidelines, eating jumbo pretzels with nacho cheese, and the next they were gone."

"Did you happen to hear what they were talking about before they left?" That might give me a clue as to where they had headed. Not only was I in need of Pop's assistance, I was worried. It was cold outside. I didn't want Pop coming down with the sniffles or worse.

"Sorry." George shook his head, sending beads of sweat flying. "I had Josie's music playing."

Josie's routine was set to a medley from *Les Misérables* that was both beautiful and loud.

George waved as his next student came into the rink. He zoomed to the sound booth to cue up music, and I pulled out my phone and dialed.

"Rebecca." My grandfather's voice came on the line. "Are the girls out of the clink?"

"I'm working on it."

"Do we need to stage a jailbreak? I've always wanted to try baking a file into a cake. I'm not sure it would work, but at least the girls would have something to snack on until we came up with another plan."

The sound of a woman's laughter on my grandfather's side of the conversation made me wonder if I was interrupting something I didn't want to think about. If so, Pop was going to need a doctor after being brained for answering the phone at a less than opportune moment. The laughter got louder. I cringed and considered hanging up. Instead, I conjured up an image of the girls behind steel bars and asked, "Where are you? I need your help."

"Is it about the case?" His voice got low and whispery. "Stan and I worked out a plan that can get you into you-know-who's basement without the you-know-whats gnawing on your leg like it's one of those fancy-shaped rawhides. Mary Anne O'Reily's dog has a rawhide that looks like a mutant chicken leg. If Amy Jo and Mark Boggs could get their chickens to grow as big as that, they wouldn't need to get a second mortgage from the bank. They'd be making a fortune selling those cluckers to Perdue."

"I'm not going to break into the Kurtzes' basement, so just—" Wait. "Amy Jo and Mark Boggs are having financial trouble?"

"Hey, don't start without me," Pop yelled as more laughter drifted through the receiver. "Sorry, Rebecca. Your father needs me to do a test shot with Nan. It's my job to make her look comfortable. Jimmy Bakersfield gave us a lift to the center in his new ride. We'll be done here in about two hours if you want to stop by and talk about our plan."

Click.

Sigh.

I put the phone in my pocket and considered Pop's words while George and his skater glided across the rink. Amy Jo and Mark Boggs had been taking care of Betsy Moore's horses when she was out of town and her house was robbed. If Amy Jo and Mark were having money troubles, they might have been tempted to snag a few items from their neighbors in order to keep their financial heads above water.

Of course, for Mark and Amy Jo to qualify as suspects, they would have to have lived here long enough to commit the crimes. Since Pop was currently too busy to stop angry hordes of senior citizens from painting protest signs, I had time to track down a new lead. The time had come for me to figure out when the Boggs family had moved to town.

Eleven

Pop's mention of chicken reminded me I hadn't eaten lunch. I hit the drive-through for nuggets, a large order of fries, and a Coke as big as my head. Then, munching on a fistful of salty deep-fried potatoes, I steered my yellow Civic to the Boggses' farm. When I pulled into the concrete driveway lined with cars, my stomach was protesting the amount of grease I'd consumed.

Slightly nauseated, I climbed out of my toasty warm car and hurried to the door of the front porch of the Boggses' two-story red-and-white farmhouse. I rang the bell, wrapped my arms around myself, and stamped my feet to keep warm as I waited . . . and waited. I rang the bell again.

Huh. I looked at the four cars in the drive and wondered if Mark tinkered with automobiles in his spare time. If so, there was a good chance no one was home.

I was about to leave when the door swung open, revealing a woman about my height with straight, light brown hair and sad eyes.

"Can I help you?"

The hitch in the woman's voice and the tissue clutched in her hand made me think this was a really bad time for a visit. "My name is Rebecca Robbins. I'm looking for Amy Jo Boggs. If this is a bad time, I'd be happy to—"

"Rebecca Robbins?" The corners of her mouth turned up. Her eyes brightened. "I'm Amy Jo. Please come in. We were just talking about you."

We? Who was we?

I followed Amy Jo down a hall, past a small office and a formal dining room, into a cheerfully painted orange and yellow living room filled with eight or nine not-so-cheerful people. I spotted my high school employee Kristin Chapman seated on the wood rocking chair next to a partially assembled Christmas tree and waved. She gave a weak smile and waved back. Next to Kristin was her mother. The rest of the faces were unfamiliar, but I could guess who they were. This was Ginny Chapman's family, who had started mourning her death on Sunday and had now learned that Ginny had been murdered.

"Rebecca, this is my husband, Mark." A tall, gangly guy with a mop of curly blond hair stood and held out his hand. I shook it while Amy Jo introduced the other people in the room. Among the mourners were Ginny's younger sister and her two daughters.

"We've been working on arrangements," Ginny's sister said. Her wrinkled eyes were red from fatigue and tears. "With everything going on, they won't let us have the wake until Sunday. Ginny would have hated to make everyone wait. She didn't like it when people went to a lot of trouble for her."

Everyone nodded.

Amy Jo sniffed and patted her great-aunt's hand. "I'm so glad you stopped by. We were going to call and ask if you might be willing to help our family." Amy Jo sat on the arm of a floral-patterned sofa and indicated for me to take a seat in the chair next to her. "My great-aunt Ginny was one of the nicest, most considerate people I've ever met. If she had just passed in her sleep as we were originally led to believe, we would still be sad, but we would understand why she was gone. But now . . ."

Mark took Amy Jo's hand. Sniffles filled the room, and my heart squeezed in sympathy. To grieve without understanding who caused the loss and why had to be unbearable. I thought about losing my mother and how that had made me feel. Great. Now I was starting to sniffle.

Taking a deep breath, Amy continued, "Besty Moore came by earlier. She said Julie Johnson hired you to look into the thefts."

"Actually," I said, relieved to focus on anything that wasn't going to make me cry, "that's part of the reason I dropped by. I was hoping you could answer a couple of questions, but those can wait until after . . ." After what I wasn't quite sure.

I started to stand, and Amy Jo waved me back into my seat with a sad smile. "Please stay. It took Betsy months to sleep through the night after the break-in. Mark and I are happy to answer whatever questions you have. Especially now that we understand what it's like to have someone take something precious from us."

From across the room, Kristen looked at me with glistening eyes. I had two choices. I could flee out the door and feel like a schmuck or sit back down while pretending I wasn't about to cry.

The chair won.

Mark raked a hand through his unkempt hair and shifted in his seat. "What Amy Jo is trying to say is that our family wants the person who ended Aunt Ginny's life brought to justice."

"The sheriff and Deputy Holmes are working to make sure that happens." Technically, the sheriff was off catching a turkey or raking leaves, but that was probably more useful than having him get in Sean's way. The sheriff was better at making reassuring statements, directing his staff, and shaking hands than at tracking criminals. As far as I was concerned, it was best to have him play to his strengths.

"We know the sheriff's department will work hard," a dark-haired woman seated next to Kristen said, "but we don't feel confident in their ability to handle a murder investigation without outside assistance. That's where you come in."

What? Wait. No. "I don't think—"

Without waiting for me to figure out what I thought, Mark said, "We know you've agreed to dedicate your time to helping solve the thefts. We don't want to interfere with that, but we were hoping you might also be able to look into Aunt Ginny's death."

"But . . ."

"We can pay you." This from a tiny woman with sharp features and steel-gray hair. "I'm willing to pay whatever it takes to see to it that my sister rests in peace." She swiped away a tear with a tissue. Lifting her chin, she added, "Please."

Gulp.

"It's not about money." I swallowed hard, and my heart hammered. All eyes looked at me with sorrow and hope. Hope that relied on me. Yikes. "I'm really not qualified."

"You solved the last two murders," Kristen said.

"But—"

"And the car theft ring," Kristen's mother added. "The sheriff's department would never have arrested the criminals responsible for those crimes if it weren't for you."

"That's not true." I didn't have a gun or handcuffs. Arresting people was not in my skill set.

Unfortunately, none of the faces looking at me seemed to believe that.

"Look," I said, trying to ignore my grease-coated lunch rolling in my stomach. "I'm really not qualified to investigate a murder." Hell, I wasn't qualified to investigate anything more than who snagged the last pretzel out of the heating carousel. Only I couldn't ignore the way Kristen's lip trembled and Ginny's sister's shoulders slumped. "I'll keep my ears open. If I hear anything I think will help catch Ginny's killer, I'll let Deputy Holmes know."

Then he'd either ignore what I had to say or pitch me into the pink penitentiary from hell. While he might be willing to let me poke my overcurious nose into a ten-year-long string of robberies, I doubted he'd be so accommodating when it came to murder. Still, if it brought Ginny's family a moment of peace, I would take whatever retribution Sean delivered.

Of course, that peace might be short-lived depending on what I learned from Amy Jo and Mark. The two walked me to the door after the family gave me a rundown on Ginny's likes, dislikes, friends, and typical activities, along with a key to her apartment at the retirement home. There was probably some kind of law about me going into the apartment without the sheriff's permission, but I figured I'd worry about that bridge when I jumped off it.

"Here's a list of our phone numbers in case you have any questions or information." Amy Jo handed me a piece of paper and gave me a small smile. "I realize you might not solve this case, but we feel better knowing someone we trust is working for Aunt Ginny."

Amy Jo was talking about trust, and I was about to ask questions that could implicate her in a decade's worth of crimes. Was I a nice person or what? Still, the questions had to be asked. Maybe I'd get lucky and Amy Jo and Mark would have information that would eliminate them from the suspect list. While that wouldn't help me solve Julie Johnson's case, I'd stop feeling like a traitor. Sometimes you had to take what you could get.

With that in mind, I changed the subject to the thefts. "Betsy mentioned that you and Mark helped feed the horses while she was away for Thanksgiving last year."

"A bunch of us try to help out with livestock when one goes out of town. Last year we helped Betsy with her horses. The year before it was the Gullifers' cows."

My fingers itched to reach for my notebook. Instead, I mentally scrolled down the victim list. The Gullifers' house had been robbed four years ago. Or maybe it was five. Whichever year it was, they were on the list, and Amy Jo and Mark not only knew them . . . they knew how to get into their house. At least they did as of two years ago. I needed to find out when they'd started the animal swap. Before I did that, though, there was something else I had to ask. Something I hoped would get them off the suspect list for good.

"When exactly did you move to Indian Falls?"

Amy Jo beamed at Mark. He beamed back and said, "Eleven years ago last month."

Well, crap.

Zipping my coat, I promised to be in touch and then headed out into the cold, wishing I hadn't come to visit Amy Jo and Mark. If I'd waited until tomorrow, Sean might have already found Ginny's killer. I wouldn't have seen the way these people were counting on me to help them. I wouldn't feel like such a complete ass, knowing that my actions might deal them another blow.

Okay, technically, if Mark and Amy Jo were behind the thefts, my actions wouldn't be the reason they ended up singing gospel songs in a pink room. Still . . .

Shivering, I hurried to my car. As I reached for the handle, I spotted a flash of fur and heard a distinctive purring sound. A moment later, Homer skittered from under a bush. Apparently, Betsy still wasn't having luck keeping him inside.

Homer chattered, stood on his hind legs, and waved his hands. The friendly gesture made me smile. Since I didn't speak raccoon, I made the assumption the little guy was hungry and dug a few french fries out of the bottom of the fast-food bag. Homer's whiskers twitched as he took a fry and began to munch. When he was done with the fry, he purred and waved his paws again, and I handed him another. While he ate, I revised my thoughts on getting a pet raccoon. Couches were totally overrated, right?

Despite the cold, I waited until Homer polished off the remnants of my lunch before giving him a pat on the head and climbing into my car. Homer ambled up the porch to the front door while I waited for my heater to kick in. After several minutes, I saw the door open and Homer disappear inside.

Seeing the furry tail twitch before the door closed made me feel lighter. Less conflicted. The welcome Amy Jo gave Homer suggested he was a frequent visitor. Anyone who welcomed a pet raccoon into their house at the risk to their furnishings couldn't be a criminal. Okay, that thinking would earn me an eye roll from anyone trained in investigative deductions, especially Deputy Sean. They'd say acceptance of a raccoon had no correlation with the guilt or innocence of a suspect. I didn't care. Homer thought Amy Jo and Mark were good people. I trusted his instincts. Now I had to prove both of us right.

The good news was that my new mission required me to do exactly what I was going to do anyway—find whoever had been robbing houses and bring them to justice. The bad news was it also required me to try to track down another murderer. The last two times I did that, I wound up with a gun pointed at my nose. I really wasn't interested in repeating that experience. Getting shot would totally ruin my day.

Hoping I wouldn't need to invest in a bulletproof vest, I motored down the street in search of a sign for the Gullifer Dairy Farm. Sadly, the Gullifers didn't appear to believe in advertising. It took me forty-five minutes, three dropped calls to my grandfather, and a lot of colorful vocabulary before I pulled up to my destination.

The sound of mooing and the faint smell of cow manure accompanied me as I walked to a house that needed a new coat of white paint. Twenty minutes later, I was back in my car, armed with a list of jewelry, small electronics, and other valuables taken by the thief five years ago. I also learned that Amy Jo and Mark had been lending a hand with livestock for the past seven years. Drat. The upside was the Boggs duo had only been given a key to the milk room and the barn. Not to the house. Apparently, attaching machines to cow udders didn't rate refrigerator privileges.

Steering back to town, I debated the next steps in my investigation. I still thought the motivation behind the first theft was the key to solving the case. With that in mind, I pulled my car into a driveway and dialed Amy Jo's number.

When Mark answered, I apologized for interrupting and asked, "Do you and your wife know Mr. and Mrs. Kurtz?"

"Seth and Jan?" There was a smile in his voice. "Of course. They were at the welcome party Aunt Ginny threw for us a couple of weeks after Amy Jo and I moved to town. Aunt Ginny was worried we weren't making enough friends, so she introduced us to hers. That's the kind of woman she was. No matter how busy she was in her own life, Ginny always looked out for her family and friends. Although I'm sorry to say the party was a disappointment to her."

"Why do you say that?"

Mark laughed. "The whole point of the party was to introduce us to people we could socialize with. While Aunt Ginny's friends were nice, they . . ." He sighed. "Well, let's just say Aunt Ginny was in her eighties and we're . . . well . . . not."

Fair point. "So you didn't spend time with Seth and Jan after that day?"

"Not much. Ginny and Seth had some kind of argument, and she stopped inviting him to her parties. I guess they must have patched things up, though, because Ginny had me deliver chicken soup to the house last year when Jan came down with pneumonia. Until then I'd only heard stories, but the stories are true. Those dogs are scary."

I agreed.

By the time I hung up, Mark and I had bonded over our fear of Indian Falls' answers to the Hound of the Baskervilles. I had also learned that while Mark and Amy Jo met Mr. and Mrs. Kurtz soon after coming to town, Mark didn't encounter their German shepherds until last year. If he and Amy Jo had broken into the Kurtz home, they would have come face-to-face with the dogs' angst ten years ago.

Of course, knowing that I was looking into the thefts, Mark could have slipped the chicken-soup anecdote into the conversation to throw me off track. The perpetrator of the Thanksgiving

Day thefts was smart and good at flying under the radar. If he wasn't, Sean would have already thrown him behind bars. Still, I couldn't get myself to believe Mark and Amy Jo were anything more than what they appeared to be—kind, good-hearted people who were grieving the loss of a beloved family member. A loss I had promised to investigate. Since I wasn't sure what my next step in the Thanksgiving thefts case was, there was no time like the present to start.

Twelve

Ginny Chapman lived in a first-floor one-bedroom condo at the Indian Falls Retirement Community. When the building next door was converted from an unused high school into the gathering place for shuffleboard and Sinatra, the town's older population held bake sales, craft fairs, and raffles. The proceeds raised were to be used to create an enclosed walkway that joined the two buildings. Pop and his contemporaries were better at eating their wares than selling them, so it took eight years and a check from an anonymous donor before the walkway was built. Since the center and the retirement community shared a parking lot, rarely did cars leave their parking spots. Who needed to drive when meals, workout classes, and entertainment were available without having to walk outside? Especially now, when the weather was so cold. It was no surprise that traffic accidents and parking tickets were down fifty percent during the winter months. I was also not shocked to discover that there was no place in the parking lot for me to park.

Since there was no avoiding a stroll in the cold, I parked at the roller rink and hoofed it the two blocks to the center. I then availed myself of the heated walkway to travel in comfort the rest of the way.

My nose was still cold when I reached the light-blue-carpeted lobby of the Indian Falls Retirement Community and heard the Canon in D blare out of my purse. Several pairs of eyes looked at me as I dug my phone out of the side compartment. So much for being inconspicuous.

HOW ABOUT BARS OF SOAP WITH THE DATE STAMPED ON THE FRONT?

Sighing, I typed back, YOUR GUESTS MIGHT THINK YOU ARE COMMENTING ON THEIR HYGIENE. Or that Danielle and Rich had raided the housekeeping carts at the local motels. DON'T WORRY. I'LL COME UP WITH SOMETHING.

At least I'd try, after I finished my current mission.

Sliding my phone back in my purse, I followed the posted signs to apartment 121. As far as I knew, there were only thirty condos in the three-story building, but I guess whoever created the numbering system was optimistic about the building's chances of expansion.

Aside from the small gold letters on the door, Ginny's apartment had no identifying markings. I considered the lack of police tape on the door a good sign. If Sean dropped by, he wouldn't be able to prove I knew entry was a no-no.

A vaguely familiar man in ratty gray sweatpants and an oversized Elvis Arthur and Hermanos Mariachi sweatshirt came out of the apartment next to me. The few gray hairs on his head were long and stretched over the top of his head in an effort to camouflage the bald spot. He peered through his wire-rim glasses and pulled a cell phone out of his pocket as I slid the key in the lock. Unless I was mistaken, the Indian Falls gossip train was leaving the station. If I didn't want to get flattened by the engine, I had to make this quick.

I closed the door behind me and squinted into the darkness. Someone, probably the cops, had closed the drapes in the living room. Being on the first floor meant a garden patio. It also meant neighbors could press their noses against the glass and get a glimpse inside.

Once I found the light switch, I looked around the immaculate kitchen and decided whoever closed the drapes didn't need to bother. There wasn't much in here to see. The white Formica countertops were free of crumbs. The black stove and microwave were devoid of fingerprints. Even the bright blue teakettle on the stove looked brand-new. Either the woman never cooked or her housekeeping skills rivaled Donna Reed's.

I did a quick inventory of Ginny's cupboards. Four plates, bowls, and saucers. Six plastic tumblers. Macaroni and cheese. Chocolate-chip-enhanced fiber oatmeal. Frosted Flakes. A year's supply of chocolate pudding and Oreos. The fridge was more of the same. A Papa Dom's pizza box. Two bottles of cranberry juice. A half gallon of milk with a seal that hadn't been broken. Two tubs of ice cream, a box of corn dogs, and a bunch of frozen meals graced the freezer. Well, one thing was certain: Ginny wasn't a health-food nut. She also didn't stash scraps of paper or scribbled-on receipts in her kitchen drawers. In fact, she didn't keep anything in here that wasn't absolutely necessary. Impressive yet disappointing.

The living room was just as streamlined. The couch was pristine, most likely due to the plastic overlaying the bright green fabric. A small basket of perfectly rolled yarn in primary colors sat next to a dust-free rocking chair. A television and DVD player rested atop a small oak cabinet. From the perfectly shelved selection of films, I'd say Ginny liked movies where people got shot, blown up, or both.

In the bedroom, I found another television, a collection of black-and-white movies, and lots of photographs. Ginny with her family. Ginny getting a scarf from Elvis Pop. Ginny and her husband on their wedding day. Pictures of her in front of a beach resort. On a small footstool next to the bed was a partially packed suitcase. A black-and-white polka-dotted bathing suit sat on top. Ginny had started packing for this year's escape from the snow.

Ignoring the slimy sensation rolling through my stomach, I pawed through her clothes, opened the night-table drawer, and poked around her jewelry box. Ginny's clothes weren't flashy. Her jewelry was minimal, and the dresser drawer was filled with a set of knitting needles, bits of yarn, and the most recent issue of *TV Guide*. I was about to close the drawer when I noticed the edge of a small book peeking out from under the magazine.

Ginny's checkbook.

Since I now knew that Ginny preferred lace panties, I figured I'd already broken all moral boundaries. No point in stopping now.

A quick flip through her checkbook told me Ginny had a balance of two thousand sixty-three dollars and ninety-one cents. She'd paid her phone, electrical, and gas bills last week, as well as her condo association fee. I flipped back a page and noticed a check for nine thousand dollars written to Florence D. Hemmens dated two weeks ago. The day before the check was written, a deposit for that exact amount was made into the account.

Huh.

I flipped through the pages, which dated back to June of this year. Ginny appeared to be as good at balancing the books as she was at scrubbing the counters. Every month she logged a direct deposit from Social Security as well as the bills she paid. If I did the mental math correctly, Ginny spent the same amount of money every month. That amount was almost exactly covered by the check she received from the government. What she didn't spend went toward the biannual property tax bill she faithfully paid and logged. Her property tax bill dropped her balance perilously close to zero, but the government deposit a week later remedied the matter.

I'd say one thing for Ginny: The woman knew how to budget. Fear of bouncing a check would have scared me into transferring money from savings into the account. Math wasn't my strong point. Ginny had either nerves of steel, complete faith in her mathematical prowess, or no savings to transfer. Of course, the nine-thousand-dollar deposit and subsequent check belied the last option.

Or did it?

My search had turned up this one bankbook. Ginny didn't own a computer, which indicated she wasn't doing her banking online. If she had a savings account, I couldn't find any evidence of it. Something wasn't adding up about the deposit or the check. Too bad I hadn't a clue what that something was.

Frowning, I tried to do a search on my phone for the recipient of the nine-thousand-dollar check. No signal. Predictable. I scribbled the name down in my notebook and slipped the bank register back into the drawer where I'd found it. Then I resumed my search.

Ginny's bathroom would also pass the white-glove test. The medicine cabinet contained several over-the-counter vitamins, a hairbrush, and an almost empty bottle of Pepto-Bismol. The last was probably due to Ginny's eating habits, which somehow managed to be worse than those of the kids working for me. Sitting on the green counter were a yellow toothbrush, a can of aerosol hair spray, and a prescription bottle for Ambien CR with Doc Truman's name listed as the prescribing physician.

A glance at my watch told me it was time to clear out. Sean had probably learned about my foray into this apartment. If so, he would be on his way. For both our sakes, it would be best to avoid that particular confrontation. Still, I couldn't help taking one last walk through the bedroom in the hopes I'd spot something more useful than Ginny's love of sugar and her talent for keeping her life uncluttered. Although I suppose the lack of clutter was interesting. Most people who lived alone, me included, didn't need lots of extra plates or bowls, yet we were compelled to stuff the cabinets with table settings for ten and enough kitschy coffee mugs to invite the state of Rhode Island to afternoon tea.

Huh.

I looked around the cabinets and frowned. Ginny didn't have any mugs on her shelves. So why the teapot? To my way of thinking, microwaves had mostly usurped the teapot's usefulness, but many coffee and tea lovers still felt compelled to have teapots on display even if they were never used. Pop did. The last time I took the lid off that teapot, I found a combination of dust and rust. Yum. Still, Pop kept the teapot as a backup in case the microwave went belly-up.

According to items on her shelves, though, Ginny didn't drink tea. Or coffee or anything that required a mug. The woman didn't appear to own anything that didn't serve a purpose. So I had to wonder—what did Ginny use the teapot for?

There was one way to find out. I moved the teapot closer, re-moved the lid, and felt my heart stop. Inside the perfectly polished teapot was money.

Lots and lots of money.

Singles. Fives. Tens. Twenties. A couple of fifties thrown in, but nothing larger. Just stacks and stacks of small bills with a couple of rolls of quarters thrown in for good measure.

Eureka! I had found Ginny's savings account.

I took a seat at the small square kitchen table and emptied the teapot's cache onto the place mat in front of me. Three recounts later, I determined the teapot-trove total. Including the two rolls of quarters, Ginny had one thousand four hundred and thirty-six dollars' worth of mad money. Not enough to retire on, but plenty to visit the riverboat casinos without fear of busting in the first twenty minutes. Especially if she played the penny slots like Pop.

I re-rubber-banded the bills, shoved them back into their steel safe, and then replaced the teapot on the stove. The sound of rus-tling paper stopped me in my tracks. I shifted the teapot and heard the sound again.

Sure enough, there was a piece of paper taped to the bottom of the teapot. Huzzah! The burner grill must have snagged on it when I put the pot down. Not exactly a skilled investigative technique, but I'd take it.

Careful not to tear the paper, I peeled the slip of lined note-book paper off the bottom of the kettle. On the paper were the numbers 8465793884 followed by WMCSA 765432. I read the series of letters and numbers again and waited for Ginny's ghost to give me some insight into their meaning.

Nope. No ghost-whisperer moment. No great inspiration. Nothing.

I put the kettle back on the stove and slipped the paper into my pants pocket. These numbers and letters were important enough for Ginny to hide. Perhaps whatever they meant was important enough to kill for. That was more to go on than I had when I arrived here.

Once all the lights were off, I locked Ginny's condo door and hurried down the hall. When I stepped into the covered walkway, I smiled. I'd made a clean getaway.

"What the hell do you think you're doing?"

Or not.

Plastering what I hoped was an "I'm totally innocent" smile on my face, I turned around. "Are you talking to me?"

Sean stalked across the worn carpeting. His face was red from being out in the cold. At least that's what I was telling myself. If my actions made his cheeks turn that color, no amount of fast talking was going to keep me from singing gospel with the Estro-Genocide girls.

"You broke into Ginny Chapman's condo?"

"I did no such thing." Hurrah for honesty.

Sean didn't look impressed. "A half-dozen people called to tell me you were spotted going into Ginny's condominium."

"Amy Jo and Mark Boggs gave me a key." I dug into my pocket and did show-and-tell. "Ginny's family said they'd feel better if I took a look around. The sheriff's department didn't have a notice on the door, so I assumed it was safe to go inside."

Sean crossed his arms. "I didn't put a department notice on the door because Ginny's condo isn't a crime scene. I also thought her family would want to select clothes for the funeral service."

"That was nice of you," I said, and I meant it. I remembered choosing my mother's clothes. I stood in front of her closet, barely

155

seeing anything through the tears. Luckily, Annette was standing next to me. She helped pull my mother's favorite blue dress from the closet and drove me to the funeral home to deliver it. I was touched by Sean's consideration for Ginny Chapman's family. Arranging a funeral was hard enough without having to worry about police restrictions.

Sean shifted his feet and shrugged, which made me smile. The man was more comfortable being a pain in the ass than a nice guy. Behind him, I spotted several of my grandfather's contemporaries watching us with avid interest.

Lowering my voice, I asked, "Did you have a chance to look through Ginny's place before her family went in?"

"I performed a walk-through Monday morning."

"So there shouldn't be any problem with me going through it today. Right?"

Sean's eyes shifted to something over my left shoulder. Our audience must be growing. "No, there's no problem." The overly cheerful tone made me wince. There was totally a problem. Something he confirmed when he quietly added, "Or there won't be if you agree to talk about this in private."

"I was just heading over to the senior center to find Pop and enlist his help in stopping the protest. Just like you asked."

A male voice behind me whispered, "Should we tell her Arthur already left, or do you think she's just trying to get away from Deputy Holmes?"

Sean smiled. I sighed and looked out the window, where the sky was a dreary gray. "It's cold out there."

He smiled. "I'm betting it'll feel even colder in jail."

Fair point.

"I'm dying for a cup of coffee," I said, loud enough for those whose hearing aid batteries had failed. "Do you want one?"

While there was a smile on Sean's face, his eyes were all steel as he put a hand on my shoulder and said, "Sounds great. Let's go."

We both smiled like idiots as we passed a group of my grandfather's adoring female fans on our way to the exit. Once we hit the sidewalk, Sean asked, "Where did you park?"

"The rink. There weren't any spots in the lot when I got here."

Sean grinned. His sheriff's department car was parked in front of a DO NOT PARK sign. Popping the locks, he said, "Get in."

As Sean cranked the engine, I sent a text to Pop, telling him we needed to talk. Then I waited for Sean to hang a right toward the rink. He took a left.

"Where are we going?" I asked. If his giving me a ride was a trick so I'd quietly go to lockup, it was going to ruin my whole day.

"We're getting coffee, as you suggested." He took the next left. "We wouldn't want the gossips to think we were lying. Right?"

He executed a perfect U-turn and parked in front of Indian Falls' source for high-octane beverages, Something's Brewing. Directly in front of another NO PARKING sign. The grin he flashed said he did it to prove he could. It was probably the same reason that, despite the forty-one-degree weather, he unzipped his coat. Because now I had a clear view of his gun.

Fun times.

Sean pretended to be a gentleman by holding open the door, and my spirits lifted as my nose caught a whiff of fresh coffee. Yum.

The store was empty, which was something of a surprise considering the popularity of Sinbad Smith's brew and the homey hunting-lodge atmosphere he'd created. A cheerful fire crackled in a stone hearth to my right. A brown leather couch and two chairs formed a conversational area in front of the fire. Three small round oak tables were positioned around the rest of the room, and a large deer head—complete with pointy antlers—surveyed the view from above. The deer creeped me out, but I supposed there were worse things in the world. My run-in a few months ago with a dust-encrusted taxidermied bear had demonstrated that.

A tall, solidly built Egyptian man with wavy dark hair grinned at me from behind a long wood counter. "Good afternoon, Rebecca. Deputy Holmes. What can I get you?" Sinbad gestured toward a plate of baked goods on the counter. "Maybe a cinnamon apple muffin?"

The muffins were the size of my head and smelled fantastic. Too bad my stomach was still on the blink after my fast-food lunch bonanza. Sean didn't have the same dilemma and ordered a muffin, two chocolate chip cookies, and a large hazelnut coffee.

"Cinnamon latte for you, Rebecca?" Sinbad asked as he filled a large cup.

Having Sinbad remember my favorite drink never got old. It was a part of small-town life I was truly grateful for. I also appreciated the way he smiled at me. As if he meant it. With the holidays approaching and his son not around to celebrate, Sinbad had every right to be bitter—and who better to take that unhappiness out on but me, who'd helped put his son away? Still, he always smiled and never screwed up my drink. How incredible was that?

Smiling back, I said, "How about a vanilla pumpkin latte with lots of whipped cream? I'm cooking dinner next week and need to get into the holiday spirit."

"You got it."

The cappuccino maker bubbled. The steamer hissed. Sinbad hummed. As he handed me my drink, he said, "There was a woman in here earlier, asking questions about you."

"What kind of questions?"

"She asked if you ever came into the store to buy coffee." Sinbad grabbed a rag and began to clean the machines. "The woman claimed she was looking to buy you a gift and didn't know if a coffee mug would be appropriate."

Weird. "Did the woman look familiar?"

Sinbad shook his head. "I've never seen her before, and I'm good with faces. Especially when the person has prominent features."

"Was her nose long and pointy?"

"That's her." Sinbad smiled. "It makes me feel better to hear that you know her. I was worried. It's one thing to tell Lionel what kind of coffee you like, but a complete stranger asking for information can be concerning. Even if the woman says she's the mother of a minister."

Bingo. Danielle's soon-to-be mother-in-law had paid Sinbad a visit. Not only was she coming by my house, she was digging for dirt on me. Why? I had no idea. Whatever the reason, I doubted it was good.

Sinbad went back into his office looking more upbeat. Meanwhile, I took a seat on the couch with a sense of unease about both the woman stalking me and the conversation Sean wanted to have. Warming myself in front of the fire, I sipped my drink and waited for Sean to start talking.

He'd polished off both cookies and half of the muffin before he asked, "So what did you find?"

"What makes you think I found something? You went through Ginny's condo. Did you find anything?"

Sean brushed a crumb off his shirt. "Do you think I'm going to tell you details about my ongoing investigation?"

"No." Hey, a girl can dream.

Sean broke off another piece of muffin and popped it into his mouth. I took a sip of coffee, and he nudged the plate in my direction. Most people would see it as the act of a man who'd eaten his fill, but I knew and respected Sean's bottomless stomach well enough to understand a peace offering when I saw one.

After taking a bite, I chewed, swallowed, and said, "There's money in Ginny's teapot."

"Enough for someone to kill over?"

As far as I was concerned, no amount was large enough, but I got Sean's point. "She had one thousand four hundred and thirty-six dollars on her stove. According to her bankbook, her checking account didn't have a whole lot more, but there was a weird deposit and withdrawal."

"Yeah, I saw that, too." He leaned back. "I checked with the bank. Ginny doesn't have a savings account, and all deposits other than the direct ones made by the government have been made in cash."

In the city, Sean would have needed a warrant to acquire that information. In Indian Falls, all that was required was a badge and a box of DiBelka Bakery doughnuts. Small-town people did more than just remember coffee orders. They cared about finding the person who killed one of their own. If they had to bend a few laws in order to achieve that goal, so be it.

"Did you find out where she got the nine thousand dollars?" I asked.

"Not yet." Sean looked over his cup at me. "Did you?"

I wanted to say yes, but we'd gotten this far without lying or juvenile behavior. There was no point in breaking the streak now. "Nope. Ginny didn't appear to have many secrets." Just the teapot trove, the bankbook, and the slip of paper. Sean knew two of the three. Since he was acting unusually rational, I decided to share the rest.

As I reached into my pocket, I heard the bells on the shop's entrance ring. The fire flickered as wind and a woman wrapped in a bright red coat and hat swept in. Still holding the door open, the woman stopped in her tracks, took one look at me, and screamed.

Thirteen

Before I could stand up or squeak out a greeting, I was tackled with all the force my former college roommate could muster. "I can't believe I finally found you. I've been driving around this town for hours."

Jasmine's exaggeration made me laugh. If an unfamiliar car and driver had cruised the downtown streets of Indian Falls for hours, I'd have heard. Especially since the driver had rich chocolate-colored skin and a current hairstyle that made it look like she'd stuck her finger in a light socket. The people in this town appreciated differences, which was obvious by their love of Pop's band, their patronage of this store, and the fondness they felt for Bryan and Reginald. Even so, as Sinbad had just attested with his concern over Mother Lucas, strangers wigged them out.

"What are you doing here?" I asked, extricating myself from Jasmine's iron grip. "I left you a message. You never called back."

Jasmine plucked the cup out of my hand, sniffed at it, and took a taste. "Wow. Can I get one of these?"

Sinbad came out of the back and fired up the steamer. While the machines worked their magic, Jasmine shouted, "I tried to call you back, but my cell phone died and I couldn't remember what bag I'd packed my charger in. Besides, it was easier to tell you everything once I got here."

"Why are you here?" I asked as Sinbad handed Jasmine her drink. "I'm happy to see you, but I thought you were going to the National Mortgage Brokers Conference in Reno."

Jasmine shrugged and took a sip of her coffee. "That was before Neil made a pass and I had to quit. A woman has a right to work without threat of harassment."

"Did you file a complaint?" Sean asked.

"He's the boss." Jasmine batted her heavily lined brown eyes at Sean before giving him one of her sexy pouts. It was an expression she'd perfected in our dorm-room mirror to elicit sympathy and protective instincts in her dates. "Unless I wanted to file an expensive lawsuit, there was nothing I could do."

I raised an eyebrow but didn't dispute her claim. As far as I knew, Jasmine was the only female employee Neil had never made a pass at. Something I envied, considering my personal experience with the matter.

Sean gave Jasmine a sympathetic nod. "A real man never intimidates a woman."

I rolled my eyes and took a drink of my latte as Jasmine sashayed over to Sean and held out a sparkly-polished hand. "I can see why Rebecca is head over heels for you. I'm Jasmine Fields, former roommate and all-around best friend."

I choked on my drink.

Jasmine fluttered her false eyelashes.

Sean raised an eyebrow. "Rebecca said she's head over heels for me?"

"Well, sure." Jasmine whacked me on the back. I pitched forward and smacked into Sean.

Sean grabbed my drink before it landed in his lap and gave me a big smile.

"Oops." Jasmine laughed. "Sometimes I'm too enthusiastic. But considering the two of you are a couple, I don't have to feel too bad. Right?"

"Wrong." I pushed away from a leering Sean, snagged my drink, and got to my feet. Walking around to Jasmine's side of the sofa, I said, "Jasmine, this is Sheriff's Department Deputy Sean Holmes."

Sean waved.

Jasmine frowned. "I thought you were dating a guy named Lionel."

"I am."

"He must be one accepting dude to let you go on dates with other men," Jasmine said. "Especially one this attractive."

"Thanks." Sean winked.

"Sean and I aren't dating," I said through clenched teeth. "We're just . . ." Just . . . Huh. I had no idea what Sean and I were. Friends was too optimistic. Enemies was too harsh. The definition of our relationship lay somewhere in the murky waters in between. "I was hired to look into a crime. Sean is working on the case. The two of us are meeting here to compare notes."

"That's not all it looked like you were comparing." Jasmine nudged me with her elbow. Then her smile faded, and she cocked her head to the side. "Wait. When did people start hiring you to look into crimes? Did someone blow another hole in your mother's rink?"

Out of the corner of my eye, I saw Sinbad flinch. Crap. "Could you lower your voice a little?" I asked.

"Why?" Bafflement marched across Jasmine's expressive face. "Everyone here has to know a psychotic bomber gave your roller rink a face-lift. That kind of thing would be big news around here."

That kind of thing was big news lots of places, including Moline, Rock Island, Rockford, and Peoria. The number of television crews filming the rink's new air-conditioning was legion. Discussing that event in this establishment was a bit insensitive, though, considering the psychotic bomber was Sinbad's son.

Since explaining that to Jasmine would only make Sinbad even unhappier, I did the next best thing. I changed the subject. "One of my former teachers decided my involvement in the past murder cases qualifies me to look into a theft that happened to her two years ago."

Jasmine turned to Sean. "Does it?"

I looked at my coffee and wished I had something stronger as Sean turned to Jasmine and said, "Tenacity and curiosity are two qualities essential to every investigator, whether part of a formal law enforcement agency or not. From what I've seen, Rebecca has both qualities in unfortunate abundance."

I tried to decide whether I was offended. Since it could have been worse, I concluded I wasn't. Outrage took too much energy.

I finished my coffee, pitched the cup in the trash, and said, "Sean, would you mind if we finished this consultation later? I haven't seen Jasmine since I left Chicago. The two of us have a lot to catch up on."

"Sure." The humor in Sean's eyes disappeared. "But the minute you learn anything that affects my case, I expect you to let me know. Deal?"

Well . . .

Sean put his hand on the cuffs dangling from his belt and smiled.

"Deal."

"Great." Sean nodded to Jasmine and headed for the door. "It was nice to meet you. Any friend of Rebecca's . . ."

The door closed before I could hear the end of the sentence. I was guessing that was a good thing.

"So, now what?" Jasmine asked. "Do you have sneaky private investigator stuff to do, or do you have time to show me the town? I want to see everything."

"You were here nine years ago." I pulled on my jacket and zipped up. "Not a whole lot has changed."

"Indian Falls didn't have this coffee shop nine years ago." She tilted her cup at Sinbad, who was wiping down the counter for the twelfth time in order to have an excuse to eavesdrop. "I would have remembered coffee this good. It's been almost a decade. Give me the grand tour. Our final stop can be the rink so I can see what changes you made after that madman rearranged the walls."

Before Sinbad could wing coffee beans at my friend's head, I hustled Jasmine outside into the cold to see the sights. The Indian Falls Grand Tour lasted forty-five minutes. The first thirty-five of them were spent at the sheriff's Department, where Jasmine argued with a sniffling Roxy about the "Welcome to Indian Falls" ticket Sean had left on her blue Ford Escape windshield. While

Sean parked in front of fire hydrants, he preferred keeping that particular perk to himself.

Seventy-five dollars and a lot of swear words later, Jasmine got her first look at the recently renovated and currently well occupied rink. "Saturday Night Fever" blared from the speakers. Skaters old and young coasted, cavorted, and cross-pulled around the shiny wood floor.

"I can understand why you decided to come back for good," Jasmine yelled over the music. "I couldn't believe you let me talk you into moving to Chicago in the first place."

"You didn't have to talk me into it. I wanted to go."

Jasmine threw back her head and laughed. "You didn't know what you wanted to do. Coming with me to Chicago was the easiest way to pretend like you had a plan." When I frowned, she laughed again. "Don't be upset. As much as I harped on you to sell this place and come back to Chicago, I'm glad you made the choice to do what you wanted. You're finally doing what's right for you. To tell the truth, I'm jealous."

A kid zipped past while making farting noises with his arm. "Why would you be jealous of this?"

Jasmine's smile faded. "You've found where you belong. You're important to the people here. I'm still looking for that. Neil wasn't the reason I left Chicago, although he did make a pass. As if he had a chance in hell." Jasmine sighed. "I'm approaching my midthirties, and I have nothing to show for it."

"Of course you do," I said. "Not only are you the best mortgage broker I know, you've got dozens of friends and a great family. What more could you want?"

"I don't know." Jasmine looked away and shrugged. For a second I thought I saw tears in her eyes.

Worry streaked through me. Jasmine hated tears. She never cried. Not when a boyfriend broke up with her or when her goldfish, Shrimp, died. Jasmine believed in expressing emotions with broken crockery and glass-shattering decibels. Tears weren't her style. That she might be feeling the need to cry now made me reach out and take her hand. "Are you okay? You can tell me anything. You know that, right?"

"I'm fine." Jasmine turned to me with an amused smile.

All signs of tears were gone, if they had ever been there in the first place. Maybe I'd seen a reflection of the disco ball.

"Strike that," she said. "I'm better than fine because I'm taking charge of my life and doing exactly what I want to do. Just like someone else I know." The music changed. "You Can't Hurry Love" echoed around the room, and Jasmine swayed to the music. "Do you mind if I take a couple of laps around the rink? I was in the car for hours today. It'd be nice to stretch the kinks out."

I got Jasmine a pair of size eights. As she joined the party, I made a beeline to the office, closed the door, and pulled out my phone. Maybe the tears were a trick of the light, but I had to make sure. If my friend needed help, it was my job to make sure she got it.

The man who was once my boss and admirer answered on the third ring. Since Neil had a habit of showering affection on any woman who was friendly, I skipped over the typical social niceties and explained why I was calling.

"Jasmine's in Indian Falls?" Neil asked. "What's she doing there? She moved back home in order to be a caregiver for her stepfather. He has cancer, you know."

I didn't know. Probably because the man was second cousin to Harvey the Rabbit. Jasmine's parents had celebrated thirty-five years of marriage last April. Jasmine must have realized Neil wasn't going to be happy with her departure and given herself an easy out. Neil was creepy but not completely insensitive. Especially where family was concerned.

Keeping with the story Jasmine fabricated, I said, "Jasmine's here for a quick visit before she heads home. She swears she's doing okay, but I thought you might be able to tell me if something other than her stepfather's illness has been bothering her. I know some people worry about their own health and go to a lot of doctors when someone they love is diagnosed with a scary disease."

"Not that I know of. Jasmine didn't log any recent personal time. She even canceled the vacation she was supposed to go on last month in order to be here for a particularly complicated closing. As far as I can tell, she was her normal self until she gave her notice."

Thanking Neil, I hung up and let out a sigh of relief. Jasmine might be mildly unhappy, but she wasn't sick. As owner of the company and all-around nosy guy, Neil would have known if Jasmine was using her benefits or popping meds. Whatever was bothering my friend wasn't health-related. Since Jasmine didn't do well being badgered about her feelings, I'd just have to step back and give her space. When she was ready to talk, I'd be here.

Since I wasn't interested in joining the rolling dance party, I booted up my computer, pulled the notebook out of my purse, and got to work.

The first order of business was a search on Florence D. Hemmens, the recipient of Ginny's nine-thousand-dollar check. Apparently Florence wasn't a popular name these days. There was a Web site for the Hemmens Theater, lots of pages documenting Florence Nightingale, and one solitary LinkedIn account for an F. D. Hemmens.

Since I wasn't a LinkedIn member, I couldn't see the full profile.

The little I could see said that F. D. Hemmens was a retired high school principal from Syracuse, New York, who had relocated to sunny Florida. Under "Education" she listed a PhD from New York University, and she asked people contact her for reference requests, getting back in touch, and real estate transactions.

Huh.

Another search gave me the name of the school Dr. F. D. Hemmens retired from ten years ago. A white pages search and a phone call confirmed her first name was Florence. Eureka! This could be my girl.

Only now that I'd found her, I wasn't sure what to do with her. The page I could see told me she had a company Web site. I clinked on the link and went to a page that advertized rental properties in Sarasota, Florida, and the surrounding area. From what I could see, Florence rented properties by the week, month, or year. Since the units that went for that much had multiple bedrooms, I was guessing the nine thousand dollars must have been Ginny and her friends' get-out-of-winter card.

Feeling sad that Ginny wouldn't get to walk on the beach this year, I wrote down Florence's phone number, e-mail address, and Web site so I could pass them along to her family. Maybe they'd be able to find out what Ginny's portion of the rent was and get a refund.

Now that the mystery of the check's recipient was solved, I pulled the slip of paper I'd taken off of Ginny's teapot out of my pocket. After smoothing it out, I wrote the numbers and letters from the paper into my notebook and studied them. The first had ten digits. Could it be a phone number? I plugged the numbers into the reverse number option of the online white pages and got the message "invalid area code." Drat.

Okay, it wasn't a phone number. What else could it be? I stared at the numbers for several minutes, waiting for inspiration to strike.

Nothing.

I moved on to the five letters in the next line: WMCSA. The letters were written in the same precise block handwriting that I'd seen in Ginny's check register. The only difference was the letters were all capitalized. In the check register, Ginny capitalized the first letters of names or companies. Unlike my check log, which had lots of scrawled, half-legible words, Ginny's had perfect penmanship. Every *i* had been dotted, every *t* crossed. Which made me think these letters were capitalized for a reason. If only I knew what that reason might be.

The six descending numbers written under the capitalized letters left me just as stumped. I hoped Ginny's family would have better luck deciphering them.

Nobody was home at the Boggses' house, so I dialed both Amy Jo's and Mark's cell phones. No answer. Not a surprise. They were probably busy. Either that or they were currently in a location where they couldn't get a signal. Our county was on the list for a cell phone tower upgrade, but since the cows outnumbered people three to one in this area, I was betting our placement on that list was dead last. Unless the bovine set became addicted to texting and Angry Birds, it was going to be a while before reception improved.

I left Amy Jo a message to call me, scribbled down the few facts Sean had given me, and frowned. I'd managed to fill the notebook pages with a respectable amount of information. Heck, I'd even dug up information Sean didn't have. That would normally have bolstered my confidence. Instead, not sharing the contents of Ginny's note with him made me feel queasy. I'd kept information from Sean before, but that was when he sneered and acted like a Neanderthal. In recent weeks, the man had taken several steps up the evolutionary ladder, which left me feeling guilty and conflicted. Two emotions I should have been better at, considering my experience with them.

Since I didn't want to go around feeling like a schmuck, I punched number 5 on my phone and waited for Sean to answer. Voice mail. I hated voice mail. After the beep, I told Sean that I'd forgotten to pass along one other piece of information and that I'd try to stop by the sheriff's department with it later today. Of course, with Jasmine around and my duties for Danielle's wedding, I wasn't sure what my schedule looked like, but . . .

Eek! I was rambling. I hated when I did that.

I said good-bye, disconnected, and contemplated whether being embarrassed was preferable to feeling guilty. As far as I could tell, it was a wash. Ignoring my humiliation, I picked up my notebook in hopes of finding a new lead. I'd yet to find one when the door swung open, letting both the dulcet tones of "Don't Go Breaking My Heart" and my grandfather inside.

"You think that would make a good song for my set?" Pop asked as he closed the door behind him. "I'm looking to add a couple modern pieces to the act for broader appeal."

"You might want to pick a song that doesn't require two people." Not to mention one that was written in the last two decades.

My grandfather unzipped his jacket and revealed a skintight, shiny, purple shirt underneath. "I'm looking to hire a chick singer. So far I haven't found one who has a flexible schedule and legs that look great in a short skirt."

"Doesn't she also have to sing?"

"That's what the short skirt is for." Pop grinned. "Of course, it wouldn't hurt if she had good pipes. It'd be nice to share the stage with equal-caliber talent."

Well, that was one challenge that could be met with relative ease. Too bad the other problems I was working on weren't as easy.

"So, what's the emergency?" Pop asked, easing his satin-clad butt into a wooden chair. "I would have gotten here sooner, but your father had some trouble with his camera. I never knew a flash could explode like that."

I wasn't going to ask. "Pop, I need you to convince your friends at the center to call off their protest of the sheriff's office."

"No can do."

I blinked. "Why not?" Pop was always willing to help. Especially when it involved shutting down something as illogical as picketing Sean's office. Not to mention the fun factor of getting to throw his celebrity status around.

"Almost every club and social group in the center has agreed to the protest. Ginny was one of the center's most popular members. Ethel and Marjorie have contacted the local media. News crews will be here first thing tomorrow morning. They've put me in charge of entertainment, which is good for networking. I might even be able to get some press for the band. This could be my big break." Pop's eyes twinkled. "Better yet, Sean will be so distracted by the protest he won't have time to get in the way of your investigation."

"He'll also be irritated enough to keep Erica, Mary, and Halle behind bars."

"You don't give yourself enough credit. You can investigate

rings around . . ." Pop's voice trailed off as what I'd just said hit home. "Wait. Why did Sean arrest Erica, Mary, and Halle? Did they roll over his foot or something?"

I guess the Indian Falls gossips had been too busy contacting the media and painting protest signs to keep up with the day's news. "The girls accidentally shoplifted a few things from the pharmacy. Worse, it was sort of my fault they did it."

"What did they take?"

"Some sleeping pills and . . . I don't remember what else." Call me old-fashioned, but while I accepted my grandfather's social life (okay, accepted was an overstatement, but I was working on it), I couldn't bring myself to use the word "condom" in a conversation with him. Before my grandfather could ask more questions, I filled him in on the whole story. "Sean said he'll spring them if I get the protest called off. If not, he's keeping them locked behind bars."

"Well, crap." Pop hiked up his pants and frowned. "I can't have the girls rotting in jail just because I want to be on television. Now I have to find a way to convince Ethel and Marjorie to call off the hounds. That's easier said than done."

"Why?" I asked. "People can't seriously believe that Sean's initial cause-of-death findings were inaccurate due to discrimination."

"No, but lots of seniors feel they haven't gotten a fair shake from the mayor on other issues. They see picketing the sheriff as a chance to move their political agenda forward."

Agenda? "What agenda?"

"Most of the folks at the center think their concerns about the environment are falling on deaf ears."

"Your friends are concerned about pollution and conservation?"

"We don't care about that stuff," Pop said. "All of us over the age of sixty-five are going to die before the world has a chance to run out of oil. Nah, the center's political board is concerned about the fountain that's being built in the park. The land it's being constructed on was originally set aside for a shuffleboard deck. Then one day, poof. The land was commandeered for the mayor's pet project without any concern for us. He could have torn up the basketball court or the baseball field, but he chose to nix shuffleboard. Old people have the right to a sporting venue, too. Jimmy even came up with a plan to turn the deck into a curling rink during the winter months. He wants to train for the next Olympics. A gold medal would be a surefire chick magnet."

So would wearing matching socks. "Aside from getting Jimmy a gold medal, how do we get the protest planners to stand down?"

Pop shrugged. "I could get Ethel drunk and have her make a couple calls. She's got a thing for White Russians."

Good to know. "Any other ideas that don't require liquor?"

"Maybe. Let me make a few phone calls and see what I can do."

Pop pulled out his phone and started dialing. When his voice dropped an octave and got all husky, I cleared out. Pop deserved a love life. I just didn't want to experience it firsthand.

A couple of George's new artistic skaters were practicing spins while the rest of the crowd boogied to "Jump, Jive, an' Wail." George was standing on the sidelines, talking to Jasmine while keeping an eye on his students. I was about to join them when my cell phone vibrated. Amy Jo Boggs was calling.

Since the decibel level was cranked to oh-my-God and my

grandfather was using my office to do his impersonation of Barry White, I headed for the quiet of the parking lot to answer the phone.

"I got your message. Sorry it took me so long to call back. The people from the adoption agency called, and when they heard about Aunt Ginny being murdered . . ." Amy Jo sighed. "Well, there is now some question as to the stability of our family. Which is why I'm hoping you might have news."

Yikes. Poor Amy Jo and Mark. I'd heard adoption was tricky, but it had never occurred to me that having a family member murdered would derail the process.

Wishing I had better news to convey, I gave her a rundown on my foray into Aunt Ginny's apartment, including my discovery of the nine thousand dollars Ginny paid for a condo rental. "I also found a piece of paper taped to her teapot. The paper had a series of letters written on it. I was hoping they might mean something to you." Shivering, I pulled out the slip of paper and squinted at the writing.

Damn.

One of the worst things about the onset of winter was how early it got dark. I moved closer to one of the parking lot lights and read the series of letters to Amy Jo, who then repeated them to her husband. While the two debated what the letters meant, I looked for a place to get out of the cold without bailing on the phone call. Being outside without a coat was not one of my better ideas.

My apartment door was locked, and the key was currently nestled in my coat pocket, but the door to the stairway was open. Being out of the wind would be an improvement over my current situation. The cold air was starting to chap my lips. While Mark and Amy Jo debated which family members might know what the letters meant, I headed across the parking lot.

The wind gusted. I put my head down to keep the worst of the cold off my face, which was probably why I didn't see the headlights barreling toward me until it was too late.

Fourteen

Tires squealed. An engine roared. White lights raced toward me. I did the only thing I could think to do. I let out a scream and ran.

Shit. My hip sang as metal struck bone. Suddenly, I was airborne. Then I wasn't. Shit. Shit. Shit.

My phone flew out of my hand as I skidded across concrete and smacked into the rink's brick wall. Pain bloomed in my leg, my arm, and my chin.

Car tires peeled rubber. Pain swirled in my stomach. The world swooped in and out of focus as I scrambled to my feet and limped for my apartment's entrance, hoping to avoid another run-in or—worse yet—death.

Heart slamming, I reached the doorway and then turned in time to see taillights disappear down the block.

The good news was I was alive. The bad news was I could barely stand. The adrenaline that had helped get me up and moving had faded. The only thing left was numb terror.

My legs trembled. My knees buckled. I grabbed the door frame for support and fought to breathe.

Tears pricked the back of my eyes, and I squinted around the parking lot for signs of my phone. Someone had just tried to kill me. I needed to call for help. I needed to call Sean.

To do that, I needed my damn phone, and it was nowhere in sight.

"Hey, Rebecca. Are you all right?" a girl yelled from near the front of the building. I squinted into the darkness at the familiar voice and saw one of my best high school employees, Brittany, waiting for me to answer.

I started to lie, to yell that everything was fine. Saying that I was hurt would just scare her. Hell, it would scare me. The car and driver were already gone. There was no reason to freak either of us out more than necessary. Right?

The world swam in and out of focus. My fingers lost their grip on the door. As the pavement grew closer, I yelled, "Call Sean Holmes."

Then everything went black.

"Rebecca? Hey, Rebecca. Sweetheart, it's time to wake up now."

My eyes felt like they were glued shut. After several tries, I managed to open them and was immediately sorry that I had. There's nothing more humiliating than waking up with people staring at you. Especially when those people include both my father and Deputy Sean Holmes.

"Hey, there's those beautiful eyes." My father's face hovered inches from mine. I could see my grandfather's face peering over Stan's left shoulder. All around me buzzed the murmur of conversations.

"You gave us quite a scare." Stan gave me a strained smile. "How are you feeling, sweetheart?"

Claustrophobic. On top of that, every part of my body ached and several parts, including my head, screamed with pain. Through the haze of agony, I did notice that someone had thrown a blanket over me, which meant I wasn't cold. That was something.

Before I could answer my father's question, Doc Truman's concern-lined face hovered overhead. "If you would all please back off, I need to treat my patient."

Stan and my grandfather disappeared. Sean didn't budge.

Giving Sean a frown, Doc turned back to me. "You've got a couple of bad scrapes, a dislocated shoulder, and a possible concussion."

Well, that explained the headache.

Doc stroked the top of my head. "Sean is going to talk to you for a minute. Then Warren and Chuck are going to take you for a ride to the hospital, where I can do a more thorough examination and treat your injuries. I can't give you anything for the pain until I run some tests and know for sure what I'm dealing with. And don't even think about giving me any lip about going to the hospital. Your mother would want you to do exactly as I say."

I hated hospitals. When I was seven, I came down with a case of pneumonia. My mother promised me I'd be in and out of the hospital in a matter of hours. They kept me six days. During that time, I tried to stage four separate escape missions and ended up being strapped to my hospital bed every time my mother left the room. The minute the doctors discharged me, I vowed never to step back into a hospital again. I'd had to break that pledge over the years, but I was never happy about it. The last time . . . well, the look of sympathy in Doc's eyes told me he remembered my most recent trip to that facility and the good-bye I had to say there. Going back to the place where Mom died wasn't what I wanted to do, but Doc wouldn't make me go if it wasn't necessary. Besides, I was more resourceful now than when I was seven. If I needed to, I'd find a way to break out.

"Are you sure you can't give me drugs before I talk to Sean? Or maybe a bottle of wine?" I asked.

Doc grinned. "No, but I can give you some water."

Whoopee!

Doc carefully shifted the gurney I was on into a semiseated position so I could take a drink. The cool water soothed my throat, but I still found myself wishing for something that could take the edge off the pain. Especially when Sean got out his notebook and started asking questions.

"Can you tell me what you remember?"

I tried. Unfortunately, other than being clipped by a car, I was fuzzy on the details.

"Did you see what kind of car it was?"

"No."

"Did you recognize the driver?"

"I didn't see the driver. All I saw was headlights."

"How fast was the car going?"

"I don't know." I remembered the roar of the engine gunning and the sound of rubber squealing on the pavement. Fear rammed into my stomach as understanding hit home. "This wasn't an accident." I choked on the words and had to repeat them. "The car hitting me wasn't an accident. The driver hit the gas when I came into view. Someone tried to kill me."

The murmur of voices grew louder. I guess my words had traveled farther than I'd intended.

"I know." Anger stormed in Sean's eyes. "And I plan to track down the person who did it and make sure they pay."

Wow. For the first time in recent memory, Sean looked ready to throttle someone with his bare hands and it wasn't me.

"Have you received any threats lately?" Sean's voice was calm despite the pulsating vein in his neck. "You've been looking into the thefts and Ginny's murder."

"You think my granddaughter provoked someone into running her down?" Pop pushed his way past Stan and stormed over to Sean. "This wouldn't have happened if you and the sheriff were equipped to do your jobs. Julie Johnson would never have needed someone to track down the thief. She wouldn't have hired Rebecca. My granddaughter wouldn't have almost just died."

"Pop." I struggled to sit upright. My body screamed. The world's axis shifted, and I lay back down. Note to self: Quick movements were a very bad idea. "Pop." Very slowly, I reached out and took my grandfather's hand. "This isn't Sean's fault. It isn't mine, and it isn't yours."

Pop's fingers tightened on mine. "But—"

"No buts." I smiled. Ouch. Even smiling hurt. "Sean's going to look for the person who hit me, and I'm going to the hospital to get drugs."

In fact, once the medication took the edge off reality, being confined to a hospital room didn't bother me much. In effect, part of me knew I'd soon yearn to tunnel out of the place with a spork, the beaten and bruised part of me was happy to have a safe place to hide.

It wasn't until I was starting to drift in and out of sleep that Lionel's face appeared next to my bedside. His hair was disheveled, and his green eyes were shadowed with concern. His smile was warm and filled me with a happy glow. Or maybe that was the drugs. It was hard to tell.

"I tried to call," I said. "Pop let me use his phone. He says mine was run over by Sean's cruiser."

"I know." Lionel ran a hand lightly down my cheek. "I was checking out a rash on one of Mrs. Riley's steers when the call came in. By the time I called back, it sounded like your grandfather was in the middle of some kind of party. I did manage to learn that you were in the process of getting a CT scan." Lionel laced his fingers through mine and sat on the edge of the bed. "So what's the final verdict? Is your head as hard as we all think it is?"

"Harder." I smiled. "I have a mild concussion, and my right shoulder is going to be pissed that I used it to cushion my fall, but Doc Truman said I should be up and running in another day or two."

"Let's keep the running to a minimum."

I gave him a smile as a wave of fatigue hit. "No promises."

The last thing I remembered was Lionel kissing me on the lips and whispering that he loved me. For the first time those words made me feel safe instead of scared.

For some reason, I'd believed recuperating in a hospital would be boring. Wow, was I wrong. Starting with the night nurse, who woke me up at midnight to tell me she was taking over my care, a steady parade of people came and went from my room. When morning came, the numbers increased. The Toe Stop staff, Stan, Annette, and Jasmine all made appearances. George assured me he would take care of the rink, and Jasmine volunteered to take a few shifts if necessary. She was going to stay in town to help me once I got out of the hospital on Friday. Pop was letting her bunk at his place until I was sprung. I was also visited by a bunch of my mother's friends, Betsy Moore, Bryan, Pastor Rich, and my grandfather, who was sporting a black pompadour wig and a dark blue satin jumpsuit with gold spangles.

"I thought I'd do my act and spread some holiday cheer in some of the hospital wards."

To demonstrate, Pop smacked PLAY on his CD player and began belting out "It's Now or Never," effectively drowning out the bings and beeps of the machines in my room. Here was hoping the equipment on other floors made louder noises, or there could be trouble.

When Pop headed out to do his holiday floor show, Halle, Erica, and Mary strolled in. The trio had gotten sprung last night after Sean received a call from Marjorie informing him that the protest had been moved to city hall and the camera crews re-routed. The curling committee was going to get its fifteen minutes of fame. Now the members of EstroGenocide were carrying large coffee cups and a take-out bag from the Hunger Paynes Diner. One sniff told me the bag contained Mabel's famous meat loaf sandwich and the diner's signature peanut-oil fries. The girls gave Pop high fives and told him not to worry. They were going to be here to protect me in case the driver from last night made an appearance.

Oh boy!

Lucky for me, Erica had brought her laptop, and Halle and Mary were excited to have an excuse to watch the afternoon talk shows, so I was able to eat the meat loaf sandwich and take a nap in relative peace. By the next day, my bodyguard was down to one and my head had stopped aching. Hurrah.

Now I just needed to get out of the backless nightgown and life would return to normal. And it better happen soon or I'd go nuts.

Thankfully, by the time I came out of the shower I was finally cleared to take on my own, Erina informed me, "Doc Truman stopped by. He said you'd be released tomorrow morning. Your grandfather said he'd be back later. A couple of patients in the children's ward weren't big fans of the King or tapioca pudding, but they had good aim."

Poor Pop. "Was he upset?"

"Nah." Erica smiled. "He's going to keep coming back until they can sing every word of 'Don't Be Cruel' or they get well. Whichever comes first."

Something told me there were going to be a lot of kids feeling better really soon.

"Since your grandfather's going to be busy singing and dancing, I told him I'd drive you home when Doc Truman gave you the all clear. We have our final fittings scheduled for the afternoon, but Tilly said she could reschedule for Saturday if you aren't feeling up to it."

Tilly treating my already injured body like a pincushion was the last thing I wanted to do tomorrow. However, with the wedding a week away, I owed it to Danielle and Rich to try to keep the appointment.

Hey. Wait a minute. Between the painkillers and the parade of visitors, I'd overlooked the fact that Danielle had yet to stop by. Rich had, but Danielle hadn't been anywhere in sight. Now that I had noticed, I was bummed. Yes, Danielle was busy with work and wedding stuff, and I was sure the mother-in-law from hell arriving a week early hadn't been easy to deal with. Still, I was supposed to be one of her best friends. You'd think I'd rate a drive-by visit or at the very least a phone call or text.

I was still sulking the next afternoon when Doc Truman finally signed my discharge papers and gave me a sling to wear and a fistful of prescriptions to have filled. I shoved the sling in my purse and, despite her recent arrest, had Erica make a beeline for the drugstore. The pharmacists watched Erica like a hawk while ringing up my order and even trailed after us when we walked to the door. Once we reached Nothing Borrowed Nothing Blue, I popped two pills, slowly eased out of the car, grabbed my bag Erica picked up for me with the appropriate undergarments and shoes, and hobbled inside.

"What are you doing here?" Danielle gasped as a tinkling bell announced my arrival.

I gave her my best it-looks-way-worse-than-it-feels smile and winced. The smile would be easier to pull off when the meds kicked in. "Doc says the bruising on my chin will fade by next week. If it doesn't, Annette vows she'll perform magic with her trusty bag of cosmetics."

"That's not what I meant." Danielle looked toward the front door and then back at me. "I mean . . ." She swallowed hard and whispered, "What are you doing here? Rich said he visited you in the hospital. He said he talked to you."

"He did," I assured her. "He even brought me flowers and a dozen of Mrs. DiBelka's chocolate éclairs. You've picked a winner. I guess he forgot to tell you that I promised not to eat the entire box of éclairs or in any way jeopardize fitting into my maid of honor gown. The last thing you need is to be worrying about the zipper not going up on my dress."

"You don't . . . he didn't . . ." Danielle let out a loud sigh. "I asked Rich to tell you that you shouldn't worry about the wedding. That you should focus on resting and getting better and—"

"You're firing me?" Being hit by a car was less painful.

"No." Danielle glanced toward the entrance again. "But I thought . . . it's just that . . . Mother Lucas thought you might be uncomfortable having photographs taken of you with bruises on your arms and face. She also said that maybe you'd be nervous about going out in public until the person responsible has been caught."

I glanced over to see what was so fascinating outside and spotted Mother Lucas standing on the sidewalk across the street.

"You're firing me." Okay, now I was starting to get angry. Mother Lucas had questioned Sinbad about me, threatened me, and now convinced my best friend to ditch me.

Did I want to go traipsing down the aisle of St. Mark's in a dress that made me look like Barbie's less fortunately endowed second cousin? No, but I wanted to support my friend. My friend who at this moment was wringing her hands and sending terrified glances in Mother Lucas's direction. Danielle wasn't easy to freak out, but I'd been scared of Rich's mother, too, when she showed up in my apartment.

Oh God.

"Rebecca." Tilly came into the showroom. The minute she spotted Erica browsing through a rack of bridesmaid dresses, Tilly's smile morphed to a frown. "I'm sorry I wasn't here when you came in, but I'm ready for all of you. Shall we start with the bride?"

I answered before Danielle leaped at the opportunity to escape. "Why don't you start with Erica since Danielle and I are just doing a final fitting? We shouldn't require much time."

Erica grinned. Tilly sighed. When both disappeared into the fitting room, I looked back out the window. Rich's mother was gone, but Danielle's fear remained. "How did Mother Lucas get to Indian Falls?"

Danielle blanched. "Rich was supposed to drive to Iowa and pick her up, but she surprised us by driving herself."

"Why did she come to my house?"

Danielle looked down at her shoes. "She asked me about the wedding plans, and I mentioned the hairstyle and Erica taking over as bridesmaid. I went to get her a glass of water, and the next thing I knew she was gone."

"Danielle." I took a deep breath and waited for Danielle to lift her eyes. "Where was Rich's mother two days ago when I was walking across the rink parking lot?"

"I don't know," Danielle whispered. "She said she was going to St. Mark's to pray, but Rich never saw her."

Holy crap.

"Danielle, dear." Tilly's voice rang out. "You're next. You can come back, too, Rebecca."

Neither Danielle nor I moved because suddenly the fear made sense. Danielle was getting ready to try on the wedding dress she would wear when she married the son of the woman who'd run me down.

Fifteen

"You think Mother Lucas ran me over?" I asked. "Why haven't you reported her to the sheriff?"

"Because I don't know for sure if she did it." Danielle ran a hand through her hair and started to pace. "She came back from praying and was the nicest she's ever been. She said the time in the church had made her reflect on how lucky she was to have a son who loved her and a daughter-in-law who was strong enough to stand by him through anything. It wasn't until we finished dinner that I got Erica's message about you being hit by a car and realized Mother Lucas didn't have an alibi for the time the attack occurred."

Danielle whimpered.

I opened my mouth to speak, but Danielle cut me off. "I don't want to believe that Rich's mother ran you over with her Chevy Tahoe, but I plan on finding out. If she did it, I promise I'll turn her over to the sheriff. In the meantime, I don't want you in harm's way. That's why I asked Rich to tell you—"

"Wait a minute." I grabbed Danielle's arm to stop her from wearing a groove in the plush gray carpet. "Mother Lucas drives a Chevy Tahoe? Was she driving that car when she went to pray?"

"Yeah." Danielle wiped her nose with the back of her hand. "Why?"

The Toe Stop's new handyman, Deke Adkins, owned a Chevy Tahoe. The car wasn't as massive as Lionel's monster truck, but it ran a close second in height and width. If a Chevy Tahoe had clocked me, emergency teams would still be peeling me off the grille.

"Your soon-to-be mother-in-law is off the hook." Although that didn't mean I wasn't going to keep my distance. The woman was scary. Still. "Unless she boosted a smaller car"—a crime that wasn't exactly unheard of around here—"she wasn't the one behind the wheel."

"Really?" Danielle asked. "You're not just saying that to make me feel better?"

I wish. Knowing the identity of the crazed motorist was preferable to wondering when they'd try again.

"No."

"So." Danielle gave me a small smile. "Did I totally ruin our friendship, or are you still willing to walk down the aisle and help me get married?"

A normal person would probably stay offended or at least make her friend grovel before relenting, but I understood how much this wedding and the life she was making meant to Danielle. Besides, I'd just had an object lesson in how short life could be. I wasn't about to waste time on anger.

Smiling, I said, "Just try to stop me."

By the time the fitting was over and I was back in my sweater and jeans, I wished Danielle had taken me up on my offer. The U.S. military could adopt Tilly's dress-fitting techniques to break prisoners of war. Hours of standing in high heels while Tilly adjusted, considered, and remeasured every centimeter of the hemline was torture. During that time, Danielle bombarded me with ideas to replace the broken table favors. Paperweights with Bible quotes (Rich had extras from the last church retreat), individual bags of potpourri, and personalized Hershey Bars topped the list. The last I thought had possibilities until Tilly reminded us that chocolate and white wedding dresses don't mix. Bummer. By the time Danielle, Erica, and I left the store, I was hungry, achy, and in serious need of a nap. The last I planned on availing myself of as soon as I reached my living room couch.

Or not.

My sofa was currently occupied by Jasmine, Stan, and Lionel. Behind them stood several members of the EstroGenocide team, Brittany, and George. My grandfather was busy talking about his band's recent rehearsal from the comfort of my overstuffed rocking chair. A colorful, albeit slightly askew, WELCOME HOME sign hung from the mantel.

When people spotted me, they broke out into wide smiles.

"There she is." Pop got to his feet and adjusted his spangled jumpsuit. "I hope you don't mind that I used my key. Jasmine and Stan wanted to be here when you got home."

"You shouldn't be alone while recovering." Jasmine gave a toothy grin and glanced around the room. "I guess your other friends had the same idea. They even brought food."

I wasn't sure why being hit by a car warranted two tuna casseroles, three Bundt cakes, and a platter of cheese, but the buffet was well appreciated by the masses. So much so, in fact, that none of them seemed to notice when I snuck down the hall with a plate of munchies and my stash of pain pills. I had started to close my bedroom door when my grandfather appeared in the doorway.

"Sorry about the party. My phone's been ringing all day with people asking how you're doing." Pop put a hand on my arm. "How are you really?"

I put my hand over his and smiled. "I'm a little sore, but I'm fine, Pop. Honest."

Pop grinned. "Good, because I've been saying that it takes more than a speeding car to slow you down and that nothing would make you happier than helping catch the person responsible."

Personally, I would argue that the speeding car did a great job of slowing me down, but the last part of Pop's statement was true. I wanted to track down whoever had decided to play a live-action game of Frogger in my parking lot. Of course, to do that, I had to figure out why someone pointed a car at me in the first place.

As far as I knew, no one had been threatened or injured during the decade of investigation into the Thanksgiving thefts. Had I hit a nerve with the thief, or was Ginny's killer concerned that I might have found something in her room? I'd been looking into Ginny's murder for only a few hours before getting sideswiped, and I wasn't the first one to go through Ginny's apartment. Surely, if the murderer were concerned about what was to be found there, he or she would have targeted Sean first. Unless my logic was faulty, I took that to mean my investigation into the Thanksgiving thefts had hit a nerve. Too bad I had no idea why, but there was one way I could think of to help me find out.

"Are you and Stan still doing a photo shoot with Seth and Jan Kurtz?"

Pop's eyes brightened. "Tomorrow at eleven. Seth wanted to do it today, but Jan is finishing up a set of mugs in ceramics class. Stan told them he'd need an hour for makeup and wardrobe and another hour to get the shots with the dogs. Seth is only bringing three of them, but that's three less you have to deal with. If you need more time, just let me know and I'll stall."

"Stall what?" Lionel appeared behind Pop.

Pop turned. "Rebecca's got a line on busting the Thanksgiving thief out of the water." Giving me a thumbs-up, he said, "I'll get the party crowd out of here so you can rest and be in top form tomorrow. Call if you need me to act as lookout. I can always ask Jasmine to be Stan's assistant. You wouldn't believe how those two have hit it off."

Pop kissed me on the cheek, gave my hand a squeeze, and then disappeared out the door. After taking a bite of cracker, I took a seat on the bed and gratefully listened to the buzz of voices fade. The front door slammed, and then there was silence. Something I'd had far too little of in the last several days.

However, with two of us in the room, the quiet was unsettling instead of soothing. Wow, one of us really didn't look happy.

"What's wrong?"

"Do you realize that your shoulder was dislocated and that the rest of your body looks as though it was used as a punching bag?"

Duh. "I had to try on a strapless gown today. Trust me, I know."

"Then why in God's name are you planning on investigating the thefts tomorrow instead of staying in bed and resting the way Doc Truman told you to? Are you trying to get yourself killed? Don't you realize the person who almost ran you over could be the same person behind the thefts?"

"I'm not stupid," I shot back. "Of course I know that."

"Then what the hell do you think you're doing?"

"My job."

The two of us glared at each other. Tension crackled in the room. This wasn't exactly the welcome home I'd been looking for.

Taking a deep breath, I said, "Look, I gave my word to Mrs. Johnson. Even if I hadn't, I'd still be asking questions because it's the only way to make sure I don't get run over again. Whatever ticked off the driver isn't magically going to disappear because I'm on the sidelines, waiting for Sean to make an arrest. I can't just sit around doing nothing."

"You can. What you're saying is that you won't." Lionel shook his head and turned on his heel. "Get some rest and don't do anything stupid."

"Lionel." I stood up too fast, got a head rush, and had to wait for it to pass. Then I hurried down the hall to reach him before he left. The slamming of the front door told me I was too late. Lionel was not only angry, he was gone.

Damn.

"Well, that was entertaining."

I jumped, felt a jolt of pain, and turned to frown at the source of it. "What are you doing here?"

Sean rose from the couch and tucked his hands in his front pockets. "Your grandfather let me in and invited me to partake of the food. I don't think he realized I'd be getting a floor show, too. Lionel was pissed."

"Your observation skills are truly remarkable."

Sean walked over and put a hand on my back. "You should get off your feet. Doc's orders were to rest."

I let Sean guide me to the couch and felt my body sigh with relief. "How do you know what Doc said?"

"Because I asked him." Sean sat on the arm of the couch. "He's fairly certain you won't follow those instructions, but he's ready to readmit you to the hospital if he gets word you're doing cartwheels down Main Street. So you might want to make sure whatever plans you've made that ticked Lionel off don't involve that."

"Did you hear our entire conversation?" I asked. The idea of running into Sean while peering through Seth and Jan's basement windows wasn't appealing.

"Just that it has something to do with investigating the thefts."

"And you're not angry?" Lionel was in the midst of an emotional meltdown, and Sean was being reasonable. What was wrong with this picture?

"Why would I be angry? You agreed to do a job, and you're doing it."

"What happened to reminding me that looking into crimes isn't my job? It's yours."

"You're right," he said. "It is my job. Ever since I turned ten, I wanted to go into law enforcement. Everything I've done since was to make sure I achieved that goal. Despite what you might believe, I genuinely want to help people."

"And you like parking in loading zones."

A boyish grin lit Sean's face. "Yeah, that part's good, too. A guy has to have a few perks. Do you know how many phone calls I get about some dog taking a dump on a neighbor's lawn or a cat getting kidnapped by aliens?"

Nope, and I didn't want to. "If it's so annoying, why are you working for the sheriff's department? The pay can't be that great."

"I do it for the same reason you're going to get out of bed to-morrow and do what it takes to track down a thief no matter how much you hurt. Because as unimaginable as it might be, the two of us are exactly alike." Sean leaned forward and picked the almost finished Sunday-paper crossword off the coffee table. "We can't resist a puzzle that hasn't been solved." He threw the paper back on the table and leaned his elbows on his knees. "It took a couple of months and a lot of antacids to understand that. I assumed Lionel would've figured that out long before me."

I shifted on the sofa and tried to ignore the way my nerves jumped. "Lionel's worried."

"There's a lot of that going around." Sean's blue eyes met mine. "Although don't think that means I'm not going to get an-gry when you stomp all over my cases, needlessly put your life in danger, or withhold information that could help me close them."

Oops. "That reminds me . . ." I pushed aside the prickly feel-ings talking about Lionel caused and then jumped into something equally thorny. "I found a note taped to the bottom of Ginny's teapot."

"You what?"

I breathed a sigh of relief when Sean stood up and stomped around the room, pontificating about withholding evidence. When he came up for air, I told him to stay put and then went to my room in search of the clothes I'd worn on my ambulance ride. My jeans were torn and bloody. Even with a good cleaning they'd be a total loss. I was just thankful the front pockets were still in-tact, as was Ginny's note.

"I thought the first ten digits were a phone number, but I was wrong." I held out the paper. "There's no such area code. Also, the letters feel familiar, but I have no idea why. I'm stumped,

which should make you feel better, right? Oh, and I should probably tell you that Danielle Martinez thought there was a chance
her almost mother-in-law ran me over with her car. Mrs. Lucas
drives a Chevy Tahoe, which takes her out of the running, but I
figured I should mention it. Just in case."

"In case of what?" Sean asked, taking the slip of paper out of
my hands.

"In case I'm wrong."

Sixteen

A long, very hot shower and twelve hours of sleep made me feel far better than I had the day before. The lack of communication from Lionel since he'd stormed out did not. I glanced at the phone a dozen times while getting dressed, waiting for it to ring. When it didn't, I punched in Lionel's number as Sean's words from last night echoed in my head. Frowning, I pocketed the phone before hitting SEND.

Lionel said he loved me. That was great, but I wanted more. I wanted him to "get" me. To understand I couldn't just wait around for things to happen. Too much of my life had been spent that way. It started with my father leaving. After Stan walked out of my life, I stopped thinking about what I wanted. Instead, I made choices based on what other people told me to do. Competing at artistic skating meets. Going to prom in a hideous pink dress. Picking a college my mother didn't feel was too far away. For the longest time, I'd told myself that Chicago was my way of breaking free, but Jasmine was right. I chose Chicago because Jasmine asked me to. Investigating the Thanksgiving Day thefts might not be the safest decision, but it was my choice and mine alone. Since danger could be involved, it would be best if I faced that danger prepared.

I rummaged through my fridge, pulled out bacon, and then found a frying pan. My stomach growled at the first whiff. I grabbed a bagel and pretended I wasn't interested in the crispy salt-laden pork. I needed all the bacon I could get if I had hopes of escaping this next adventure with all my limbs intact.

George was in the middle of the rink, teaching eight toddlers how to coast. Parents on the sidelines waved. A few asked how I was recovering from my "accident," and I assured them of my recuperation as I waited for class to end. When it did, George zoomed over and instructed me not to worry. Everything at the rink was under control and I should take the next several days off. If there was a problem, he'd call. The guy was the best nonmanager ever. Maybe he'd finally let me give him the official title as a Christmas present.

The sun was shining. According to my dashboard readout, the temperature was hovering in the midfifties. It was a beautiful day for breaking and entering.

A Santa scarecrow greeted me as I pulled into the Kurtzes' driveway. The car clock read ten minutes past eleven. I cut the engine and listened for the sounds of angry growls. Nothing. Maybe Seth decided to take all the dogs with him after all. A quick call to Pop burst my burgling bubble. Seth, Jan, and their three favorite furry friends were getting ready for their close-up. The rest of the canine clan was still in residence. If I went through with this, the bacon was going to come in handy. If not—well, I'd get a BLT out of the deal.

Before I lost my nerve, I strode to the side of the house in search of a basement window to peer through. The first three window wells I came to were filled with dirt and the dried remains of this year's crop of annuals. Apparently, Jan and Seth thought window boxes were passé. I circled to the back of the house and frowned. The two windows that weren't being used to cultivate flowers were painted black. The only way I was going to find out what was hidden in the basement was to get inside.

The back door was locked, and Seth and Jan didn't appear to be the key-under-the-mat or the fake-rock type of people. Now what?

I walked to the front of the house and glanced up and down the road. No cars were in sight. The only farmhouse within shouting distance was Bryan and Reginald's place. No one was around to report my actions. Time to start testing the locks on windows and pray Stan and my grandfather were right about the lack of an alarm.

All the first-story windows in the front were secured. The trend continued around the rest of the house. I glanced at my watch. Yikes. It was almost noon. Pop and Stan expected the photo shoot to take two hours tops. That meant I had one hour remaining.

I considered my options while standing in the backyard. Unless I wanted to break a window or tunnel through the ground, I was going to have to declare defeat. Unless . . . I looked at the second-story windows and gnawed on my bottom lip. Living in a second-story apartment gave me a sense of security. Rarely if ever did I lock my windows. Pop always made sure his first-story windows were secure, but he never remembered to lock the ones upstairs. The higher altitude made it easy to be complacent. After all, anyone breaking into the house would have to haul around a ladder. It was hard to stay inconspicuous when dragging around ten to twelve feet of metal.

Hoping Seth and Jan were just as lax about their upstairs security, I made a quick trip to the old pump house behind their home. Eureka. An eight-foot ladder. Not tall enough to get to the second-story windows, but high enough to get me safely into the large oak tree on the right side of the house. Conveniently, the tree had a thick branch that extended near a back window.

I used my left arm to carry most of the ladder's weight since my right shoulder was still feeling cranky. Leaves crunched under my feet. I unfolded the ladder under the tree and adjusted my purse strap over my neck so it wouldn't get in the way. After rolling out my shoulder, I took a deep breath and began to climb.

When I was in grade school, I had a crush on a boy who loved to climb trees. To impress him, I learned to hoist myself into willows and elms. Of course, I was a whole lot smaller and lighter then. Branches that were thick enough for me to scamper across seemed a whole lot smaller now. Especially the one I was kneeling on twelve feet above the ground. Tamping down the rational part of me that said this was a bad idea, I started crawling the four feet of lumber that separated me from my destination.

One inch.

Two inches.

Three.

My heart threatened to leap out of my chest. My breathing came fast and furious. The healing injuries on my legs complained with every movement.

The branch slanted downward, taking my stomach with it. I stopped, took several deep breaths, and crawled the last three inches that separated me from the window. Now for the moment of truth.

I centered my weight, put my fingers on the ledge, and pushed upward. The window moved, and I pitched forward.

Yikes.

I hung on to the window ledge for dear life as the branch beneath me dipped and swayed. The world stopped as I waited to fall. When I didn't, I shook off my panic, found my balance, and pushed the window up, up, up.

Crap. I'd forgotten about the screen. The good news was Seth and Jan hadn't thought much about it either. The screen was dented and bent and had several tears. It took only a little finagling and the screen popped into the room beyond. It clattered to the floor seconds before I climbed inside.

Phew. I'd never realized how good it felt to have both feet on solid ground. Or in this case, faded mauve synthetic carpet fibers. In the middle of the bedroom was a brass bed covered with a blue quilt and a heap of pillows that looked incredibly inviting. For the first time, I understood why Goldilocks curled up on Baby Bear's bed and risked being eaten to catch a few z's. At least Seth and Jan wouldn't eat me if they caught me snoozing on the bed. The worst that could happen was . . .

A throaty growl made the hair on the back of my neck stand on end. Slowly, I turned. Brown eyes blinked at me. A tail flicked. A mouth filled with teeth hung open as though anticipating its next morsel. In my delight to be alive and inside, I'd somehow forgotten about the Kurtzes' three less than photogenic dogs.

The dog took a step forward and let out another growl. Gulp. This was bad. A line of drool fell from the dog's mouth to the ground. Very, very bad.

Careful to keep my movements slow and nonthreatening, I reached for my purse and pulled the bacon Baggie free. The growling stopped, and the dog's nose began to twitch. I snapped off a small piece of bacon and threw it on the bed. The dog leaped onto the mattress, and I bolted for the hallway door.

A bark from behind told me that Rin Tin Tin had finished his snack and was looking for more. Or maybe he was telling his friends about the salty smorgasbord I had clutched in my hands. I broke off another piece and threw it behind me as I dodged two potted plants and ran down the stairs into the living room.

The barking behind me stopped as chewing commenced. One dog down, but the sound of yips, growls, and scrambling feet to the left told me the rest of the pooch posse was headed my way. Doing my best impersonation of Hansel and Gretel, I scattered bits of bacon and limped through the kitchen to the basement door.

Ha! I slammed the door behind me and leaned against the wall.

Nails scratched. Excited woofs and yaps told me the dogs would be waiting for me on my return. I just hoped the bacon I had left would be enough to get me out of this place before the dogs started snacking on me.

Pushing away from the wall, I reached for the light switch and then realized the lights were already on. Judging by the moisture, a humidifier was running, too. Weird.

I walked down the cement steps, reached the bottom, and stopped in my tracks. The entire room was filled with silver tables. Above the tables, long, white fluorescent lights illuminated row after row of plants with distinctive, spearlike, green leaves.

Holy shit. Seth and Jan Kurtz were growing pot. From the sophisticated look of the operation, I'd guess they'd been doing it for quite sometime.

A large, sturdy wooden desk stood on the far end of the room. I did a quick inventory. Phone. Scale. Zip-close bags. Bubble wrap. Packing boxes in a variety of sizes. Shipping labels and envelopes. Seth and Jan weren't growing cannabis for long winter nights and backyard barbecues. They were selling it. Packages that hadn't yet been sent to customers were neatly stacked and addressed. Florida. New Mexico. Wisconsin. Utah. The widespread geography of the Kurtzes' clientele and the slick organization of the packing system suggested this wasn't a new endeavor. If I was right, I had just found what the Thanksgiving thief would have stolen and the Kurtzes wouldn't have reported.

Of course, now that I had the information, I had no idea what to do with it. Reporting my discovery wouldn't capture the thief. It would only get Seth and Jan arrested. Their clients might get arrested, too.

Were they breaking the law? Sure. Even so, having two of my grandfather's contemporaries and their mail-order friends thrown in jail made me feel icky. I'd never been a fan of sparking up a joint and getting mellow, but I wasn't morally opposed to the people I knew who were. Laughing hysterically at bad jokes was silly, not dangerous.

To ease my conflicted conscience, I scribbled down the names and addresses of Seth and Jan's business associates in my notebook. If I changed my mind, I could always—

Yikes. I caught a glimpse of the small clock on the Kurtzes' desk. Pop and Stan would finish their photography routine in four minutes. I still had to get past the dogs, clean up evidence of my unauthorized presence, and get my car out of the driveway before Seth and Jan returned home. Even if I hadn't been battered and sore, I might not have been able to make that happen. I needed more time. Good thing I knew someone who could help with that.

I pulled my cell phone out of my pocket, pushed Pop's number, and hit SEND. The phone beeped, and I looked down at the screen. CALL ENDED. No bars. Crap. I wandered around the room, looking for a signal. Nope. The room might as well be covered with tinfoil, and the phone on the desk had no dial tone. This was perfect.

Clutching my bag of bacon, I made my way toward the stairs and paused to listen to the sounds from above. There wasn't any barking or growling. Dare I hope the dogs had slipped into a bacon-induced coma?

I put one foot on the stairs and heard the sound of nails scraping against linoleum. The natives were up there. In a minute they would once again be restless.

Stealth wasn't going to fly. The only thing that was going to save me was speed. I reached the top of the stairs, flung open the door, and threw the bag of bacon to the right. When the dogs scampered after the bag, I slammed the basement door behind me and bolted. The sounds of dogs battling for pork accompanied my flight up the stairs to the bedroom where I'd entered. I grabbed the screen, considered my likelihood of getting it back in place from the outside, and stashed it under the bed. Seth and Jan would have to put it back in place themselves. I was out of here.

Several harrowing minutes later, the window was shut and I was back on the ground, vowing never to do anything that stupid again. I stashed the ladder back in the pump house and heard a car door slam and dogs yip. A peek around the garage told me what my gut already knew. Unless I could bluff better than I did in Lionel's weekly poker games, I was busted.

Grabbing my notebook, I flipped to a blank page and sketched the back of the house. The drawing sucked, but hey, there was a reason I didn't play Pictionary. Thank goodness this particular ploy didn't require the *Mona Lisa*.

Studying my drawing, I walked around the side of the building while doing my best to pretend I wasn't aware of the five pairs of eyes staring at me from the front porch. I fiddled with my pen, made a few expressions of intense concentration, and looked up as one of the dogs began to growl.

"Hi." I waved and winced. My shoulder wasn't happy. Smiling, I yelled, "Sorry to drop by unannounced. I wanted to get a look at the layout of the house so I could compare it to the others that have been broken into. The two of you look really great. Did you go to a spa?" Seth frowned while Jan flushed with pleasure. The dogs took a step forward, and I decided to clear out. "I should let the two of you get inside. It's cold out here. I'll be in touch if I have any other questions. Thanks!"

I kept a manic smile plastered to my face until the Kurtzes' house faded from my rearview mirror. Unless the dogs sucked up every crumb of bacon, Seth and Jan were going to know someone had been inside. Guess who their first choice for home invader was going to be? However, due to the nature of their basement science project, I was pretty sure they weren't going to report their suspicions. Too bad that was the only thing I was certain of. Though my foray into breaking and entering had given me a motive for the initial theft, I still didn't have a clue who was behind it. I was determined to find out, though. What I needed was someone who could tell me who Jan and Seth might have shared their sideline with. I needed my grandfather.

I pulled over at the first cornfield with cell reception and dialed. No answer.

A quick drive-by of Pop's house told me my grandfather wasn't home but my father was. Although not for long, since he was waiting for a ride to take him to my grandfather's gig in Des Moines. Pop and the band were performing for a Red Hat convention. Jasmine had gone along to help with setup. Apparently, she'd always wanted to be a roadie.

"It's a big gig for the band. Your grandfather decided to drive up early. He's going to walk the stage and take photos with the candidates for Ms. Red Chapeau. He's hoping to get some press out of it." Stan grabbed two beers out of the fridge, popped the tops, and took a seat across from me at the kitchen table. He slid a beer toward me and put his hand over mine. "How are you feeling, sweetheart? Don't try to lie. I can spot a fib a mile away."

"I'm fine."

Stan's eyebrows rose. His grip on my hand tightened. "Really?"

The old Stan would have embraced the lie because it was easier. He wouldn't have feigned interest, and if pressed into a conversation, he'd have come up with an excuse as to why he couldn't talk. Stan insisting on a real answer made my heart flip.

I swallowed down some beer along with the lump in my throat and said, "I'm feeling a little bruised, especially after the morning I had."

Stan leaned forward. "You got in?"

"With the help of a tree and some bacon."

"Did you get into the basement?"

I nodded. I could see he was waiting for more information, but

I kept my mouth shut. Stan was showing signs of turning over a new leaf. I wasn't about to tempt him to regress with a bumper crop of marijuana.

"So now what?" he asked.

I put the bottle on the table. "I don't know. Seeing the basement gave me an idea of why the robberies started, but not who's behind them. The worst part is that I'm not sure I'll be able to figure it out before the thief strikes again." I didn't want to fail Mrs. Johnson, the town, or myself. I was in danger of doing all three. Up until now my ability to solve crimes involved dumb luck, not any real skill. And for some strange reason, I was admitting my inadequacies to the most unreliable person I knew.

My father nodded. "You know more about the thefts after a week of investigating than the sheriff's department learned in ten years. That's nothing to be ashamed of." He patted my hand. "But you're right. Whoever's behind the robberies knows this town. They know how the sheriff's department does things, and they've had a lot of time to cover their tracks."

I took a big drink. "That doesn't make me feel any better."

"It's not meant to."

Once again I was reminded of the reasons heart-to-hearts with my father weren't a good idea. You'd have thought I would have learned.

"Well, thanks for the beer." I pushed my chair back. "I should get going."

"Wait." Stan leaned forward. "What I was trying to say is the thief has been one step ahead for years. The only way to catch up is to do something unexpected."

I scooted my chair back in. "Like what?"

My father smiled. "Most good cons who get caught do so because they get complacent. The thief has a pattern based on what's succeeded in the past. He doesn't expect things to change. If they do, you'll catch him."

Three honks came from a car outside.

"That's my ride." My father glanced at his watch and stood. "Oh, and I hope you don't mind, but I invited one more for Thanksgiving. Alan's parents aren't going to make it home in time. I didn't want the poor kid feeling all alone. I hope that's okay."

Alan was a nineteen-year-old kid whose parents bought an RV and took off to see the country, leaving their son home to tend to the family business—a motel on the outskirts of town. When my father met him, the motel looked like it belonged on the set of *Psycho*. Since then Alan's family business had gotten a fresh coat of paint and a lot of new clients thanks to the duo's creative marketing. I'd been jealous when Stan started devoting time and attention to the then-unknown teen. Who could blame me? Stan had never bothered to give either to me. Still, despite my version of sibling rivalry, I found myself liking Alan and admiring my father for his dedication to the kid. Especially now that their business association had ended. "Tell Alan I'd love to have him come to dinner."

Although now that I did the mental math, I realized I no longer had enough knives, forks, and plates to serve my guests. This was a problem.

"Great." Stan gave my arm a pat. "I hate to do this, but I've got to run. If Eduardo is late to the gig because of me, your grandfather will short-sheet my bed for the next two months. Do you know how cold it gets upstairs? I promise I'll be around later if you want some help. Okay?"

"Sure," I said as emotion stormed in my chest. Stan was good at sounding sincere even when he intended to forget the promise he made. That quality made him a great salesman and a crappy father. I knew better to buy into it.

"Hey, Dad?" Stan turned with his hand on the doorknob, and I smiled. "Thanks."

My father's eyes met mine. Regret and hope glistened. "Any time."

I watched Stan disappear out the door, took another sip of beer, and decided my father was right. The thief was good at this. His method of breaking into houses had succeeded for a decade. Unless he relocated or kicked the bucket, he was going to try again. Up until now, I'd been trying to uncover the thief's identity without success. Just like the sheriff's department. If I wanted to catch the crook before another house was hit, I had to change my methods. I had to make the thief come to me.

Seventeen

Now that I had decided to be proactive, I had to figure out how to go about it. In order to catch the crook, I first had to know which house or houses were being targeted. Then I could be there to yell "surprise." To do that, I needed to determine which citizens of Indian Falls were going to be out of town on Turkey Day and, of those people, who had the best stuff to boost. Since my main source of gossip was bringing the bright lights of Vegas to Des Moines, I went to the next best hub of information—the diner.

Only a couple of the red Formica tables were occupied when I walked into the Hunger Paynes Diner. Diane Moore, daughter of sheriff's department receptionist Roxy Moore, was holding a coffeepot while laughing with the half-dozen teenagers occupying the booths in the back. She waved as I slid onto a stool at the end of the counter and grabbed a faded menu. The smell of grilling meat reminded me that I'd skipped lunch. This whole investigative thing really screwed with a person's schedule.

I ordered a Diet Coke and a bacon burger with a side salad and waited for Diane to shout the order back to Sammy before asking, "How are things going?"

Diane beamed. "I've gotten two college acceptances. Mom's hoping I go to Northern, but I'm still waiting for U of I to make a decision. Their admissions standards are tough, but I think I have a chance."

Roxy bragged enough for me to know Diane was not only hardworking but had a 4.0 grade point average. Diane was smart, she was observant, and she had a great memory for details. Three reasons I was here today.

"Do you have a minute to talk?" I asked, looking around the diner. "I don't want to make your customers mad."

"I just gave everyone refills." She handed me my soda and hurried around the counter to take the seat next to me. "Do you need help with something? My mom thinks getting run over should have taught you to leave investigating cases to Sean and the sheriff. Actually, she's just upset Sean turned down her offer to buy him dinner."

I stifled a surge of glee and lowered my voice. "Do you know anyone who's leaving town on Thanksgiving?"

Diane glanced over her shoulder and then whispered. "Well, most people are staying home because of the . . . well . . . you know. Anyone leaving town used to contact the sheriff's office so the department could send extra patrols by."

Huh. "I didn't know that."

"The sheriff and Deputy Holmes try not to make a big deal about it. Most of the houses hit have been on the department's watch list."

Talk about a public relations nightmare. "Did your mother mention if anyone's contacted the department this year?"

"She was out sick last week, so she hasn't been in the loop, but from what she's said, no one is leaving town." Diane shrugged. "Personally, I think not telling anyone is the smart way to go. If Mom and I had to leave for the holiday, I'd turn on the lights and the television and leave one car parked in the driveway so everyone would think we were there."

Yep—the girl was smart. "Has anyone in the diner mentioned leaving town?"

"Melissa Abbott's going to her dad's house in St. Louis, but her mother will still be here. Mrs. Schaffer is going to her daughter's house, but I'm pretty sure her son will be at home." Diane frowned. "I don't think that's the kind of information you're looking for, though."

It wasn't. Or maybe it was.

Sam dinged the bell in the kitchen window, and Diane scurried back around the counter to get my food. By the time I'd polished off my burger and eaten enough of the salad to make myself feel virtuous, I had the beginnings of a plan.

Roxy Moore's sneeze greeted me as I walked through the door of the sheriff's department. Her nose matched the magenta hue of her lipstick. Balled-up tissues were scattered across the reception desk. She added one more to their number and frowned as I crossed to her.

"How are you feeling?" I asked. "Sean said you were sick. He was worried about you."

"Really?" Roxy's tired eyes narrowed. "If you're here to see Deputy Holmes, you'll have to wait. He's in a meeting with the mayor and the sheriff."

I ignored the less than welcoming tone and asked, "Has anyone asked the sheriff to patrol their neighborhood while they're out of town this Thursday?"

She frowned. "That information is confidential."

Roxy sneezed. I handed her a tissue. "I'm not asking to see the list. I just want to know if there is one."

If Roxy didn't tell me, I was pretty sure Sean would, but I'd rather not have to ask him. Sean's out-of-character behavior was starting to wig me out.

Roxy sneezed three more times and glared from behind her tissue. "The sheriff decided it would be more productive to use methods other than a list of residences to assign the additional Thanksgiving patrols."

In other words—no.

Armed with the knowledge that our thief might be hard up for targets, I got in my car and headed for the only people I knew were hitting the road for the holiday.

"We're not going." Bryan's bottom lip trembled as he hung an ornament on the Christmas tree he said he was decorating to make himself feel better. Unless the ornaments were made out of Seth and Jan's happiness-inducing horticulture, I didn't think the tree was going to do the job.

"What happened?" I asked.

Bryan's shoulders slumped. A lone tear streaked down his face. "Reginald's family doesn't like me."

"Did Reginald tell you that?"

"No." He sniffled. "He came in from his trip, ignored the fresh blueberry muffins I made, and told me we were staying here for the holiday."

I'd had Bryan's muffins. They were exceptional. If Reginald passed up the chance to eat one fresh from the oven, something was wrong.

"Do you want me to talk to Reginald?" I asked. "He might be more willing to tell me what's going on."

Armed with a steaming mug of coffee and a plate of muffins, I headed to the back of the house, where Reginald and Bryan had set up their office. Growing up, I'd seen a bunch of farmhouse offices. Most of those were comprised of scarred wooden desks, a phone, an out-of-date computer, and heaps of paper. Reginald and Bryan's office looked like it had been designed by NASA. A large, sleek, circular, black desk equipped with a laptop, two flat-screen monitors, and two phones sat in the middle of the room. Behind the desk was a bank of televisions. Some displayed numbers or colorful graphs. Others streamed images captured by the video cameras set up in the enormous greenhouse Reginald and Bryan had built out back. In essence, anyone looking at those monitors was subjected to the excitement of watching grass grow. Oh, boy.

Reginald sat in the leather chair behind the desk. His signature dreadlocks were fastened by a white rubber band at his nape. A pair of glasses perched on his nose as he glanced from monitor to monitor and talked into a headset. When Reginald spotted me hovering in the doorway, he waved me into one of the sleek red visitor chairs and finished his discussion about next year's green manure.

Ick.

I sipped at my coffee and put the plate of muffins on the desk. Discussion of manure was an effective appetite suppressant.

When Reginald's call was finished, I felt compelled to ask, "What do you feed the cows to turn the manure green?"

Reginald looked baffled and then started to laugh. His laugh was deep, warm, and infectious. At least it was after he explained that green manure doesn't come from cows. It's created out of crops grown specifically to plow under for the nutrients they'll add to the soil. Huh. I learned something new every day.

Since we weren't discussing cow patties, I handed a muffin to Reginald and took one for myself. "Bryan said your trip to see your family for Thanksgiving was canceled. He's convinced your family hates him."

"They don't hate him." Reginald took the earpiece off and threw it on the desk. "They're mad at each other. My brother learned that my sister was——" He sighed. "It doesn't matter. I decided we should sit this Thanksgiving out. Bryan's too sensitive to deal with my family in the middle of open warfare."

"You should probably tell him that. Bryan thinks this is his fault."

Reginald peeled the paper off his muffin with a sigh. "Bryan was so excited about spending the holiday with my folks. He's always wanted to belong to a big family. His disowned him when he came out on his eighteenth birthday, and he has built my family up in his head, which is why I haven't told him the crap that goes on back home. I didn't want to burst his bubble."

"I think it's popped."

"Yeah." He frowned. "I hate to see him upset. We used to spend Thanksgiving with friends when we lived in the city. Once we moved, we spent the holidays alone. We try to convince each other it's romantic, but it's not. It's lonely. I wanted this year to be different."

"Then it will be," I said. "You have family here in Indian Falls. You should spend Thanksgiving with them."

"I think whatever gave you that bruise on your chin knocked something loose. Bryan and I don't have family here."

"You have me." I smiled. "I'm cooking dinner for Pop, Stan, and a bunch of our friends. We'd love for you to join us."

Reginald swallowed hard. His eyes glistened. Straightening his shoulders, Reginald cleared his throat and nodded. "Bryan and I would be honored. We think of you as family, too."

Bryan wasn't as dignified in his acceptance. He laughed. He cried. He promised to bake all week to make sure we didn't run out of pumpkin pie. "I can also bring whatever else you need. Stuffing? Cranberries?"

"How about plates and silverware?" I suggested. "I don't have enough place settings for everyone invited." Apparently, my mother had never cooked for more than a dozen people at any one time. Mom was smart.

"Plates and silverware it is." Bryan also vowed to tell everyone in town that I was the nicest person he'd ever met.

"About that . . ." I said. It was time to transition to my real purpose for dropping by. "I need you to do me a favor."

"Anything." Bryan beamed.

"Don't tell anyone you're coming to my place on Thursday." Before Bryan could worry that I was embarrassed to have them eat dinner at my table, I explained my plan to trap the thief. "If we know which house he's going to rob, there's a good chance we can catch him in the act and put him out of business for good. You just need to let one or two of the gossips know you're leaving town and let nature take its course."

For the next hour we ate muffins, decorated the Christmas tree, and discussed strategy. Since Bryan was the more excitable of the two, he'd report their leaving town to the sheriff's department and request that additional patrols swing by the house.

Reginald would be point person for quietly spreading news of their out-of-town adventure at the diner and market. My gut told me the thief had gotten wind of the sheriff's lists in the past. If I was wrong, Reginald asking those he told about the trip to keep it a secret would do the rest. Indian Falls' gossips wouldn't be able to resist. They never had before.

Promising I'd be in touch, I hung one last bell on the tree, took my bag of take-out muffins from Bryan, and hit the road. I took the long way back to town to avoid driving past Seth and Jan's. The extra miles gave me time to consider whether to run my real-life version of *Mousetrap* by Sean. For the plan to work, I'd need Sean and his gun to be at Reginald and Bryan's house for the moment of truth. However, extending him an engraved invitation to my catch-a-crook party might not be my best option. Sean wasn't the type to go along with someone else's plan, no matter how good it might be. Even if he did go along, he'd probably find a way to cut me out of the action and rake in the glory. Getting credit for the arrest didn't matter to me, but I did want to be there when the thief was unmasked. For that to happen, I'd have to come up with a ploy to get Sean to Reginald and Bryan's for the moment of truth.

I stepped on the brakes and stared at the house blazing with light in the distance. While I'd been thinking about trapping the thief, my subconscious had done some trapping of its own. Instead of steering toward town as I'd intended, I'd driven to Lionel's house. He hadn't called since walking out the door last night. I wanted to believe a goat had eaten his phone, but something told me the goat hadn't been that cooperative. Lionel was still mad. Since I was stopped on the street instead of pulling into his driveway, I guessed I was angry, too.

I started to drive away, but then I remembered the way Lionel looked at my hospital bedside. On edge. Scared. Did that give him a right to yell, storm off, and make me unhappy by not calling? No, but fear made people do strange things. I was adult enough to understand that this experience had left us both unhappy. If I wanted to untie those emotional knots, I had to go to him.

I turned up the drive and cut the engine before I could chicken out. Muffins in hand, I looked from the house to the barn. Both had lights on. I decided to check the barn first. If nothing else, I'd get nuzzled by a camel. The world was a happier place when a dromedary loved you.

The smell of hay and animals greeted me as I walked through the barn's door. Sheep bleated. A cow chewed its cud, and several horses whinnied. The simple, rustic atmosphere was balm for my jittery nerves, as was the Chicago-Bears-ball-cap-wearing camel I found sitting on the hay in his double-wide back stall. Elwood made a throaty sound and scrambled to his feet in an effort to score attention. I was more than happy to oblige.

Elwood made happy camel sounds as I petted his neck. Then I scratched his ears with one hand while with the other I fed him part of a muffin. When he'd devoured his snack, Elwood's velvety nose bumped against my shoulder and his cheek rubbed against mine. The uncomplicated, undemanding affection of a camel broke down the barrier I'd constructed between me and fear, uncertainty, and pain. Stripped of my defenses, I did the only thing I could do. I wrapped my arms around Elwood's neck, buried my face in his coarse brown fur, and cried.

My shoulder ached. The bruises and scrapes on my legs and chin throbbed, and the stress and worry that I might not live up to the trust Mrs. Johnson and the entire Chapman family had placed in me made me want to burrow in the hay. Unfortunately, hiding in this barn wasn't a good option. The animals wouldn't object, but the owner might. If he didn't, I still wouldn't be able to stay. Annoying as it might be, Sean was right. I needed to solve the puzzles. So far, I'd made good progress on the robberies. Now it was time to focus on finding Ginny's killer.

I gave Elwood one last hug, took a step back, and wiped the tears from my eyes. Crying wasn't going to solve the problem. Looking for answers was.

I turned and felt my breath catch. Lionel was leaning against the stall doorway with his arms crossed. Automatically, I reached up to fix my hair and then stopped. Between the swollen eyes, tear-streaked makeup, and bits of camel fur stuck to my cheeks, my hair was the least of my concerns.

Lionel jammed his hands in his jeans pockets. "I was just about to call you."

"Really?"

My disbelief made him laugh. "Yes, really. I'd intended to wait until you contacted me. Then I talked to my mother, who informed me that my reasoning was flawed."

"You told your mother we had a fight?" I had yet to meet the woman and she already hated me. Oh joy.

"She called to ask if she and Dad could come a few days early. She also wanted me to ask if she could help cook on Thanksgiving. That's when I mentioned we might not be joining your hardheaded self for dinner."

I cringed.

Lionel shrugged. "I expected my mother to take my side, especially when I explained what had happened. Instead, I got a kick in the ass. My mother said that any man who picked a fight with his girlfriend on the day she was released from the hospital was doomed to go single for the rest of his life. She also told me if I was holding out for you to come to me, she hoped you were a smart enough woman to let me wait until hell froze over. And if by some miracle you did make contact first, I was to beg for forgiveness and convince you to marry me because you were a better woman than I deserved."

Wow. "Your mother sounds . . ." Intimidating. "Impressive."

"She is." Lionel smiled. "So what do you think?"

"About what?"

"What my mother told me to do."

My mouth went dry. Butterflies whacked my stomach. If Lionel proposed, Bryan's blueberry muffins were going to make a reappearance.

Not that I was opposed to the concept of marriage. My grandfather and grandmother had provided an envious example of two people who were happier together than apart. Still, though I was delighted to help my friends enter into legally committed relationships, I felt faint at the thought of being in one myself. Until that changed, I wasn't ready to consider marriage. Especially not after the fight Lionel and I had had yesterday. As it stood now, we'd be divorced before the honeymoon.

"I'm not sure what to think." My answer had the advantage of being both honest and vague.

Lionel closed the space between us. "I'm sorry." His fingers laced with mine, and his thumb rubbed circles on my palm. "Hearing that you'd been hit by a car scared the hell out of me. As I drove to the hospital, I thought about how empty my life would be without you and I panicked. That's why I overreacted last night. I'd almost lost you once. It's hard to accept that you want to continue down a path that might make someone hurt you again. You are the most important part of my life."

Eek. Here it comes. What would I do if Lionel proposed? Between the camel and the man, there wasn't much room to run. I could pretend to faint. The hay looked soft enough to keep me from doing any major damage when I went down and . . . I realized Lionel wasn't talking. He also wasn't sinking to the ground or producing an overpriced piece of rock in a velvet box. He was just standing there, looking at me with those sexy green eyes—waiting.

"That's it?" I asked.

Lionel grinned. "I can get down on my knees and beg for forgiveness if you'd like."

"Kneeling isn't necessary." In fact, it would make me pass out.

"Good." He took a step closer. "I'll save that for next time."

Next time?

His mouth lowered to mine, and all thoughts of future fights, proposals, and criminal investigations disappeared. Warmth spread through my sore muscles. I wrapped my arms around Lionel's neck and leaned in. The bag of muffins dropped to the ground. As tempted as I was to have us join them, I had to ask, "Does this mean you're okay with me continuing to investigate?"

Lionel sighed and took a step back. "As my mother eloquently pointed out, I don't have a choice. Besides, once the thief is caught and Ginny's murderer is behind bars, this won't be an issue anymore. After all, how many crimes can one small town have?"

More than you'd think.

Music began to play. Lionel dug into his pocket for his phone. When he was done with the call, he gave me an apologetic kiss and headed out to help with a llama emergency. I watched him go as Elwood swallowed the last of Bryan's baked goods.

Before Elwood could add more fiber to his diet, I grabbed the paper bag, threw it in the trash, and drove back to the rink. The Toe Stop parking lot was packed thanks to "buy one pizza, get one free" night. As I parked my car, I noticed people standing in clusters around the exterior of the rink. Their signature hot pink-and-silver jackets made no secret of their identity. The Estro-Genocide girls were here. I climbed out of my car and was immediately flanked by J. K. Fouling and Dharma Gheddon. As I started walking toward the rink, Erica the Red fell into position in front of me while Anna Phylaxis brought up the rear. Once again the women of derby had decided I needed protection. Part of me was annoyed. The wimpy, incredibly sore parts were relieved.

When we reached my apartment door, the girls waited for me to go inside before hurrying back to their patrol of the parking lot perimeter. The president of the United States had the Secret Service. I had girls wearing faux satin. There was no contest. I'd take my protection detail over his any day.

I sagged against the door. Not only was I tired, I hurt. I needed medication, a long, hot bath, and twelve hours in which I didn't think about thefts, murders, Danielle's wedding, or my less than stable love life. One night with no stress. Was that too much to ask?

As I kicked off my shoes, I spotted a small white box with a jaunty silver bow atop my coffee table and smiled. Pop must have left me a get-well gift. Feeling happier than I had in the last week, I pried open the lid and dug through the paper.

Ouch. A dot of blood bloomed on my index finger. Just what I needed. Another injury. After setting the box on the table, I yanked the tissue paper out of the box to reveal the contents—and went completely still. Sitting in the middle of the box was a syringe tied with a shiny red ribbon. Attached to the ribbon was a note that read KEEP OUT OR YOU'RE NEXT.

Pop hadn't left me a gift. Ginny's killer had.

Eighteen

I sucked in air. My heart skidded in my chest and then picked up speed. Ginny's murderer had been in my home. My life had just been threatened for the second time this week.

During my hospital convalescence, I'd decided the driver of the car was reacting to my investigating the thefts. Knowing someone had tried to run me over was scary, but I'd dulled the fear with the knowledge that the perp was a thief. Not a killer. Now I was prepared to panic.

"Hey, are you okay?"

I jumped, turned, and went flying as my foot hooked on the bottom of the chair. Oof. I narrowly avoided smacking my head on the coffee table and hit the carpet with a thud. Ouch. Ouch. Ouch.

"Wow, I didn't mean to freak you out. I thought you heard me come in." Jasmine grabbed me by the waist and hauled me to my feet. "Some of the band guys dropped me off on their way home. Your grandfather stayed behind to party with the Hat Queen.

That man is a force. You should've seen the way the women threw their clothing at him."

No. I was already teetering on the edge. Seeing that would have sent me right over.

"Your grandfather wants me to consider joining the act."

"Can you sing?" I asked, ignoring the potential instrument of death taunting me from five feet away.

Jasmine grinned. "Not well, but that doesn't stop your grandfather." She looked down at the table and raised an eyebrow. "What's with the needle?"

"It's, er, um," I said cleverly.

She picked up the box. "It's kind of creepy with the bow and the . . . holy shit." Jasmine's smile and carefree attitude disappeared. "Where did you get this? Who gave this to you? First you get run over by a car, and now this? What kind of town are you living in?"

All good questions. I wished I had equally good answers.

"The box was waiting for me when I got home. I was just about to call Deputy Holmes when you came in." The last part probably would have been true had my mind been capable of thought. To prove my ability to function like a normal human being, I got out my phone and dialed. Five minutes later, Sean walked through the door looking disheveled and more than a little dangerous.

"You figure Ginny's killer left this for you?" he asked, looking up from the note.

I nodded, swallowed hard, and tried to channel Wonder Woman. Nothing scared her, not even riding in an invisible plane.

"Was the front door locked?"

I thought back to walking up the stairs. The derby girls were talking as I let myself inside. I'd had the keys in my hand, but did

I use them to get in? I was pretty sure I did. If not, one of the derby girls would have noticed and said something.

Sean examined the door and then checked every window in the place. All the windows were locked. There was no sign of forced entry. The murderer either could walk through walls or had a key. I wasn't fond of either option.

While Jasmine babbled about thinking she'd left this kind of crime behind, Sean did his cop impersonation. He asked for the exact location where I'd found the box, my whereabouts for the day, and anything I might have done to prompt this latest threat. I gave Sean my itinerary without embellishing on the details. No reason to confess to tree climbing and puppy payoffs if I didn't have to. From his expression, Sean knew there was more to my story than outdoor property surveys and muffins, but he didn't call me on it. I guess he figured I was beat up enough.

When he closed his cop book, I asked, "Is there any way I can convince you to keep this to yourself?" The last thing I needed was Lionel hitting the roof or the derby girls building bunkers in the parking lot.

Sean glanced at Jasmine then back at me. "Can we speak in private?"

Jasmine stopped her crime-is-everywhere monologue and plopped her hands on her hips. "Rebecca and I don't have secrets from each other. Whatever you have to say can be said in front of me. Right, Rebecca?"

Um . . . Jasmine was fun. She was feisty and loyal and about as subtle as a rampaging cow in . . . well, just about anywhere. If Sean wanted something kept secret, he had better say it out of Jasmine's hearing.

Pulling Jasmine into the kitchen, I said, "Sean doesn't discuss open cases in front of civilians. The only reason he's talking to me is because I've been hired by one of the victims."

She glared in Sean's direction and blew hair off her forehead. "I guess that makes sense. But I want a full report after he leaves."

Jasmine grabbed the remote and plopped onto the couch. Then I nodded for Sean to follow and walked down the hall to my room.

I closed the door behind us and Sean asked, "Did anything else happen today that I need to know about?"

I bit my lip, and Sean sighed.

"Okay," he said. "The only way to keep you safe is if I know what's going on. So let's do this. For the next few minutes, I'm going to pretend I don't have a badge. Tell me."

To his credit, Sean didn't yell or stomp or turn various shades of red. He just listened as I confessed to balancing on tree branches and throwing bacon-flavored confetti. His voice was calm when he asked, "Did you find anything in the Kurtz house to help the investigation?"

A picture of Seth and Jan behind bars popped into my head. "Are you still pretending not to be a cop?"

Sean closed his eyes. He took two deep breaths and then opened them. "Consider me Joe Civilian."

"Good." Before Sean could change his mind, I told him about Seth and Jan's basement business.

"Seth and Jan are in their seventies."

"I guess they found a way to supplement their Social Security." An ingenious, albeit illegal, way. "Those plants could be the reason the thefts began. We just have to figure out who knew about them and wanted a piece of the action badly enough to risk arrest."

Sean pursed his lips, walked across the room, and stared out the window.

"You think my theory sucks."

He turned. "I think it's the best lead the department has had since the robberies started." He smiled. "For the record, I still plan on taking credit once the perpetrator is caught."

I rolled my eyes. "So now what?"

"Now I run down the people Seth might have told about his basement crop. With a little luck, we'll catch the robber in the next day or two."

Hearing him say "we" would catch the crook made me smile. Then again, I noticed that, while he gave me credit, he didn't give me an assignment. "What should I do?"

"Stay safe." Sean held up a hand. "I'm not saying you should barricade yourself inside this place, although I'd suggest it if I thought there was a chance in hell you'd listen. Instead, I'll settle for a promise that you won't go anywhere by yourself. The killer will think twice about attacking if you have someone sleeping here at night and going around town with you. I'm sure Lionel will be happy to volunteer for the job."

"Happy" wouldn't come close to covering Lionel's emotional state if he heard about this most recent threat.

Sean must have guessed my thoughts since he added, "I'd volunteer, but I'm not the one spending time in your bed. Although I wouldn't say no if circumstances changed."

I waited for Sean to laugh or smirk, but he didn't look amused. Sean wasn't having fun at my expense. Sean was serious.

Gulp.

Suddenly, I became very aware of my surroundings. Closed

door. Fluffy bed. Sean stepped toward me as though he intended to make use of both. My heart swooped. My palms sweated. If this was a move designed to make me uncomfortable, it worked.

"I like Lionel," Sean said. "I respect him. More important, I respect you. Which is why I'm not going to make your life more difficult than it already is by acting on what I feel. But if you decide Lionel isn't the guy for you . . ."

Sean raised his hand and lifted my chin. Nerves, fear, and—holy crap—a strange kind of attraction jangled my stomach as I waited for him to kiss me.

He didn't. He ran a thumb along my jaw and said, "I'd be interested in seeing what kind of sparks would fly if we explored being more than friends." Dropping his hand, he turned toward the door. "Keep someone with you at all times, Rebecca. If you don't, I'll have to assume you want me to handle the job personally."

Eek!

Sean walked out the door, and I sat on the bed. I heard Jasmine shout good-bye, followed by the front door closing. Sean was gone. Part of me wasn't sure I'd wanted him to go.

All the pain must have caused a severe chemical imbalance. Hell, I'd probably hallucinated everything that just happened. Sean couldn't be interested in dating me. He got his kicks from yelling and yanking my chain. If I were being truthful, I'd admit I was also entertained by our skirmishes. Sean kept me on my toes whether I wanted him to or not. I'd thought of him as the annoying, know-it-all big brother who made me want to stick out my tongue. Now . . .

I pressed my hand to my stomach and took several deep breaths. The way my insides were jumping made me feel very adult and more than a little stupid. Sean and I were friends on the best days and combatants on the worst. Lionel, however, was smart, sexy, and kind to both people and animals. He was everything I wanted in a man. The only reason I was reacting to Sean now was because he'd taken me by surprise. The suggestion the two of us would in any scenario make a good couple was laughable. Sean and I would forget this conversation happened, and life would continue as it was supposed to. Me with Lionel, and Sean . . . well, Sean would be Sean. End of story.

A quick call told me Lionel's llama issue was more complicated than originally anticipated. Thank goodness Jasmine was delighted to take up residence in the guest room and to be my shadow for the next several days.

"Aren't your parents going to be upset you haven't come home?" I asked.

"Nah. I wasn't sure what my plans were, so I didn't give then a specific date of arrival. I'm happy to bodyguard for as long as you need me."

Fun times.

Despite the upheaval in my life, I slept like the dead. When I woke, I glanced at the clock and sighed. I'd missed church services. I'd never win awards for my faithful attendance, but this week I'd promised Danielle I'd be at St. Mark's in order to listen to Rich's final sermon as an unmarried man.

I sent a text to Danielle apologizing for oversleeping. She sent back DON'T WORRY ABOUT IT. Then she sent a reminder about the errands I'd promised to take part in this week. Then she sent WE NEED TABLE FAVORS. NOW.

Damn. I'd forgotten about the favors. Between solving favor problems, visiting the florist and caterer, decorating the hall, and going to the rehearsal dinner on Wednesday, let alone grocery shopping and cooking for Thanksgiving, there wasn't going to be much time left in my schedule for investigating. I had to get a jump on it now.

My aching body protested as I hopped out of bed, grabbed my purse, and tiptoed down the hall to the extra bedroom I used as a home office. I longed for coffee and a bagel as the computer booted up, but I stayed put. If Jasmine knew I was awake, she'd want to help. My friend had lots of fabulous qualities, but being sneaky was not one of them.

TV cops were always talking about motive, means, and opportunity when investigating murders. Since they managed to capture their perps in less than sixty minutes, I decided to take my cue from them and did a search on the murder weapon to see how hard it was to obtain insulin without a prescription.

Yikes. Not hard. Though many types of insulin were obtained by prescription, several older versions were available over the counter. So much for narrowing my search.

And so much for focusing on means. Maybe I'd get further on motive. As far as I could tell, the only hint of motive lay in the numbers and letters Ginny had recorded on the teapot note. Flipping to that page in my notebook, I studied them and hoped for an epiphany.

Nothing. So much for wishing the medication affected not only pain but also my extrasensory abilities. Since I wasn't qualified to answer phones for the Psychic Friends network, I flipped back through my notes and read from start to finish. By the time I got to the end, I was just as baffled and more than a little disheartened. When I walked into Ginny's wake tonight, her family was going to ask if I was any closer to catching the killer. I was going to have to tell them no. Maybe it was time to admit I wasn't a real investigator and give up.

I threw my notebook on the desk and swore as it knocked over a picture frame. After setting the picture upright, I studied the photograph. It was a picture of my mother and me. The photograph was taken when I was sixteen, after my last meet as a solo artistic skater. I'd taken second, which wasn't bad considering how frustrated I'd been during my practice session. A double toe loop combination that I'd typically done with ease had given me fits. Bad landings, falls, and aborted jumps plagued me as I practiced the maneuver again and again. To no avail. I was about to throw in the towel when my mother told me to start the routine over. To go back to the beginning and figure out where I'd gone wrong.

Wait a minute. I grabbed my notebook and headed for the door. I knew what I had to do. I needed to go back to the beginning and determine what Ginny had been doing and who she had seen in the minutes leading up to her death. It was time to pay a visit to the scene of the crime.

Nineteen

Senior center activities were kept to a minimum on Sunday afternoons in deference to the population's need for after-church eggs, bacon, and hand-dipped milkshakes at the diner. I guess they believed attending services gave them special dispensation for cholesterol and calories. The few who hadn't attended church or didn't believe in the miracle of divine diet intervention were watching football in the same television room where Ginny had taken her last breath.

Jasmine started to go inside, but I shook my head. "Not yet. We have a reenactment to perform."

Taking slow steps, I walked down the hallway to the recreation room where Danielle's shower had been held. It took a minute and a half at most to cover that ground and just over that time to walk from the crime scene to the covered walkway or the front door. Those were the three most-used entrances to the building and the ones most likely utilized by the killer.

"I bet the murderer used this door." Jasmine pointed to an exit on the opposite side of the building from the parking lot. "Then he could get in and out without being seen."

"It's for emergency exit only." I pointed to a sign warning an alarm would sound if used.

"Those signs are all phony," Jasmine said. "People in the city use them all the time to make people think twice about—"

Before I could stop her, Jasmine pushed open the door. A loud siren whooped and wailed. "Huh." Jasmine plugged her ears and yelled, "I guess that's another difference between this place and Chicago. The signs mean what they say."

It took fifteen minutes before someone shut off the alarm. In the meantime, people who couldn't turn off their hearing aids went next door to watch the game, which gave Jasmine and me free rein to look around the room where Ginny had died. The game was still on the television. Jasmine cheered for a field goal while I walked to the chair where Ginny had been seated.

The heavy blue chair was designed with a high back and stuffed armrests and was angled toward the television. A person seated in the chair should spot, in her peripheral vision, anyone coming into the room through the lone door. I could test that theory, but I wasn't keen about sitting in a chair where someone had died. Things were dangerous enough in my life. There was no need to tempt fate.

I positioned myself next to the chair, squatted so I was at the same level as someone sitting, and asked Jasmine to tear herself from the game long enough to walk through the door. Yep. Even with my eyes glued to the television set, I saw Jasmine sashay into the room. Unless Ginny had been sleeping, she saw her killer approach. Since there weren't any signs of a struggle, I had to believe Ginny assumed she had nothing to worry about when the other person pulled out a syringe.

My research said a person could fall into a coma within ten to thirty minutes of the overdose and potentially slip into death sometime after that if nothing was done to counteract the drop in blood sugar. Sometimes death was known to take even longer. Not exactly the most efficient way to kill someone. So why use it? And how? Even if Ginny was friends with her attacker, she wasn't going to sit still while they jabbed her with a sharp, pointy object. Friends just don't let friends do that.

Maybe Ginny was like Pop and took catnaps during the day. A sleeping Ginny wouldn't have noticed her attacker or the syringe. However, even in his deepest sleep, Pop would notice if someone stuck him with a needle. Once he clocked the perpetrator, he'd call Doc Truman for help. Since Ginny did neither, I had to assume she'd been oblivious to the problem. Why?

To get that answer, I pulled out my phone. Sean picked up right away. "Did Ginny have any medication other than the insulin in her system?"

"The autopsy listed traces of zolpidem in her blood," Sean answered. "Doc said that was to be expected since Ginny had problems with insomnia."

I thought back to the prescription bottle of Ambien CR in Ginny's medicine cabinet and signaled for Jasmine to follow me.

"Where are you now?" Sean asked as Jasmine shouted one last string of insults at the refs.

"I'm just leaving the center, and don't worry—I'm not alone."

"I can hear that. Why the drug question?"

"Just trying to decide why Ginny would let someone nick her with a needle. I think you answered that. Thanks."

I was about to disconnect when Sean said, "Wait a minute."

His tone turned softer. Deeper. Sexier. Yikes. "You're being careful, right?"

"Sure thing. Talk to you later." Click.

Phew.

Doing my best to ignore the spike in my pulse, I led Jasmine through the covered walkway to Ginny's condo. Nothing looked like it had been moved since my last visit. I told Jasmine to stay in the kitchen and made a beeline for the bathroom. Sure enough, there was the prescription bottle I remembered. The prescription was for twenty pills, filled two weeks ago, and instructed the user to take as needed. I popped the top and found seven pills inside. Unless Ginny had chosen to hibernate her way through the last week of her life, I was guessing someone had helped himself or herself to some of Ginny's pills and slipped them into her food or drink. Once she was asleep, giving her a shot would have been easy, albeit rude.

I returned to the kitchen and examined Ginny's front door. There weren't any signs of tampering or forced entry. Either the killer got top marks in lock-picking or Ginny opened the door and let him in. I'd bet the bank it was option B. Ginny wasn't killed by a stranger. She was killed by a friend she trusted. Now I had to figure out who.

I steered Jasmine out of the condo before she could start rummaging through the fridge. As I locked the door, the diminutive Ethel Jacabowski stepped into view.

"Oh, Rebecca. It's so good to see you. We've all been so worried since the accident. Pastor Rich even added you to the prayer list during this morning's service. I know some people don't believe prayer can help, but it certainly doesn't hurt, does it?" Ethel shifted a foam container stamped with the diner's logo in her hand. "What are you doing here today? People are saying you're helping the sheriff find the person who killed Ginny. If so, I'd like to do whatever I can to help. Ginny was one of my very best friends."

The sheen of tears in Ethel's eyes made my throat tighten. Swallowing hard, I asked, "Could you tell me who Ginny's other friends are?"

"Oh, goodness." Ethel dug into her coat pocket and pulled out a frilly pink handkerchief. "Everyone loved Ginny. I guess her best friends are me, Joan and Marty McGoran, and Alice Peppinger. Joan and Marty are talking about canceling their trip to Florida this year. They can't imagine being there without Ginny. Ginny loved our annual trip south. It's just not going to be the same without her."

"You still plan on going?" I asked.

Ethel sighed. "It's what Ginny would want. She was a founding member of our group. The Winter Migration Club, we called ourselves. Over the years we've had members pass or move away, like my Paul, but we never considered not going. The club has always felt the best way to celebrate those we love is to live life to the fullest. So I'm going to put away my leftovers and get some packing done before the wake. Ginny would approve."

The simple dignity in Ethel's voice made me want to cry. Before I did, I asked, "Did you see anyone in the hallway last Sunday before you found Ginny?"

"Not that I remember." Ethel frowned but then brightened. "Wait. I do remember Jimmy Bakersfield sneaking into the kitchen. He'd been around before the shower, making eyes at the petit fours. I figured he was going to swipe a few. Doc Truman keeps warning Jimmy that diabetics have to watch their sweets intake, but you know men. They never listen."

Ethel gave me a small smile and shuffled down the hall with her takeout. As we headed to the exit, Jasmine said, "This investigating thing is exciting. Timing how long it takes to get from the exits to the crime scene. Looking through the victim's apartment. Questioning witnesses. I feel like I'm in one of those old black-and-white movies. So, what do we do next? Rough up a witness? Run down a suspect? What?"

I looked at Jasmine's four-inch-heeled boots and tried to picture her outrunning a suspect. An image of her five-foot three-inch frame sprawled on the sidewalk sprang to mind. I made a mental note to take her shopping for Reeboks and headed for my car. Meeting Ethel had been a stroke of luck. Without meaning to, she had given me a suspect who was near the crime scene and, since he was diabetic, had access to the murder weapon. It was time to pay a visit to Pop's friend and my first investigative client, Jimmy Bakersfield.

Jimmy wasn't home. He also wasn't at the center or the diner, which was bad for the murder investigation but good for my stomach. After inhaling the aroma of Ethel's takeout, I was ravenously hungry. Since the after-church lunch crowd had thinned, Jasmine and I were able to snag a booth in the back.

While we filled our stomachs with fried chicken and mashed potatoes, several of the diner faithful stopped by to say hello and meet Jasmine. Outsiders were always of interest, but outsiders with dark skin, gold-tipped magenta nails, and a laugh loud enough to rival Farmer Richardson's donkey made jaws drop and people stare. Reginald hated the attention being different garnered. Jasmine thrived on it. She smiled, cracked jokes, and asked dozens of questions about the town, the people, and me. By the time our plates were cleared, Jasmine had a good shot at running for mayor and winning.

Since everyone in town would be at Ginny's wake, I decided to forgo another stop at Jimmy's house. Instead, I steered toward home and changed into a long-sleeved, navy blue, knit dress and my most track-worthy black boots. When Jimmy paid his respects tonight, I'd be ready.

Jasmine met me in the living room. "What?" she asked as I stared at her fitted neon orange top and even tighter brown-and-gold pants. "Do these pants make me look fat?"

Truth? The shape of the pants wasn't slimming, but I wasn't about to tell Jasmine. I'd taken a kickboxing class with her. What she lacked in control, she more than made up for in power. I'd had my ass kicked enough this week, which was why I took another tack. "You look great, but you might attract too much attention in that outfit. Investigators need to blend in."

Jasmine laughed. "Rebecca, I'm a black woman in the middle of a lily-white town. There ain't nothing going to make me blend in."

Fair point.

The Restful Repose Funeral Home was located on the east side of town in a two-story colonial building. The first floor consisted of two viewing parlors located on either side of a large foyer; both were decked out for the holidays. Straight ahead was a hall that led to a roomy eat-in kitchen perpetually stocked with sandwiches, water, and cookies. The scent of lilies and Pine-Sol filled the air just as it did during Mom's wake. The memory of that day hit me square in the chest. Taking several deep breaths, I signed my name in the register, hung up my coat, and walked into the viewing room.

Amy Jo waved at me from the front, where a large picture of Ginny stood on an easel next to a small silver urn. Ginny's wishes had included cremation and one final visit to Florida to have her ashes spread on a beach.

"I'm so glad you felt well enough to come." Amy Jo took my hand and held it tight. "We've been worried. Deputy Holmes assured me that your involvement in Aunt Ginny's murder investigation had nothing to do with the accident, but I'm not sure I believe him."

Obviously, I wasn't the only one who needed to work on my fibbing technique. Once I assured Amy Jo I was fine, I asked, "Did you find the money in the teapot?"

Amy Jo smiled. "Yes. We can't thank you enough for telling us about that. Otherwise we would have had to dip into our savings to pay for the service."

"Why? I would have thought the bank would have let you use Ginny's account to pay for this." That's how it worked for my mother's funeral. I just had to fill out a couple of forms and the bank cut a check.

Amy Jo sighed. "The bank told us Aunt Ginny closed her savings account two years ago, and the money in the checking account is barely enough for us to pay her association dues and monthly bills. I still don't know where she came up with her portion of the money for the rental or the cash in the teapot, but if Aunt Ginny had the will, she'd find a way."

The more I heard about Aunt Ginny, the more I liked her.

Pachelbel's Canon in D rang out from my pocket. Danielle

really needed to work on her timing, and I needed to remember to turn my phone to vibrate.

"I'm so sorry," I said to Amy Jo as I pulled the phone out and read Danielle's message. Mother Lucas was offering to help select new table favors. Unless I wanted to solve another murder, we needed to come up with them pronto.

"You look worried. Was that information about Aunt Ginny's murder?"

"Danielle was texting about wedding stuff. She's concerned about her table favors." I was the queen of understatement.

Amy Jo smiled. "I remember my favors. I thought the bottle opener with our names on it was wonderful, which is good because at least two dozen people left theirs behind. Danielle's lucky to be having her wedding so close to Christmas. It means she can pick favors like holiday candy or decorations."

Huh. I'd been trying so hard to ignore the pre-Thanksgiving decorating that I hadn't considered using the impending season for inspiration. Now that I had, I knew how Danielle could avoid spending her honeymoon in lockup.

Smiling, I started to grab my phone to text Danielle. Then I remembered one last question I needed to ask. "Has Jimmy Bakersfield been by yet?"

Amy Jo nodded. "He brought flowers. He's very kind."

Kind or guilty? I guessed it was up to me to figure out which.

I paid my respects to the rest of Ginny's family, waved to my grandfather, who had joined the line, and hurried out the door in search of my suspect. Eureka! I found him in the kitchen, balancing a plate of cookies. Skirting around a couple of kids and three of Pop's most ardent admirers, I tapped Jimmy on his flannel-clad shoulder and said, "Hey, Jimmy, can I ask you a few questions?"

Jimmy smiled, handed me his plate of cookies, and bolted.

Wow, for all that girth in the middle, the man could move. He was out of the room and halfway down the hall before I could ditch the plate and give chase. Drat. I dodged a lady with a walker and almost tripped over a toddler crawling out from behind a chair as Jimmy disappeared out the front door.

Ignoring the shouts and gasps behind me, I raced through the lobby, out the door, and smack into a fluffy fur coat. The coat, me, and the person draped in fur hit the ground in a heap. I didn't have to look up to know that the sound of squealing tires signaled the escape of my quarry. Crap. Crap. Crap.

I apologized profusely to the woman I'd flattened, scrambled to my feet, and helped haul her upright. I was about to give her my contact information in case her coat needed dry cleaning when Lionel appeared at her side. "I see the two of you have met."

"Not exactly," I said. Since she might want to sue me for personal injury, it seemed like a good idea. Holding out my hand, I said, "Rebecca Robbins. I'm Lionel's girlfriend."

"Sandy Franklin," the stylish, brown-haired woman said with a smile. "I'm Lionel's mother."

Twenty

This was bad. My main suspect in Ginny's murder had fled the scene, I was outside in the cold without a coat, and I'd knocked my potential mother-in-law on her ass. Things couldn't get much worse.

"Does anyone need help here?"

Or maybe they could.

I turned and plastered my best nothing-to-see-here smile on my face as Sean Holmes strolled up the walk. "We're fine," I lied, praying he'd take the hint and go away.

No such luck.

Sean stopped walking. "I thought I saw you both fall. Are you sure everyone's okay? I can call the paramedics or see if Doc Truman is inside."

Once we had assured him no one was in need of medical attention, Sean left to pay his respects, leaving me to apologize once again.

"I'll say one thing for you." Lionel's mother laughed. "You

know how to make an impression. Not that I wasn't already impressed. My husband and I have heard a great deal about you from our son."

I cringed. She laughed again. The sound was warm and bright and reminded me of my mother's laugh.

"Don't worry," Mrs. Franklin said, patting my arm. "Everything we've heard has been good. We appreciate being invited to spend Thanksgiving with you. Please let me know if my husband or I can help in any way. Lionel said you're cooking for quite a crowd. We'd be happy to pitch in if it gets to be too much for you."

A sane person who had never cooked a turkey solo in her life would have accepted the help. However, after this initial meeting, I felt like I had something to prove. "Thanks, but you shouldn't be spending your time here cooking. I have everything under control."

If only that were true.

Lionel ushered us both inside. When he and his mother walked into the viewing room, I went on the hunt for Sean. Less than two months ago, Sean would have sneered at my investigative deductions, and I would have gone off half-cocked to confront the suspect on my own. Today, I planned to pass along my suspicions and trust Sean to take care of the rest. Funny how time and potential death changed a girl's perspective.

Surprise, surprise. I found Sean snarfing cookies in the kitchen. Snagging a snickerdoodle, I waved for Sean to follow, grabbed my coat, and headed to the only place I could think of where we wouldn't be overheard. Outside.

Between bites of cookie, I gave Sean an update on Jimmy's diabetes, his being in the center during the time of Ginny's murder, and how he turned track star the minute I appeared. With a promise to keep me informed, Sean escorted me back into the safety of the funeral home. He then stalked off into the darkening night to serve truth, justice, and the Indian Falls—if not American—way, leaving me wishing I could go, too. Not that I needed to be in on the arrest. The whole confronting-bad-guys thing was highly overrated. But I wanted to be there because, while I understood the means and opportunity for killing Ginny, I still didn't know why Jimmy had taken her life. Not knowing was driving me crazy.

"Is Sean off to arrest Jimmy?"

I turned at the sound of my grandfather's voice. My grandfather gave me a wide, albeit slightly askew, smile. Pop must have skimped on the denture adhesive today.

"Everybody inside is talking about you," Pop said.

Big surprise.

"They're saying you fingered Jimmy as the thief, and he ran when he realized the jig was up." Pop shrugged. "I told them there was no way Jimmy was sneaky enough to break into all those houses without getting caught and that you were just running for the bathroom. Pain meds wreak havoc on the bowels."

Time to change the subject. "You were right. I don't think Jimmy is the Thanksgiving Day thief." I thought he was something much worse. "Was Jimmy good friends with Ginny?"

Pop cocked his head to the side. "Jimmy asked Ginny on a couple of dates, but she never said yes. She told him he'd have to get a better car and new tube socks first. Of course, that was before his VW Bug was stolen and he had to get new wheels. Since then, Ginny steered clear just in case he called her on that promise. She didn't know she had nothing to worry about. Jimmy hasn't sprung for new socks since Nixon was in office."

I made a mental note to fumigate the rental roller skates Jimmy used and asked, "So they didn't have a fight or a falling-out?"

"Not that I know, and I'd probably know." Pop pulled a pair of gloves out of his pocket and shoved his hands into them. "Ginny played things close to the vest, but Jimmy's an open book. The man can't keep a secret for nothing. How you fell for that 'doctor won't let him go in the dunk tank' routine two months ago is beyond me. The red face and sweaty palms should have been a dead giveaway."

The sweaty palms and crimson face were exactly the reason I'd agreed to take over Jimmy's dunk-tank duty. He'd looked like a man ready to have a heart attack. Now I understood why.

Pop cocked his head to the side. "You don't think Jimmy knows something about Ginny's death, do you?"

Yes. "No, but don't you think it's strange that Jimmy went racing out of here when I asked if he'd be willing to answer a few questions?"

"Yeah, that's weird." Pop frowned. "Could be he knows who did it and doesn't want to rat them out. Jimmy's a softy. He won't step on a bug if it can be avoided."

Clearly not because he was worried about the state of his socks.

"I've been busy with the band," Pop said, "so I haven't been around much this week to notice if Jimmy's been acting off. Give me a little while to ask around. If Jimmy's been worried about something, someone here will have noticed."

By the time Pop, Jasmine, and I went back to my place, we'd learned that Marion Poste had bought her girdle a size too small, that construction on the park's fountain was delayed yet again, and that no one noticed anything strange in Jimmy's behavior—until Thursday.

"What happened Thursday?" I asked, sliding a bag of popcorn into the microwave.

Pop rummaged through my fridge and came out with three bottles of beer. "Got me. Three people saw Jimmy at the Scrabble tournament on Wednesday. He said he was winterizing his new car and picking up his suit from the dry cleaners to wear to Danielle's wedding. The next day he freaked out when someone noticed *The Price Is Right* was giving away a car that looked like his. He left the center, and no one saw him again until he showed up at the funeral home today."

When Sean called with an update, I learned that no one had seen him since. Jimmy wasn't at home. His cell phone went right to voice mail, and his car was nowhere to be found. In essence, Jimmy had vanished.

Sean wasn't concerned. "I've notified all law enforcement agencies to be on the lookout for his car. There's a good chance someone will spot it and we'll get to the bottom of Ginny's murder."

There would have been a better chance of spotting Jimmy's old car. Too bad it had been blown to bits.

"Now what?" Pop asked after I passed along Sean's message. "We're not going to let Sean be the one to haul Jimmy's ass to jail, are we?"

That was the general idea.

"Do you have a better option?"

Pop blinked. "No, but I'm not the hotshot private investigator. I'm sure you have a plan for tracking down Jimmy and sweating a confession out of him."

I did. It involved eating the entire bag of popcorn while sitting on the couch. Sean would catch the crook and grab the glory. If Jimmy was the murderer, there was a good chance he'd also played hit-and-run with me in the rink parking lot. I wasn't interested in a rematch.

"I think it's better to let Sean handle the murder case while I focus on the Thanksgiving Day thefts," I said, dumping the popcorn in a bowl.

Pop grabbed a handful of my snack and munched. "Not a bad idea. If the thief thinks you're busy working on the other case, he might get sloppy. What did you find in the Kurtzes' basement? Stan didn't want to tell me."

"That's because I didn't tell him. I'm not going to tell you either." The last thing we needed was Pop and his fans sparking reefer refreshments after a gig.

"You don't want me to help?" Pop's shoulders slumped. "Why? Is it because you think I'm old?"

"You are old, Pop." Admitting it out loud made my heart hurt. I didn't know what I would do if I didn't have Pop around.

"I helped with investigations in the past, including this one." He walked into the living room and plopped down on the sofa with a frown. "Look how well that turned out."

A vision of Nurse Eleanor clad in skintight black leather with a rose dangling from her mouth sprang to mind.

"Look." I swallowed a handful of popcorn and sat down next to my grandfather. "I'm not saying I don't need your help investigating." Who else would supply me with all the Indian Falls gossip? "But if news of what Seth and Jan have in their basement gets out, people will wonder how someone learned about it. They'll realize someone broke in and start looking for that person. How long do you think it'll be before everyone in town figures out it was me? Sean won't have any choice but to put me behind bars."

This wasn't my real reason, but that didn't make it less true.

"That doesn't mean you can't help," I said, and Pop's eyes brightened. "I'm working on setting a trap to catch the thief, and you're just the man to help me do it."

Jasmine, Pop, and I snacked as I explained about Reginald and Bryan's travel plans. "They've already called the sheriff's office to request additional patrols go by the house."

Pop nodded. "You're hoping someone at the sheriff's department gossips about the list and the thief hears about it. Normally, that would work—Roxy likes people to think she's in the know—but Roxy knows Sean really wants to close this case. Unless she's given up on her relationship hopes, she's going to guard that list like it's Fort Knox."

"This Roxy person has the hots for Sean?" Jasmine asked.

"Yep." Pop took a swig of beer. "It's been going on for years. Took a while before Sean clued in. Now that he has, he pretends he doesn't notice when she hits on him. It's pretty entertaining if you know the backstory. Anyway, that's the reason she'll keep this off the gossip airwaves."

"That's where you come in," I said. "If you tell one or two of your friends that you stopped by the station and heard Roxy talking about Bryan and Reginald, I'm betting they'll share the news. You could even drop in a line or two about Reggie and Bryan's expensive electronics equipment."

"Oh, that's good." Jasmine turned to Pop and smiled. "I never knew how good she was at this sneaky stuff."

Pop grinned. "I taught her everything she knows."

I wasn't sure I was comfortable with being "sneaky," but I'd been called worse.

"I'm betting Reginald and Bryan's house will be an irresistible target. All I'll have to do is show up and catch the thief in the act."

I waited for Pop to cheer. Instead, he chewed popcorn and said, "There's only one problem."

"What?" Without calling in the FBI, the plan was as good as it was going to get.

"You're cooking a dinner for twenty people on Thursday and planning to stake out a house on the same day. How do you figure on being two places at once?"

Damn. Pop was right. This was a problem. Unless I could come up with an answer, I'd have to choose between disappointing hungry holiday guests or letting down Mrs. Johnson and allowing a criminal go free.

This was bad.

Twenty-one

"*So what do I do?*" I asked.

By the time I'd finished the bowl of popcorn, we hadn't come up with an answer. Now since Jasmine and Pop were asleep on the couch, they weren't in a position to help problem-solve.

I grabbed spare blankets from the closet, tucked them both in, snagged a soda, and headed for my room. Going to bed at ten o'clock made me feel lame, but it'd been a rough week. I'd have to let my subconscious work on the problem. Maybe when I woke my worries would be over.

I took a quick shower, changed into my pink flannel pajamas, texted Danielle about my idea for table favors, and was about to climb into bed when the phone rang. Lionel.

I said hello and asked, "How's your mother?"

"She's glad the two of you ran into each other." Lionel laughed. "My father's sorry he missed meeting you. I thought maybe we could arrange for all of us to get together before Thursday. Do you have time for dinner tomorrow?"

I mentally scrolled through my calendar. "I'm helping Danielle decorate the church." As were half the members of Estro-Genocide.

"How about Tuesday?"

"Danielle's having a bachelorette party." "Party" was probably too strong a word since the event was taking place at the Toe Stop, but Danielle was determined to have some fun. "Then Wednesday is the rehearsal, followed by dinner."

Lionel sighed, and I heard the telltale sound of calendar pages flipping. "My afternoons are packed since I'm taking Thursday and Friday off. Well . . ." His voice turned deep and sexy. "We can always meet for breakfast. Want to come over?"

"Your parents are staying with you!"

"So?"

"I can't sleep over with them there," I squeaked. "What would they think?"

"They'd think we have sex, which will probably make my mother happy since she wants grandchildren."

Eek.

I wasn't ready to have kids. Hell, half the time I had a hard time believing I wasn't still a kid myself. I mean, look at me. How could I help a child figure out who they were and what they wanted to be when I barely understood those things about myself?

"I can't have sex with you if your parents are in the next room." Grandchildren aside, the thought of sleeping with Lionel with his mom listening in made me feel icky.

"Okay," Lionel said. "Then why don't I spend the night with you?"

"What will you tell your parents?"

"That I'm spending the night with you."

I gnawed on my lower lip.

"Let me guess, you don't like that any better."

"Not really," I admitted. "Besides, Pop and Jasmine are camping here tonight."

Lionel sighed again. "Well, we'll see you at the funeral tomorrow. Why don't I check in with you after that and see what your schedule looks like? My parents and I can always meet you for coffee if there isn't time for anything else. I want them to know and love you the way I do."

A girl couldn't ask for any more than that.

A YOU'RE A GENIUS text from Danielle was waiting for me when I woke the next morning. My lack of ability to solve either of my cases made me feel like I hadn't earned the title, but the compliment bolstered my spirits as I got out of bed.

Jasmine was still conked out on the couch when I went into the living room. Pop was nowhere to be found. Either he'd decided to walk home while I was asleep or he'd called one of his friends for a ride. I hoped it was the latter since the radio announcer said overnight rain and dropping temperatures had caused patches of ice on the roads. Worried, I placed a quick call. I heaved a sigh of relief when Pop answered—despite the sound of a woman's voice in the background asking if he wanted breakfast in bed.

Hearing the word "breakfast" made my stomach growl. My mother always swore a hot breakfast helped a person think more clearly. Since I needed all the clarity I could get, I decided to heed her advice.

Sadly, sweetened carbohydrates and salty protein didn't fix my investigation problem. Mom's theory was a bust. Cooking a large breakfast also took longer than anticipated, which is why Jasmine and I walked into St. Mark's Church for the funeral just as Pastor Rich was taking the pulpit.

The large sanctuary was filled to capacity, a testament to Ginny's popularity. I slid into a back pew and scanned the crowd for any sign of Jimmy Bakersfield. I spotted Pop and Ethel near the front. Sean was leaning against a pillar on the right side of the sanctuary. Sheriff Jackson was positioned on the left. Jimmy was a no-show.

The funeral was short but touching. Pastor Rich talked about Ginny's love of bingo, warm weather, and family before reading a familiar Bible verse, one that was also used at my mother's funeral. Tears filled my eyes as "Amazing Grace" began to play. My nose started running. I reached into my purse for a tissue and came up empty.

I felt a drip from my nose land above my lip. Then another.

With no tissue in sight, I had only one choice. Trying to appear casual, I lifted my arm up to my nose, wiped, and spotted Lionel's mother sitting in a pew about three rows up—watching me.

Was I making a great impression or what?

When the funeral was over, Jasmine and I hopped in my Honda and joined the procession of cars to the cemetery. Grass crunched under my feet as I walked over to stand under a tree next to Pop. He had one arm around a weeping Ethel and his other around his former girlfriend Louise Laggotti.

Wind whipped our coats. People stomped their feet in an attempt to stay warm as Rich said a quick prayer and told everyone to join Ginny's family at the senior center for lunch. Normally, all things funeral made me sob, but I was too busy being cold to get upset. Next time.

I spotted Lionel helping his mother into the monster truck and walked over. I leaned up and gave him a quick kiss. "Do you want to sit together during lunch? That would give your parents and me a chance to talk." Plus, being surrounded by a hundred other people would make it difficult for Lionel's mom to ask embarrassing questions.

"We can't. Dad has a conference call, and I have an appointment with a goat."

Jimmy also didn't attend the lunch. Either he also had an appointment with a goat or he had advance knowledge of the menu. No amount of salt and pepper could make the flavorless chicken and pastelike mashed potatoes appetizing. Although no one else seemed to have a problem with the food. Gossip about Jimmy's disappearance and speculation as to why he might have killed Ginny must have added enough spice to make it taste good.

Since I was still stuffed with French toast, I moved through the hall, hoping gossip would clue me in on a motive for Ginny's death. An hour later, I'd learned that Barna Donavan thought Jimmy had been possessed by aliens, Lorna Theiss was sure it was due to the too-small size of his tighty whities (that damn elastic can really mess with a person's circulation), and Eleanor thought Jimmy was being framed. The last was the only sensible comment I'd heard, which prompted me to ask, "Why do you think that?"

Eleanor shrugged. "I'm not supposed to say."

"Why not?"

Eleanor glanced over her shoulder and whispered, "I'm not allowed to talk about the medical condition of a patient. Especially when the patient is still alive."

Since Ginny had just been laid to rest, Eleanor had to be talking about Jimmy. I considered pressing Eleanor for information, but I didn't want to compromise her medical ethics. Instead, I grabbed a cup of coffee, added lots of cream and sugar, and walked into the hallway to think. There were two reasons Jimmy was a suspect. First, he was wandering around the center during the time Ginny was given the shot of insulin. Second, he was diabetic, which meant he had access to the murder weapon.

Or maybe not.

I walked back into the hall and found Pop surrounded by a group of admiring fans. A few gave me dirty looks when I pulled him away.

"What's up?" Pop asked. "I was just about to tell them about the time Miguel forgot to wear a belt onstage. The pants were two sizes too big, and he'd run out of clean underwear. The audience went wild."

Miguel was only five feet tall, but what he lacked in height he more than made up for in girth. He was also coated in a thick layer of black hair. The idea of seeing him go commando was enough to make me want to faint. No doubt a number of the audience members did.

Pushing the image of Miguel's hairy butt out of my head, I asked, "Do you know what kind of diabetes Jimmy had?"

Pop frowned. "He had type 2, like your grandmother. Jimmy didn't like to talk about it, though. He said chicks didn't like hearing about a man's weaknesses."

"Grandma never took shots for her diabetes."

"Nope." Pop's eyes grew misty. "Doc said she might have to switch to shots someday, but she didn't live long enough for that to happen."

Pop took my hand and held it. No matter how many women he dated or how many gigs he performed, Pop still missed Grandma. I did, too.

When Pop strolled back to regale his fans with stories about Miguel's bared butt, I thought about Jimmy. Maybe the reason I couldn't discern a motive for Jimmy killing Ginny was because he didn't do it. Maybe he bolted from the wake because he thought I'd learned he was behind the thefts. I had a hard time believing Jimmy was a long-term criminal mastermind, but what other answer was there?

So far, Jimmy was under suspicion for Ginny's murder because he had means and opportunity. Take away means and the probability of him committing the crime would drop like a rock. I needed to know if Jimmy treated his diabetes with pills or insulin shots.

"I can't talk to you about Jimmy's care," Eleanor said as I slid into the seat next to her. The rest of her tablemates had table-hopped or gone home for a nap.

"I know," I said, "but if Jimmy still takes pills for his type 2 diabetes, you could be right about his being framed. Giving that information to the sheriff's office could get Jimmy off the hook."

"You think so?" Eleanor's wide eyes told me I'd scored a direct hit with my information. Standing, she said, "I'll talk to Doc and see what we can do."

I felt a stab of triumph followed by a swell of disappointment. I no longer had a primary suspect in Ginny's murder. Technically, Jimmy could have gotten his hands on some liquid insulin to do the job, but my gut told me he hadn't. And I still had no idea who had.

I didn't have time to find out either. The minute lunch ended, Danielle cornered me with Rich's SUV keys in one hand and a large to-do list in the other. It was wedding time.

Since Jasmine took bodyguard duty seriously, she came along.

I performed introductions between the two as we climbed into the car. Rich's SUV had heated seats. I was appreciating the toasty-warm quality of my butt cheeks when I noticed Jasmine and Danielle watching each other in the rearview mirror. Both were frowning.

Uh-oh.

I realized the problem a second too late.

"Holy shit," Jasmine yelled. "I know you. You're the hooker."

Oh God! I'd been so distracted by the murder and the thefts I'd forgotten that Jasmine and Danielle had crossed paths back in Chicago when Danielle was ringing the male half of the crowd's bells at our former boss's holiday party.

I could see Danielle remembered Jasmine, too. Her eyes widened, and her foot slammed on the brakes. We must have hit one of the slick spots the radio announcer had been talking about, because instead of stopping, the car skidded for a second before it spun out of control.

Twenty-two

Danielle and Jasmine screamed. I opened my mouth to join the chorus, but fear closed off my throat. All I could do was grab the oh-shit bar and hang on for dear life. The car careened to the left, spun in a circle, and then hopped the curb. Smack. We smashed into one of the new saplings that had been planted at the beginning of fall as part of Mayor Poste's town beautification plan and came to a stop.

The tree wasn't so beautiful now. What had once been a three-foot-tall, two-inch-wide sapling now resembled a broken toothpick. The tree was toast, but none of us inside the borrowed SUV was hurt. Thank goodness for seat belts and malfunctioning air bags. Danielle should recommend her fiancé have the latter looked at, but for now I was glad I wasn't being suffocated by an oversized punching bag. Danielle's expression, however, suggested she'd rather be unconscious than deal with the person who was currently hyperventilating in the backseat.

"She has to leave town," Danielle said. "Or she'll ruin everything."

"Why do I have to leave town?" Jasmine sat up like a rocket. "It's not like I'm the one who dressed up like Santa's skanky helper and let people unwrap my present before Christmas."

"No one unwrapped anything," Danielle shouted. "I was an exotic dancer, not a hooker."

"What's the difference?"

Yowzah! Before Danielle could jump Jasmine, I yelled, "Enough. Jasmine isn't going to tell anyone that you were an exotic dancer because she wouldn't want to screw up your wedding or the rest of your life. She understands what it's like to want a new start. Right, Jasmine?"

Jasmine let out a huff.

I took it for assent. "And Danielle isn't going to run you out of town, Jasmine, because she knows what it's like to leave Chicago under less than ideal circumstances. Right, Danielle?"

The bride crossed her arms and pouted. Neither said a word, but the shifts in their body language told me the worst of the shouting had passed.

"Now, unless you want people wondering why the pastor's fiancée mowed down one of the mayor's trees, I suggest we talk about this somewhere less conspicuous." The last thing Danielle needed was to have her driving mishap viewed as a political statement.

Danielle must have agreed since she threw the SUV into reverse. Minutes later, we were safely parked in the bakery parking lot, in desperate need of éclair therapy. I ate two while Danielle gave Mrs. DiBelka the cake topper her mother-in-law insisted they use on the five-tiered wedding cake. The bride-and-groom statue had been in Pastor Rich's family since the early 1900s. Wow, did the thing look its age. The peeling paint on the bride's face made her look like a molting snake, which was almost pleasant next to the groom's resemblance to Quasimodo. A better maid of honor would accidentally smack the knickknack out of Mrs. DiBelka's hand and put an end to the current and all future brides' misery. I snagged an apple doughnut instead.

We emerged from the bakery with a box of pastries and headed to the photographer. While we drove, I explained to Jasmine how Danielle used the money she earned as an exotic dancer to pay her way through college. Once she had her degree, she quit dancing but discovered how difficult it was to leave the stigma behind. Which is why she moved here.

When Danielle pulled into our destination, I frowned. "Why are we at Pop's house?" I hoped Danielle hadn't changed her mind about using a DJ. If Mother Lucas had a problem with me, wait until she got a load of Pompadour Pop.

"Russell White fell out of his hayloft and broke his arm yesterday," Danielle said, cutting the engine. "I called around and got lucky when your father agreed to handle the photography."

"Lucky" wasn't the word I'd have chosen. The only photos I'd seen my father take were from my childhood. Those were either blurry or had thumbs in them. He'd had more practice since then, but still . . . I wasn't about to let his new get-rich-quick scheme ruin one of my best friends' wedding day.

I planned on telling him that, but I stepped into the kitchen and stopped cold. Scattered around the room were boards filled with photos. Pop in his Elvis getup. Ethel grinning while holding Jimmy Bakersfield's hand. Ginny reclining on a chair with a book in her lap. Agnes Piraino curled up with six of her cats. Not only were the photographs not blurry, they were good. Very good. I'd been wrong about my father's skill. As we drank coffee and created a list of photographs Danielle wanted in her wedding album, I was forced to wonder what other things about my father I'd misjudged.

After an hour, Stan glanced at his watch and rose from the table. "I hate to cut this short, but Ethel, Jack, and LouAnn want a few pictures taken before they leave town Friday. Feel free to call or leave me a note if you come up with any other ideas. Oh, and, Rebecca, would you mind if we moved up the time for dinner on Thursday? My date's worried about being away from home after it gets dark. Between the thefts and the murder . . . well, you understand. Thanks, honey."

With a wink, Stan scooted out the door, effectively cutting off any chance of protest. Just when I thought Stan had changed, he was back to his self-centered ways. Here I was cooking dinner for almost two dozen people and Dad wanted me to shift the time because of a woman whose name I didn't even know? Moving the time for dinner up would give me less time to cook and . . .

Wait a minute. Maybe Dad was onto something. Moving up the dinner would eliminate cooking time, but it would free up my afternoon and evening. Ha! I knew how I was going to host Thanksgiving and catch a crook.

Danielle sighed, cutting off my triumphant moment. "What's wrong?" I asked. Had my father's early departure upset her?

"Rich was hoping Ethel would postpone the Florida trip until after the wedding. He thought it might pull her out of the depression she's in. I'm probably not supposed to say anything, but he's been counseling her for the last week. Ginny's death hit her hard."

"She probably fell for the nonrefundable ticket scam," Jasmine said. "The airlines charge so much less for those tickets hoping you'll end up in traction and cancel. Then they walk away with your money and get to sell your seat to someone else for twice the price. It's a racket. That's why I won't travel by plane."

"I thought it was because you were afraid of heights," I said.

"Well, yeah. There's that," Jasmine admitted. "Although, even if I weren't, I still wouldn't give the airlines my money. Unless I was going to Paris. Then I might have to reconsider."

While Jasmine and Danielle discussed travel destinations, I mulled over my new plans for Thanksgiving. Over the next several hours, we stopped by Tilly's for our dresses, then drove to the mall to pick up engraved beer mugs, decorations, and the new table favors. For our last stop, we tooled into the bank parking lot five minutes before closing. Did we know how to have fun or what?

"I need to start changing all my account information into my married name," Danielle explained. "You wouldn't believe how much work it is."

I did after watching Danielle write down her new address, name, and ten-digit account code more than a half-dozen times . . .

Holy smokes. Ten digits. I pulled out my notebook and looked at the numbers I'd copied off Ginny's teapot note. Yep. There were ten digits in the first set of numbers. I asked the teller, Mrs. Flax, if the numbers belonged to a bank account and was told she couldn't give out that information. If I wanted to know the answer to my question, I'd need to bring a warrant or, at the very least, Sean and his badge.

The good news was that all those hours running errands had given me time to think about my Thanksgiving Day logistics problem. By the time a dozen St. Mark's Women's Guild and Estro-Genocide volunteers had unloaded the dozens of bags of decorations into the St. Mark's fellowship hall, I'd made a phone call for reinforcements and was ready to put my plan into effect.

Pop strolled into the hall five minutes after Papa Dom's delivered twenty large pizzas. The man might not have the best singing voice, but no one could fault his timing.

While women wrapped chairs with white slipcovers and purple bows, Pop piled pizza on a plate and shuffled over to me. My grandfather popped a piece of pepperoni in his mouth and winked. It was time to start the show. "Have you talked Bryan and Reginald into changing their minds about Thursday?"

"Shhh." I glanced around the room as though concerned we'd be overheard. Several people were angling their heads in our direction. Perfect. "We don't want people to know they're leaving town. I feel bad enough as it is. If anything happens to their house on Thursday night, it'll be all my fault."

Pop frowned. "You told them leaving town is a bad idea."

"Yes, but they made their plans after I was asked to track down the thief. They believed in me, and I haven't gotten any closer than Sean or Sheriff Jackson has. I did convince them to wait until the last possible minute before hitting the road. If they turn all the lights on, there's a chance no one will ever know they left home."

Pop patted my arm and gave me a glee-filled smile. "I'm sure you're right, Rebecca."

"Thanks, Pop," I said, hoping the hushed whispers and lack of work in the room meant that I was completely wrong. Now all I needed was to notify my guests that dinner had moved to noon and have Bryan and Reginald confirm their phantom travel itinerary to one or two unsuspecting gossips and my trap would be set.

Pop grabbed another slice of pizza and flashed a smile at a group of women hanging white Christmas lights. "I'll tell your father and the Pilgrims about the time change for Thursday's dinner."

I blinked. Pilgrims? "What Pilgrims?"

"For Thanksgiving dinner. I mentioned them last week. Folks dressed like Pilgrims bring all sorts of authentic Thanksgiving food like corn bread, duck, and roasted pumpkin to people's houses. Then you get to take photos with them before they head off to deliver stuff to the next house. I was lucky I could get them on such short notice. I figured with all the people coming to dinner, we could use the extra grub."

Not a bad plan. Besides, I already had half the town coming. I might as well add Pilgrims to the mix.

Once the hall was decorated and the pizza consumed, Pop was nice enough to drive Jasmine and me to Slaughter's Market so I could get food for Thursday's Pilgrim-enhanced meal. Once the mountain of grocery bags were safely in my apartment, Pop headed out for a date, which left Jasmine and me to wonder how come my grandfather was off to score and we were putting on pajamas. Life was strange.

The sky was gray and soggy when I woke. A bad day for going outside, but a great day for cooking. Thank goodness Jasmine was willing to hang around and help out.

"Are you sure?" I asked as she tied an EstroGenocide apron around her waist. "One of the derby girls can come keep me company if you want to go home. I've kept you away from your family long enough."

Jasmine shook her head. "I'm not leaving until I know who killed that woman. This is like a real-life version of Clue. I gotta know if it was Colonel Mustard in the television room with the spatula."

Fair enough. Although from the way Sean talked when he called, Colonel Mustard would be an easier catch. Jimmy was still in the wind. No new leads had emerged. The case was stalled. The only encouraging news came from Pop, who said the gossips were spreading the word about Reginald and Bryan. If the thief was listening, he'd have heard the house would be empty after five o'clock. Only it wouldn't be, since I planned to have the cavalry there to jump him.

Three pans of stuffing, four containers of cranberry chutney, and eight pies later, we showered, changed clothes, and headed downstairs for Danielle's bachelorette party. Since Danielle was marrying a minister, barhopping and sexy lingerie prewedding rituals were out. Roller skating was in.

My new disco ball sparkled. Strobe lights flashed. Music blared as twenty women, half wearing EstroGenocide jerseys, rolled, laughed, and stuffed themselves with junk food. Danielle beamed as she did the Hokey Pokey decked out in white jeans, a purple shirt, and a BRIDE baseball cap complete with veil. Jasmine tripped and fell when she tried to turn herself all about. As I reached down to help her up, I noticed Pastor Rich's mother standing in the rink's entrance, watching me. The next time I turned myself around she was gone.

Twenty-three

Creepy.

Mrs. Lucas acted equally creepy at the rehearsal the next night. Or maybe I was just imagining her staring at me as I stood next to the altar and ate overcooked steak at the Elks Club. Peeling potatoes for hours leading up to the rehearsal could cause anyone to hallucinate. Right?

Had Mother Lucas arrived in Indian Falls before the murder, I'd have been completely wigged out. Still, I made sure to stay close to Erica the Red just in case.

As we were about to call it a night, Danielle gave me an even better gift to go along with the engraved picture frame. "Mother Lucas insists on cooking tomorrow. She says there is no reason Rich and I should spend the holiday with people who aren't family. Sorry."

I'd have performed a happy dance, but I figured Danielle might take my happiness as a commentary on our friendship instead of an expression of delight that her scary mother-in-law wouldn't crash the party and try to poison me. Now if only a few more people canceled, I might be able to serve my Thanksgiving meal at a table that would fit in my dining room instead of on the one I'd enlisted George to set up on the rink floor.

Even without Danielle's mad mother-in-law to worry about, I tossed and turned all night. With a massive dinner to prepare, a murderer on the loose, and a trap to catch thief to be sprung, who could blame me? When the clock hit 4:00 A.M., I gave up on sleep, donned jeans and an oversized sweater, and cranked the oven. It was time to stuff vegetables and herbs into turkey butts, which looked way easier on Food Network demonstrations than it turned out to be. Once the birds were in the oven, I gave my attention to the dozens of other things on my list. If I managed to finish all of them, it would be a miracle.

By the time Jasmine rolled out of bed around nine, the long table stationed in the middle of the rink floor had been set with table cloths and flowers. Another table, next to the wall that divided the wooden floor and the sidelines, was filled with pies, cakes, and whatever else didn't need to stay warm.

After cleaning up a cranberry spill, I put the potatoes on to boil and called Bryan and Reginald to go over the plan once more. At 10:30 A.M., Pop would pull his Lincoln Town Car around to Bryan and Reginald's back door. Bakery box in hand, Pop would walk around the house to the front door, where Bryan would greet him. Meanwhile, Reginald would open the back door and help Pop's bass player sneak out of Pop's backseat into the house. Bryan and Reginald would then take the band guy's hiding place in the car, and Pop would walk out the front, warning the boys to stay home tonight. Bass-playing Carlos would spend the day guarding the house and turning lights on and off so people would think Bryan and Reggie were still home. Since Carlos was originally from Mexico, he didn't mind missing the day's festivities, especially since Bryan had promised to stock the fridge with gourmet munchies and beer.

Pop would then bring Reggie and Bryan through the rink's back door so they could celebrate Thanksgiving with us. Once our Thanksgiving lunch was over, Stan would drop Reginald and Bryan back home so they could make a very large production of loading up their car. At five o'clock, they'd drive off. By then I'd be staking out the house from a spot Bryan swore was impossible to see from the road. Since Thanksgiving had put me in a sharing kind of mood, I planned on giving Sean Holmes a call while en route. I wasn't interested in playing hero. The man with the badge had signed up for that job. I was more than willing to let him do it.

When I went downstairs with a steaming tray of stuffing, Bryan and Reginald met me at the door. Phase one of Operation Catch a Turkey was complete, and I'd added several helping hands to the meal's preparation. Holiday planning didn't get any better than that.

Or maybe it did.

"What do you think?" Bryan asked as he began setting the table with the china he'd brought. "Are they fabulous?"

Fabulous wasn't the word I'd use. The white china was rimmed with a gold scalloped edge. That's where the plates' tasteful appearance ended. In the center of each was a turkey sporting a Pilgrim's hat, a wide smile, and a large shotgun. The turkey looked like he was delighted to have just shot his annoying bird cousin and was waiting for me to serve him up.

"I couldn't believe the store had these marked down to half price," Bryan said.

I couldn't believe the store hadn't reduced them further. Still, the plates had three things going for them: They were large, they were sturdy, and, as long as I didn't burn anything, the picture of Terminator Turkey would soon be covered by heaping mounds of food. Which is why I could say, "The plates are wonderful," to Bryan with a straight face.

With the table set, I raced back upstairs to perform my duties as chef. While Bryan and Reggie set food on warming trays, opened wine bottles, and selected dinner music, I removed the turkeys from the oven, scooped mashed potatoes into a large chafing dish, and slid a tray of green beans and peppers into the space once occupied by the birds. So far, I hadn't burned anything. Hoping that streak would continue, I grabbed a cookie sheet filled with rolls, turned toward the oven, and caught sight of my reflection in the stainless steel refrigerator.

Holy crap.

Strands of hair were coated with flour, mashed potatoes, or both. A streak of something orange (sweet potato, I hoped) lined my forehead, and the rest of my face was flushed and sweaty. I was a wreck.

"Is there anything I can do to help?"

I turned and spotted Lionel's mother standing in the kitchen doorway. Her perfectly pressed deep red blouse and gray trousers made her look as though she'd just stepped off the pages of a fashion magazine, and I looked as if I'd been in a food fight. My ability to impress never ceased to amaze me.

Tucking a strand of food-caked hair behind my ear, I said,

"Almost everything's ready. I was about to change clothes so I don't scare my guests."

Mrs. Franklin laughed. "You should see my family's Thanksgiving photos. This is the first time I've looked presentable in thirty-nine years. I think mashed potatoes in the hair is a rite of passage."

I searched for signs that she was humoring me and smiled at the genuine warmth in her eyes. Smiling back, I said, "I'm sorry I haven't had more time to spend with you and your husband. Things have been a bit crazy with Danielle's wedding and this dinner."

"Not to mention your investigation into a string of break-ins and a murder."

I cringed. "I know those kinds of activities could make you worry about your son's involvement with me."

"Are you kidding?" She laughed. "Lionel's always looked for safety above excitement. Even when he was a little boy. If the rest of my children were hanging upside down from tree branches, he'd be warning them of the dangers with his feet firmly on the ground. My son thrives on order—sometimes too much so. Being a large-animal vet allowed him to move to a community where everyone knows everyone and life is mostly predictable. After he came here, I worried that he was getting too set in his ways. Too afraid to explore the possibilities of life or hang upside down from a tree. Then you came along and changed all that." She took my flour-crusted hand in hers. "I couldn't be happier."

"Really?"

"Really." She laughed again. "The worst thing my son could do is spend his life with someone predictable. He almost did that, and it broke my heart to stand by and smile as they made wedding plans. I hated that he was so unhappy when she refused to move away from Chicago and broke off the engagement, but I was re-lieved, too."

A timer dinged. Mrs. Franklin picked up a pot holder and headed for the oven to rescue the rolls before they went up in smoke. I was glad she did. Otherwise the Indian Falls Fire Department would have gotten a call—because I was too stunned to move.

Lionel had been engaged. More important, he'd never told me.

"Go get cleaned up," she said, sliding the pan onto a trivet. "I'll keep an eye on things here while you put something on that'll make my son's eyes pop."

From the way I was feeling, that wasn't the only thing Lionel was going to feel pop. Once this holiday was over, he had some serious explaining to do about his almost-marriage. I was lousy at dating and love, but even I knew you were supposed to share that kind of information.

Fifteen minutes later, I reappeared in black stretchy pants, a tight-fitting V-neck tunic sweater, and black leather boots and found Mrs. Franklin, Lionel, Jasmine, Stan, and Erica the Red standing in the kitchen, waiting to haul turkeys and the rest of the trimmings downstairs. Lionel gave my appearance an apprecia-tive smile before grabbing a foil-wrapped bird. Tray by tray, the food disappeared down the stairs. By the time I carried the basket of bread and container of butter down to the rink, all of my guests had arrived.

With Mozart playing quietly on the sound system and sprays of colorful fall leaves adding to the ambience, the firearm-fowl plates looked almost charming. Letting out a relieved sigh, I put the last of the serving trays on the buffet table and grinned. I did it. Nothing had been dropped or burned. Dinner was actually served.

"Should we wait for the Pilgrims to arrive?" I asked Pop.

"Nah." He handed me a glass of white wine. "Let's say grace and get this show on the road."

Pop asked everyone to take a seat. I slid into a chair next to him and looked around the table. Lionel and his parents. Stan and his date, a lovely blonde I thought worked in the high school office. Reginald and Bryan. Annette. George, Erica the Red, Typhoon Mary, and Halle Bury. Alan from the Presidential Motel. Eleanor's son, Joey. Agnes Piraino. Pop's band. Jasmine, who gave me a wide smile and mouthed "I have a date" as she pointed to the guy grinning from the seat next to her. Sean. His patrol shift wouldn't start for another five hours. Jasmine had convinced him to spend that time with us. I should have been surprised, but . . .

A strange group. Yet each had become part of my family. They would never fill the void left by my mother's death, but in their own ways they made me feel needed, cared for, and loved. They were the reason I'd chosen to adopt my mother's dream for this rink as my own. It was because of them I wanted to stay here in Indian Falls. This town and these people might not always be a comfortable fit, but it was where I belonged.

Pop said grace, and a stampede for the food began. People were going back for seconds when four Pilgrims walked through the door. Each carried a box and was wearing an overly chipper smile. The guy with the tallest hat and pointy shoes bellowed, "Happy Thanksgiving," and everyone applauded as Pop's contribution to the day unloaded their offerings onto the buffet table.

While Pop snapped shots of me and the costumed delivery

folks, the head Pilgrim apologized for being late. "Denise got a little lost driving here."

"It's not my fault." Denise tugged at her white bonnet. "The car of Pilgrims we passed distracted me."

"Friends of yours?" I asked Denise.

"Not that we know of," the head dude answered. "Our contract with the Pilgrim Program says this is our territory. No other restaurants are allowed to deliver to this area. The program either screwed up or someone went rogue."

The idea of rogue Pilgrims made me smile through dessert and the start of cleanup. Or maybe it was the glass of wine I consumed and the steamy kiss that Lionel stole behind the concessions counter that made me feel so giddy. Then I looked at the clock, and nerves set in. The rest of cleanup had to wait. We had to finish setting the trap and discover whether the thief was going to spring it.

Once Bryan and Reginald left with my father, I waited fifteen minutes and then grabbed my coat and purse and headed to the parking lot. I'd originally planned on bringing Jasmine with me, but she was busy flirting with Sean. I didn't want to tip him off until I was on my way. Sean had been more reasonable lately, but I sincerely doubted he'd let me come along on a stakeout with him. Even if he did, I wasn't sure my nerves were up to a night of the two of us sitting alone in the dark. Especially after watching Sean flirt with Jasmine throughout the meal. Not that I'd been paying attention.

Since I was thinking about Sean, I decided to get out my phone and clue him in on the sting. I was almost to the farm. There wasn't much he could do to put a stop to my plan.

"You're just telling me this now?" he yelled.

Whoever said turkey mellowed a person's mood was totally wrong.

I listened to him rail as I steered along the roads toward Bryan and Reggie's house. Sean's voice cut in and out depending on the reception, but I got the gist. He was on his way. He was a real law enforcement agent. He was angry. Story of my life.

I put the phone in my cup holder and then squinted into the dimming night. The small gravel path where Bryan had instructed me to park was a hundred feet from the driveway and hidden behind a line of mostly leafless bushes. Cutting the engine, I pulled out the binoculars I'd borrowed from Pop and waited. From this vantage point, I could see both the front and back of the house. If the thief decided to strike, I would see him. If I didn't, Carlos the bass player would.

The front lights went on. Ten minutes later, Bryan and Reginald drove off in their truck as planned.

Showtime.

Taking a deep breath, I peered through my binoculars and waited for something interesting to happen. Leaves blew in the wind. A squirrel scampered across a woodpile. No burglar. No Sean doing a drive-by. Nothing. Yep—this was a lot like watching grass grow. Consuming turkey hadn't seemed to alter Sean's energy level, but it was having a decided effect on mine. Sitting in the dark wasn't helping either. If things didn't get more interesting, I'd end up fast asleep.

Since turning on the interior car light wasn't an option, I decided to keep my mind alert by mulling over Ginny's murder case. The more I thought about it, the more convinced I was that the ten-digit number belonged to a bank account. With all the cooking and prewedding activities, I hadn't had time to ask Sean if he'd checked that possibility. If I was right, the other numbers and letters on the paper had to be associated with that account.

I grabbed my cell phone and, by the light from the screen, flipped through my notebook for the letters and numbers.

WMCSA 765432

Maybe the letters were an abbreviation for whatever name was on the account. Organizations used acronyms all the time, right? Maybe it was something like the Women's Mountain Climbing and Scuba Association. Of course, we didn't have mountains or oceans around Indian Falls, so that was probably a bust, but the abbreviation idea made sense.

Especially when I read the final set of numbers again. Because of the popularity of ATMs and online banking, every account required a PIN number. A fact I lamented whenever I needed to access the savings account my mother opened for me when I was a kid. I rarely used it. When I did, I could never remember where I put the paper on which I wrote the PIN. Ginny was probably smarter about keeping that number handy, and, if not, descending consecutive digits would be easy to recall.

Hot damn. My Spidey sense jangled. I just had to figure out what the letters meant and I'd be a step closer to catching the killer. Ginny wasn't the type to spend money on extravagant things. In fact, other than the yearly trip to Florida, I hadn't seen any expenditures that indicated . . .

Wait a minute. I sat up straight and shook off the tryptophan fog. The annual Florida trip. Ethel said Ginny and the rest of the group began their yearly trip a decade ago, and the group had a name—the Winter Migration Club. WMC: the first three letters of the acronym on the account. Coincidence? I doubted it. This account must be where Ginny got the money to pay for the group's Florida condominium. If I was right, Ethel, Joan and Marty McGoran, and Alice Peppinger would all have access to this account. The McGorans were retired soybean farmers. Alice Peppinger used to work the counter at the pharmacy. Unless one of them had hit the lottery or made a killing in the stock market, there was no way they could afford to spend several months a year for the past eleven years at a beachfront condo. So where did the money in this account come from?

I peered through the binoculars to look for the thief and felt them fall into my lap as my brain connected the dots. The Winter Migration Club had traveled to Florida for eleven years. Almost the exact amount of time the Thanksgiving Day thief had been in action. Money, jewelry, and small, easy-to-sell electronics were taken year after year. Selling them wouldn't yield a lot of money, but it would provide enough cash to rent a condo and cover travel expenses—and who would suspect a group of senior citizens? No one, especially since those seniors weren't around to question immediately after the thefts took place.

Holy shit! Ethel, Ginny, and the rest of the Winter Migration Club were the Thanksgiving Day thieves. Only now Ginny was dead. Unless I was totally whacked, one of her longtime criminal partners had killed her.

And I knew who.

I grabbed the phone and dialed Sean's number. Direct to voice mail. Damn. My phone had reception, which meant he was in a bad spot. Hoping he'd get the message, I said, "Sean, I know who killed Ginny and who's behind the robberies. If you're around—"

The back door on the driver's side opened and light filled the car, momentarily blinding me. I spun in my seat, expecting to see Sean climbing inside. Instead, I came face-to-face with a Pilgrim-attired Ethel Jacabowski, who was calmly holding a syringe against my neck.

Twenty-four

Shit! Shit! Ow.

"Please don't move, Rebecca. Otherwise you'll be sorry. Insulin doesn't kill instantly, but by the time someone found you out here and got you to a hospital . . ." Ethel reached over and plucked the phone out of my hand. "Let's just say it would be best if that doesn't happen. Trust me when I say I really don't want to hurt you."

The syringe pricking the side of my neck was evidence to the contrary, but what did I know?

"Why are you here?" I asked, trying hard to keep very, very still.

"Because I need you to do something for me. I need you to understand what I did." Ethel shifted, and the needle poked deeper into my neck. Yeouch. I whimpered and bit my lip. My eyes watered, but I didn't move. Death wasn't on my agenda.

Trying to think my way out of this, I said, "You've been robbing houses for ten years."

"Technically, eleven, but yes." Ginny sighed. "Your grand-father was positive you'd figure out who was behind the thefts. I wanted to believe he was wrong. I wanted to believe a lot of things."

Ethel's Pilgrim-clad shoulders slumped. Her eyes looked tired. Worn. Incredibly sad. Nevertheless, the needle didn't falter against my throat. No matter how unhappy and fatigued she was, Ethel meant business. I was screwed.

"You've probably figured out most of it by now. Arthur told me you would." Ethel smiled. "Of course, he didn't know I was partially responsible."

"You're also responsible for Ginny's murder."

The smile disappeared. "Ginny was my best friend, but yes. I killed her, and you probably want to know why."

The needle edged deeper into my flesh. Something wet trick-led down my neck. Sweat or blood, I didn't know, and I didn't care. A little blood wouldn't kill me. It was a press of the plunger that would do that job. I had to hope Sean had seen the light in my car go on and would feel inclined to come over and yell at me. Until that happened, I needed to say whatever Ethel wanted to hear in order to keep me alive.

Since Ethel said she wanted to explain, I said, "I would like to know. I assumed it had something to do with the thefts."

Ethel's bonnet shifted over her forehead as she nodded. "Twelve years ago, my Paul got sick with cancer. They tried every-thing, but nothing took away the pain or stopped the disease. A friend gave him a drug to help with the pain."

"Seth Kurtz. I found the marijuana plants he grows in the basement."

She let out another sigh. "Paul helped Seth turn those plants into a business that would help other people like him. There's so much pain in the world. We couldn't see the harm in growing something that could take the pain away. Seth promised to rent a place with the profits so we could spend the winter together with all our friends in Florida." Tears shimmered in Ethel's eyes. "Paul hated the cold. He didn't want to spend the end of his life in the snow. Only, when the time came, Seth backed out of the deal."

"So you and Paul broke into the Kurtzes' house to get what was owed to you."

She smiled. "Paul read an advertisement in the paper about Pilgrims who would deliver Thanksgiving dinner to you for a fee. He thought that would make the perfect cover, since the Pilgrims have to carry boxes in and out of houses. If someone spotted us, they'd see the costumes and assume we were strangers. None of our friends would ever believe it was us. My Paul was smart. Even when he was in pain, he liked planning for every contingency." She smiled at the memory. "Paul asked Ginny to make the costumes, and her husband, Walter, sneaked Jan's spare key out of the silverware drawer when she wasn't looking."

Well, that explained the costume Ethel was wearing and the renegade Pilgrims who had been spotted zipping around town today.

The interior light clicked off, cloaking everything in darkness. Suddenly, the needle felt sharper, the possibility of death more real. I told myself to stay calm, but my body wasn't listening. My heart slammed in my chest. My breathing was shallow, and the rest of me was clammy with sweat. "How did you get past the dogs?" My voice was hollow with fear.

"Walter and Ginny had steak laced with sleeping pills in their delivery boxes. When the dogs fell asleep, Paul and I went downstairs and took the cash from marijuana sales that Seth had yet to deposit. It wasn't as much as Paul had expected, so we filled the empty boxes with other things to make up the difference. We didn't think Seth and Jan would call the cops, but Jan mentioned the theft to her son and he insisted. Thankfully, by the time we returned from Florida, the police had stopped investigating the case. Paul was so sick by then I doubt they would have considered questioning us even if they'd thought of it."

Okay, I almost understood the first theft . . . but the second? "Why did you rob Mr. Donovan's house the next year?"

"Because Paul wanted to. Planning the theft of the Donovan farm and reading books about picking locks were the only things that kept him going. I still have the tools he ordered. He loved helping me learn how to use them." Ethel wiped a tear off her cheek. "When he passed that October, the rest of us decided to go through with the robbery as a tribute to his memory."

That was both screwy and sweet.

"We created an account for money we received after selling the things we took. Ginny and I worked it out so that every year a different member would access the account and pay the rent on our winter condo. That way no one would wonder how any one person could afford to pay so much. Social Security isn't all it's cracked up to be, you know."

The needle shifted, and I let out a small yelp.

"Oh, I'm sorry, dear," Ethel said. "I can't remove the syringe or you'll run away, but I'll try to keep still so I don't hurt you any more than necessary."

Call me crazy, but that didn't make me feel any better.

"If you and Ginny were in this together," I asked, "why did you kill her?"

"Because after all these years, Ginny wanted to end the club."

Ethel sniffled. "Ginny's granddaughter began having nightmares about the robberies. She was scared someone was going to come into her house and hurt her family. Two weeks ago, she wrote an essay for her English class about how the Thanksgiving thief had not only taken possessions but also stolen the warmth and joy of the holiday from everyone in this town. Ginny's granddaughter got an A on the paper, and Ginny told me we had to turn ourselves in. She wanted the town to feel safe spending Thanksgiving with their families again."

Wow. After a decade of crime, that had to have been one heck of an essay.

"Ginny didn't care that we'd go to jail. She wasn't scared, but I was. The idea of being confined in a cell terrified me. I asked her to wait a few days before talking to the others, just in case she changed her mind. I knew she wouldn't, though." The syringe trembled against my neck. "She didn't have the right to make that kind of choice for all of us, but she was going to. Unless I stopped her. I slipped three sleeping pills into her cranberry juice before we walked over to the center for Danielle's shower. She started feeling woozy during one of the games, and I convinced her to go down the hall and put her feet up. She was asleep when I went to check on her. If she'd been awake, I wouldn't have done it. I couldn't have. But I was scared and ashamed, and I put the needle in her arm and gave her the shot of my insulin. I thought I was making everything better." Ethel's voice hitched. Now that my eyes had adjusted to the dim light, I could see the tears streaming down her face as she whispered, "I was wrong."

My heart squeezed with sympathy even as it pounded with fear. "So now what?"

Ethel took a deep breath and sniffed back tears. "Now you can tell the sheriff what I did and why. You should also tell Jimmy not to leave his keys in the car and that it's not his fault you were hurt."

"You ran me down?" Why that should surprise me after what I'd just heard, I wasn't sure, but it did.

"I didn't intend to do more than scare you. You were supposed to recognize the car and think Jimmy was behind it all. The sheriff would eventually let Jimmy off the hook, and by that time the rest of us would be in Florida. Only I'm not supposed to drive at night, and I misjudged the distance. The one thing I actually did right was picking your lock. My Paul would have been proud of me for being able to do it so quickly." Her hand trembled. "He would be so disappointed in everything else. I should have thought things through before acting. That's what I've been doing the last couple of days—thinking. Which is why I know I'm doing the right thing. The truth won't bring Ginny back, but it might give her family peace of mind."

"What about you?" I swallowed hard. "Will confession help you find peace?"

"No." Ethel shook her head. "But this will."

Before I could register her movements, Ethel lifted the syringe from my neck, pushed it against hers, and depressed the plunger.

"Oh my God." I fumbled to release my seat belt and scrambled between the seats into the back of the car. Ethel gave me a sad smile as I felt around the seat for my phone. It had to be here somewhere. Insulin took a while to hit the bloodstream. If I called for help now, there might be a chance to save Ethel. She might not want to live, but I sure as hell wasn't going to let her die. I needed my phone.

Got it. More important, I had a signal.

I dialed Doc's number, begged him to get here fast, and then called Sean. Doc lived just over a mile down the road. Sean was parked up the block. As I waited for them to arrive, I tried to coax Ethel into drinking some of the soda I'd left in my car last week. It was flat and probably tasted terrible, but it had sugar in it. Ethel needed sugar to counteract the insulin. No matter how I begged or the tears I shed, Ethel refused. Taking my hand, she gave me a small smile and told me everything was going to be okay now. I heard the echo of sirens and hoped she was right.

My hair was molded to my scalp. My purple taffeta dress was hideous but fit perfectly. Standing across the room, Annette adjusted the veil on Danielle's head while Erica the Red sniffled. The smile on Danielle's face was brighter than the rhinestones that glittered at her neck and ears. She looked perfect. Everything looked perfect. It almost made it possible to forget everything that had happened less than twenty-four hours ago.

Annette had waved her makeup magic wand and made the red syringe mark on my neck vanish, but she couldn't take away the ache from the wound or the concern that Ethel wouldn't pull through. Doc said there was a chance she'd come out of the diabetic coma, but all the medicine in the world couldn't give a person the will to live. Maybe knowing the rest of the Winter Migration Club had gotten out of town before Sean and Sheriff Jackson arrived to arrest them would ease some of the guilt she was trying to escape. I planned on filling her in when I visited tomorrow. Today was about Danielle and Rich.

It was standing room only in the sanctuary as I gave Danielle's hand a squeeze, took my bouquet of daisies, and walked slowly down the aisle behind Erica the Red. Rich was beaming. When I turned to watch Danielle walk toward him, I smiled, too.

I blinked back tears as Danielle and Rich exchanged vows, and I saw lots of people reach for tissues when Rich slipped the ring on Danielle's finger. Only Mother Lucas looked unmoved by the ceremony. Her lips formed a thin, almost disinterested smile throughout the service. Until, of course, she looked at me. Then she frowned. Oy! I had no idea what her problem was, but it was starting to irk me.

When the ceremony ended, the guests went to the reception hall. The rest of us stood for a seemingly endless number of photos. As Stan posed Danielle and Rich, I noticed Mrs. Lucas glaring in my direction and decided to find out why.

"I don't like you," she said, adjusting the daisy corsage on her beige dress. "You've pushed your taste, or lack of, onto my son's wedding and encouraged Danielle to defy her new family at every turn. I don't appreciate that kind of behavior."

Personally, I didn't appreciate her trying to make Danielle feel bad for having friends and opinions, but I decided to keep that to myself. Danielle was going to get enough grief being related to this lady. Instead, I said, "Danielle's my friend. I had her best interests at heart."

Stan asked for Mrs. Lucas to come up front for a photo op. She smiled at him and then turned back to me. "Danielle isn't what I wanted for my son. He deserves the best, but he fell in love with her. I can tell she's trying to be a good pastor's wife, so I will do my best to accept that she is one of us." She stood, adjusted her skirt, and smiled. "I don't, however, have to accept you."

The woman's attitude was irritating but strangely refreshing. It was nice to have someone dislike me without threatening to kill me.

When Stan finished clicking the final photo, we trucked down to the hall for the cocktail hour. With lights dimmed and candles glowing, the room looked lovely. Lionel greeted me at the door with a glass of wine.

"How are you feeling?" he asked, brushing his fingers against the wound on my neck. His gentle touch made my heart flip.

"I'm fine." Or I would be after I finished this glass of wine. "This is a happy day. Did your parents go back home? I feel bad I didn't get the chance to say good-bye."

"They left this morning, but they plan on coming back for Christmas. You'll have your chance to see them again." Lionel shifted his weight. "Before they left, my mother said she was worried she might have upset you. She said . . ." His handsome face flushed as he reached for the right words. "She thought I'd told you . . ."

"That you started planning one of these bashes for yourself."

Lionel winced. "I was going to tell you, but it never seemed like the right time. There was always something getting in the way."

Car explosions. Death threats. Dead bodies. Yeah, over the months, lots of things had gotten in the way.

"Are you mad?" he asked.

"Not really." My initial anger had faded. Almost watching someone die had put things in perspective. "Although I guess when things get back to normal you should tell me about it."

Lionel smiled and wove his fingers through mine. "It's a date."

Food was served. People oohed and aahed over the silver bell ornaments Danielle had set next to every plate. On each was a small tag tied with a ribbon that read RICH AND DANIELLE'S WEDDING, along with the date. The cake was cut—though I was sad to see the horrible cake topper survived to ruin another bride's day—and the DJ cranked out tunes while the entire town danced. Erica the Red beat out Jasmine in the bouquet toss and got to dance with Lionel, who winked at me when he caught the garter. While they danced, I spotted a uniform-clad Sean watching me from the doorway and headed over.

"Ethel?" I asked as we stepped into the hall.

"She's holding her own. Her coconspirators are missing, but we were able to freeze the bank account and found the records they kept on the items they stole and who they sold them to. There's a chance we might be able to locate some of the items and return them to their rightful owners."

I thought about Julie Johnson and smiled. "Did you find Jimmy Bakersfield?"

"The cops in Dixon spotted his car parked outside a motel and called it in." Sean leaned against the wall. "Jimmy's relieved to know he wasn't responsible for your injuries."

"Why did he run when I tried to question him?"

"Jimmy's having memory issues. When he saw the dent in the hood of his car and realized the car wasn't where he remembered parking it, he panicked. I'm guessing he'll be seeing Doc first thing on Monday morning to make sure this kind of thing never happens."

Poor Jimmy.

"What about Seth and Jan?" I asked.

Sean shrugged. "Hearing Ethel and the rest of the winter migration club were behing the thefts must have spooked them. By the time I got to their house, the basement was empty."

"So now what?" I asked.

"Now I keep searching for Ethel's coconspirators and try to

run down as many of the stolen items as I can." Sean smiled. "Want to help?"

Help? "With what?"

Sean pushed away from the wall and sauntered toward me. "Making calls. Tracking down jewelry and family heirlooms. Reuniting victims with their possessions."

"You want me to work for the sheriff's department?"

"No." His eyes met mine. "I want something different. The sheriff thinks you'll be an asset, though. He'd like you to work part-time to help close out this case. After that, you'll be back to ordering concessions and renting skates while those of us who are trained to catch bad guys do our jobs."

Wow. "I don't know what to say." About the job. About Sean and what he wanted. About any of it.

"Think of it this way," Sean said. "After all the work you've put in, wouldn't it be nice to get paid?"

I pictured Mrs. Johnson's check. It was still stuck on my fridge with a magnet, where I'd put it the day she wrote it. The check had made me feel guilty because I didn't believe I'd be able to help. But I did. And maybe, just maybe, I'd be able to do a whole lot more.

"Yes," I said, giving Sean a smile. "Yes, it would."